BLOOD COUSINS
PART 1

OMAR D. HARDWARE

OMAR D. HARDWARE
Copyright © 2012 Author Name

ISBN-10: 197467956X
ISBN-13: 9781974679560

To everyone who was waiting for something different.

OMAR D. HARDWARE

BLOOD COUSINS
CONTENTS

OMAR D. HARDWARE

ACKNOWLEDGMENTS

This page is dedicated to everyone who made it passed the cover. I appreciate you, whether you purchased a copy, borrowed a copy, or however you stumbled upon this. Your effort means more to me than you think! It's a blessing to be able to create an alternate universe for your entertainment. I want to thank God and both my parents for this massive imagination of mine. A special thanks to my older sister Latoya Grant and my best friend Jessica Victor for proof reading my work. I couldn't have done this without them nor the help I received from my editor Vanessa Josephine Ragusa. Thank you for having patience with the process and teaching me how to structure my first book. I also want to thank my illustrator Maryam Ismali for help bringing my vision to life. I drove that man crazy! I also have to thank my good friends Saieve Al Sabah for inspiring me to write and Edward Orelus for encouraging me to continue, after reading my first few paragraphs. This book would not have been possible if it weren't for the encouragement I received from all my family and friends, managers, doctors, and all my co-workers at Rockland Endocrine & Diabetes P.C!

Enjoy.

CHAPTER 1

West Philadelphia, PA

"I bet they got over 30k in their safe!" Isaiah says, as he inhales his blunt. "And its illegal money, so they can't even call the cops if dudes run up in there."

"I don't know why you always bring this up when I drive pass here." Ruben replies as he stops at the stoplight. "You have no guns, no goons and everybody in the streets know you're broke. If you ever did succeed in robbing them, the streets would automatically know it's you, just by how a brother like you spend money."

"A brother like me? The streets never met a brother like me!" he replies, amped up. "And fuck you, you know how small the hood is, it's easy to find guns if I really wanted to." He inhales the blunt again, breathing out a big cloud of smoke.

"Man, stop smoking that shit like we're in California! These Philadelphia cops don't play. If I get pulled over they're towing my car downtown. And I can't afford that! We're already driving while black, let's not draw any more attention to ourselves. But back to the topic, if it's that easy for you to find guns, why haven't you ended this beef with Leo yet?"

"Pussy!" Isaiah replies as he puts his blunt out in the ashtray. "I'm not going to shoot Leo over pussy. I don't understand weirdos like him, willing to look the blind side of his girlfriend being a hoe! Like seriously, I'm not his bitch! I'm not the one he should be mad at. And truthfully he's too old to care this much about her."

"He's only 20." Ruben laughs.

"Yea! And I'm 17! Sleeping with girls older than me. He's a hater!"

The light turns green and Ruben continues to drive. Isaiah looks over Rubens baseball cap keeping his eyes on the laundromat, what now looked like a hangout spot for all the local homeless civilians. As Ruben drives further down, Isaiah fixes himself in the seat and continues, "I don't need no team behind me to rob that punk ass spot. I just need your scary ass!"

"Come on bro, I don't get like that! And please don't get me involved in your suicide missions. I have people at home that actually love me."

"Must be nice." Isaiah glances out the car window as the two enter their apartment buildings.

CHAPTER 2

Peekskill, New York.

"How many times do I have to tell you, stop taking my car if you're not going to put gas in it Hakeem!" Says Camille, Hakeem's mom. She walks into the kitchen and approaches him at the counter, while he closes the jar of mayonnaise.

"I was going to, but I ended up spending more than I thought I would on my date ma," Hakeem 33gives her a kiss on the cheek. "Let me live this time please." He pleas.

She laughs a little and shakes her head. "Ok, but don't let this become a habit or Amber will have to be your transportation from now on."

Hakeem takes a bite of his sandwich. "You win ma, it won't happen again. And you know what else won't happen again? Me asking to borrow 60 dollars!" He smirks. "Payday is Friday, I'm going to pay you back, I promise, and I'm going to learn how to save my money."

She looks him in his brown eyes and gives him an uncertain facial expression. "What do you need money for this time?"

"Me and Amber are going to the movies and maybe the bowling

rink after."

"You and that girl Amber!" She shakes her head. "You two make a cute couple, but I still think Taryn is the right girl for you."

"She's my best friend mom, she's like family."

"No." She straightens her face. "I never gave birth to a daughter. I raised one son. The both of you just so happened to have become friends from an early age. In a world where my opinion matters, I think it makes more sense to be with the girl who claimed you as a friend when you were ugly."

Hakeem laughs as he shakes his head. "Yea, let me get that 60 though mom." The Doorbell interrupts the two. "Speaking of the devil. Can you get that for me? It's Taryn, I have to finish getting ready." He tries to fit the whole sandwich in his mouth while walking out of the kitchen and upstairs to his room.

The doorbell rings again. "I'm coming, I'm coming!" Camille walks over to the door and opens it. In front of her stood a 5'4, slim Caucasian teenager. Her long dark hair laid comfortable over her shoulders. She wore light make up, but just enough to cover the scar on the left side of her face.

Taryn lays her blues eyes on Camille and smiles. "Hey Ma!" She leans in and kisses Camille on the cheek.

"Hey Taryn, he's upstairs getting ready for his date with Amber. You know I tell him every day he should break up with her and be with you."

Taryn laughs trying not to blush. "Please ma, we wouldn't be any good for each other. And I don't need any distractions from my school work." She walks in the house, puts her purse on the living room table and goes upstairs, and without knocking walks into Hakeem's room.

Hakeem was standing in front of the T.V putting on a t-shirt. "Hurry up and shut the door, I have to tell you something!" As she closes the door, he wastes no time approaching her from behind and lifts her in the air. The two laugh, as he carries her to his bed.

"Are you sure you have time for this?" She whispers in his ears.

"No, but I'm going to make time." He kisses her neck lightly. She hides her smile, turns around and kisses him on the lips. He lifts her up again and lays her down on top of his pillows. As he unbuckles his belt, she places her hand on top of his head and caresses his wavy hair down to his cheek bone. She couldn't help noticing, he was wearing the earrings she brought him last Christmas and kisses him again.

He drops his jeans low enough for him to be able to take his hard penis out of his boxer hole comfortably. She grabs on to it tight and slides her sweatpants down. Once her pants were at her ankles, she pulls her underwear to the side and tries to place his manhood inside.

"Not like this." He leans back and grabs his television remote. He changes the channel to a hip-hop station and blasts the volume. "Turn over!"

As she turns over to her stomach and arch's her back, he pulls her ass closer to the end of the bed by grabbing her thighs. She moans as he slips his penis inside of her. Placeing a pillow under her face, he spanks her ass and penetrates her hard. Minutes go by as Camille walks upstairs to check up on the two. She couldn't hear anything through the door due to the loud music so she continues to her room.

After he came, the two of them began to fix their clothes when she looks up at him and asks, "why were you so horny punk, shouldn't you be saving your energy for Amber later?"

Hakeem adjusts the volume on the T.V and replies, "honestly, I don't know what's up with her, it's been a few weeks since we had sex. I don't know how much more patience she expects me to have."

She giggles. "Maybe you're not pleasing her enough. I swear if you weren't my best friend I'd feel like a hoe for letting you use me."

"So, you're going to act like you didn't use me after you broke up with Chris! I love how you always make me sound like the bad guy." He shakes his head. "I need to leave though, I'm meeting her at the movies."

CHAPTER 3

Isaiah

"Damn, dad really didn't fill the refrigerator before going on that damn trip. How the fuck does he expect me to survive?" Isaiah paces back and forth from the kitchen to the living room then takes out his cell phone to dial.

"Hello?" A calm female voice answers.

"Erica, please tell me you have some food at your crib." He rubs his stomach. "I'm fucking starving!"

"You don't have to use food as excuse to come see me Zay."

He smirks. "I'm coming over in a few, have something ready for me to eat. You down to smoke too?"

"Yea, I have some dutches. Hurry up, I don't know what time Leo is coming over tonight."

"Say no more." He hangs up the phone. Before walking out of the door, he looks around the dirty apartment again, then looks back down at his cell phone. He scrolls through his contacts to "pops," and decides to give him a call, but the call goes straight to voicemail. "Dad, what's good with you? It's been three days and you haven't returned any of my calls. I'm running low on cash and grub. I know you and uncle Will are out taking care of business, but don't forget you have a son back home!" He ends the call, frustrated. Then puts his phone in his back pocket.

Walking out of his apartment building, he mumbles to himself "I wonder who got weed? Tyreik!" He continues walking through the apartments until he reaches a fence at the end of the parking lot. He uses an empty garbage can as a stoop, to help him hop the fence and land in the backyard of what looked like a broken home. As soon as Isaiah lifts his head, two pit bulls chained to a tree growls at him. "Shit!"

The dogs began barking and tries to chase after him. If it weren't for the chains, they would've caught him. He runs around the front of the house and crosses the street. "I fucking hate dogs!"

He walks up to a tan house with the number 17 on it and knocks on the door. "Yo, Tyriek, open the door, its Zay!"

The doorknob turns and as he hears the lock being unlocked, the door finally opens. "Didn't I tell you to call before rolling up to my crib?" Tyriek barks holding the door.

Isaiah rolls his eyes. Tyriek lives by himself, so Isaiah feels no need to give him advanced notifications. "I didn't have time, I still don't have time. Just give me a dub bitch." He reaches into his pockets and pulls out 18 dollars.

"Watch your mouth bro, I'm not Leo." Tyriek points at him and walks inside to grab the weed. When he comes back to the door, he looks down at Isaiah's hands. "You're missing two dollars."

"Hold me down, its only two dollars!" Isaiah continues to mumble, "you act like you're starving."

"Stop watching my pockets, you're always two dollars short!" He hands Isaiah the bag of weed.

Isaiah looks down at it then looks him in the eyes. "So, everybody in the hood knows about Leo hating ass huh!"

"If that's how you want to put it." Tyriek shrugs. "The way I'm hearing it, your sneaking around with his girl." Isaiah lets out little laugh. "If I was you I'd take it easy. Leo has a reputation of ending people he feels disrespect him. Now, I put in work with you before but Leo got real thugs with him. You have to know how to pick your battles."

Isaiah gives him a handshake, unbothered. "Good looks on the advice, but I win all my battles!"

"If only you believed that yourself. Hold on, come inside real quick!" Tyriek walks in the kitchen and opens the draw. He hands Isaiah a loaded gun. "You know how to use one right?"

"Yea, my father trained me how to use any weapon." He examines it. "It's about time you came through for me. I was just talking about getting one earlier."

"Just don't make me regret this. You know the rules, if you get jammed up in the streets, that gun never came from me!"

CHAPTER 4

Hakeem

As Hakeem parks his mother's car in the movie theater parking lot, he notices a little boy racing his father to their minivan. The excitement in the child's voice brought a smile to his face and a warm feeling to his heart. Before turning the car off, he takes out his cellphone, scrolled passed Amber and calls his father.

It's been three days since they last spoke. Even though his father told him his phone may cut off on the trip he's on with his uncle. William usually finds a way to check in with him and his mother, either with a different number, email, fax, something. Something wasn't right.

The phone call goes straight to voicemail, so he leaves a short message. "Hey dad, I hope you're enjoying yourself with uncle Jason. I haven't heard from you, so I'm just checking in. Later."

Amber approaches the car door and knocks on the window. "Are you coming out anytime soon? Let me know if I should wait or not!"

"I'm coming!" He turns off the car and puts his phone in his pocket. Amber waits with her arm crossed, as he gets out of the car.

"I had to tell everyone to stop calling me, I'm with my wife tonight." He wraps his arms around her short petite body and rests his hand on her butt.

Ambers fake attitude turned into a smile. Her yellow cheeks turned light red as she gave him a kiss on the lips. "You taste like mango babe."

"I had some mango fruit before I left! But you taste like everything I imagine you would." He covers his nervousness smoothly. "I should have washed my mouth after kissing Taryn." He thinks to himself.

"I better not hear you saying that to any girls tomorrow, I know how you seniors are!" Amber squints her eyes at him, then grabs his hand to head in to the theater.

"I'm all yours baby!" He replies, popping a mint into his mouth. The two enter the theater just in time to catch the previews.

The moon was high in the sky by the time the movie ended. Everyone walked out the theater gossiping in excitement over how much they loved the film. "That movie was pretty cool." Amber threw her fountain drink in the garbage and wrapped her arms around Hakeem's arm.

"Yea it was cool, but I think I'm over these zombie movies."

"Why? Do the zombies scare my little baby!" She touches him playfully.

"No!" He laughs. "They always end the same. These movies are too predictable."

"Hmm." She made a light sound.

"I have about three zombie movies back at home that ends the same way! Let's ditch the rink, go back to my spot and compare them." He tries to put on his seductive voice.

She smirks and shakes her head. "I know where you're going with this and I'm going to have to decline the offer."

He sighs in disappointment.

"I love you Hakeem, I hope you don't think I changed on you. I just don't want our relationship to be based on sex. Can you give me some more time?"

"Yea, I know you love me." He replies sarcastically. "I could save the world and you still wouldn't be ready for me."

"You haven't saved anyone yet." She laughs. "But seriously, I want our bond to be as strong as you and Taryn's is. I don't want to sound jealous, but I kind of envy the friendship between the two of you. I want to be your best friend too."

He shakes his head as the two stop walking. "Amber you're my girlfriend. Me and Taryn are friends, nothing more! You're the only person I think about when I go to sleep and wake up in the morning. There's no comparing the two of you. She's been my best friend for as long as I could remember. As a matter of fact, I believe I friend zoned her the first 24 hours of our friendship. Scouts honor!"

Amber couldn't hide her white teeth as she laughed. "You're stupid. I understand she's been your friend for years, I respect that, I just don't want to compete for you."

"Don't think like that! There's no competition." He looks around, then whispers in her ears. "If I was only with you for sex, this relationship would have ended the first night I got you out of your favorite baby blue panties."

"Stop it!" She blushes.

He smiles at her and kisses her on the lips. "I love you."

"I love you too."

He keeps his eyes on her as they make their way to the parking lot. "Wow she really cares for me! I could see it in her eyes. Is she crazy? How did I become so lucky? I need to stop fucking Taryn. I can't ruin this, she doesn't deserve that!" He thinks to himself.

As they approach Amber's car, an average height man in a tall black trench coat with a fedora covering his face walks in between the two bumping into their shoulders. Hakeem looks over his shoulder to respond but was at a loss for words. For a few seconds, he was paralyzed as if he was in a daze he couldn't break free of.

By the time, he snaps out of it all he could hear was Amber shouting "I hope the next person you bump into fucks you up!"

"Babe, I think I'm going to call it a night, I'll see you in school tomorrow?" He places his hand on his temple.

"Are you okay? What's wrong?" She asks worried.

"Yea I'm ok, it's nothing. I just need some rest."

"Ok then." She looks at him puzzled. "I guess I'll go home too. Get home safe baby. I'll see you tomorrow." She gives him a kiss then gets in her car. He walks away once she drives off.

CHAPTER 5

Leo

"I can't wait to get my hands on that little dread head Zay! That boy has a death wish!" Leo says, taking a gulp of the cognac liquor. "Dude really think he could talk to my girl and get away with it." He paces back and forth in the small living room.

"Since when does drinking get the problem solved?" Dimitri asks, taking the bottle from him and taking a swig himself.

"Do I look like I need a fucking counselor?" Leo takes out a cigarette from the pack on the table and lights it.

Before Dimitri replies, he grills Leo from the top of his nappy cornrows to the bottom of his baggy jeans. "Nah, I'm not your counselor, I'm your mother fuckin' dog!" He points at him. "What you need to do is worry less about finding this dude and more about keeping your bitch in check!"

Leo crushes the fresh cigarette and grabs him by the collar, almost spilling the alcohol.

"Don't you ever call Erica a bitch! You hear me?" He paused. "Follow me, I'm going to have a word with her."

Isaiah

As Isaiah approaches Erica's house, he looks around the neighborhood to see if anyone was watching him. Once he notices the coast is clear, he pulls the gun out of his pants and places it inside the recycling bin. He then walks up the driveway, heads to the corner of the house and into the backyard.

He calls her on his cellphone to open her window as he begins climbing her fire escape ladder, but it was already open. He climbs through it, one foot at a time. When he stands up straight, he realizes she was already waiting for him.

She stood next to her bed, hair wet wearing nothing but a towel. He smirks. "You're overdressed."

"Dinner is ready." She snickered, dropping her towel.

Isaiah takes off his shirt as she lays down on her bed. He wastes no time attacking her body with kisses from her neck down to her vagina. He lifts her leg over his shoulder and strokes her with two fingers. As she moans, Isaiah places his other hand over her mouth and fingers her faster, leaving his fingers soaked.

As he removes his hand to take his penis out, she moves his other hand and pulls his head in closer, by his dreads. In a low but horny voice, she asks, "do you have a condom?"

"Yea, it's already on." He rolls his eyes, lying. After the two came, they cuddled together on the bed. He takes the weed out of his jean pocket that was next to the bed and takes the tobacco cigar off the dresser. As he began rolling, he mumbles, "just because I ate your pussy don't mean I'm not still hungry!"

Knowing what he meant, she lets out a long moan and crawls out of bed. As she walks by him, he reaches his hand over and smacks her ass. She laughs, "don't make too much noise while I'm gone, my parents will kill me if they find out I had someone other than Leo over."

"I won't if you hurry up with that food!"

She shakes her head then walks out of the room. He leans his back against the bed frame and stuffs as much weed as he can into the cigar and doesn't wait for her to return before lighting it.

As the ash on the end of the joint grew longer, he realizes he needed an ashtray. He gets off the bed and searches for one. As he looks over the dresser, he accidently drops ashes everywhere. He opens the top draw and spots a coconut shell. He takes it and goes back to the bed. As he began getting comfortable, the sound of footsteps disturbed the silence. The footsteps weren't coming from the hallway, but from outside. Becoming suspicious, he takes another hit of the joint and reaches for his jeans.

As he looks over to the window, he notices a man with cornrows attempting to climb through head first. He instantly knew it was Leo. When Leo gets half way through, the two make eye contact, before he screams, "oh, hell no!"

Isaiah's eyes shot open with surprise. He looks around him for a weapon and finds nothing, but Erica's pillow. He takes it and throws it at him as he struggles to climb through the window. By the time Isaiah could get his jeans on, Leo forces his entire body through the window making enough noise that even the neighbors could hear the chaos.

As Erica made her way upstairs with the food, her parents met her halfway in the hallway concerned. "Don't worry about it guys, I left my laptop on the corner of my dresser it must have dropped!"

Her parents look at each other with disbelief. "Do you smell that?" Her mother asks. Her father gives her a disappointed look then walks toward her room door. As he reaches for the doorknob, the whole door falls on him, with Leo and Isaiah crashing through. Erica drops the plate of food in shock, as her mother screams in fear. Isaiah rolls over, stands up and kicks Leo in the face. He then runs downstairs and opens the front door to leave.

Within three steps out the door, he gets smacked in the face with a bat, which forces him to land hard on his back. Dimitri stands over him and throws the bat on the floor. He lifts Isaiah by the collar of his shirt and punches him multiple times. Throwing him back down, he kicks him in the stomach and taunts him.

Isaiah rolls over in an attempt to shield himself from anymore blows, and spits out blood from his busted lips. "Oh yea?" He yells back, trying to get back on his feet. Dimitri throws another punch, but misses. Isaiah counters it, with a punch to his stomach followed by a knee to his face. Dimitri backs into the parked car in the driveway, while Isaiah rushes him with a mix of jabs and uppercuts.

Just as he began to smirk, Leo hits him in the back with Dimitri's bat. Isaiah falls onto one knee, groaning in pain. "You piece of shit!" Leo points the bat at him. "I told you, I don't want to see you around these streets or my girl, but here you are! Smoking in her fucking room!"

"Technically I'm outside!" Isaiah replies sarcastically.

Leo kicks him in the chest, "I don't fucking care where you are!" He paused. "You got a mouth boy." He paces over him. "I'm going to tear it right off your fucking face!"

Isaiah grounded once more, rolls over on his stomach and tries to get up. "Just be careful where you put it, your girl is going to want them later." He replies. Leo tightens his fist as he walks closer to him. Dimitri tosses him a pocket knife, so he throws the baseball bat in the grass. "That's how we playing?" Isaiah looks at them puzzled. "Over a girl?" Leo quickly slides the blade out and taunts it. Ignoring the pain in his rib cage, Isaiah forces himself to get to the recycling bin at the beginning of the driveway.

"That's my wife! You're going to respect what's mine!" Leo points the blade at him. "You have no place in her life or in these streets!"

Isaiah wipes the blood off his lips and replies, "weirdo."

"You think this is a joke?"

Isaiah turns around and takes the gun out of the recycling bin. "You're the only joke here!" He waves the gun in their direction. Leo and Dimitri freezes. "You're quiet now huh lover boy!"

"You don't have it in you to pull the trigg..." The gunshot stops Leo midsentence. Dimitri quickly ducks and sprints to the backyard trying to avoid bullets. "Fuck!" Leo screams grabbing his shoulder, where there was a fresh gun wound. Isaiah smiles then shoots him in the leg. He falls onto the cement driveway, bleeding out.

"Stop!" Erica cries, running outside.

"Get the fuck back inside! Don't make me madder than I already am!" Isaiah waves the gun at her. She stops in her footsteps, then slowly back pedals back to her house, covering her mouth. He continues toward Leo, with the gun aimed to his forehead. "All over pussy." He shakes his head. Leo wipes the tears coming down the side of his eyes, as he stands over him. When he opens his mouth to say something, Isaiah cuts him off and pulls the trigger. Leo closes his eyes, but there was no sound. The gun head jammed.

Isaiah was shocked, as Leo opens his eyes relieved. He looks down at him with a grin then smacks him with the gun.

"That's enough! That's enough!" Erica runs back outside and tries to push him away. Isaiah looks down at Leo one more time then finally runs away.

CHAPTER 6

The following morning.

Hakeem

"Good morning America! This is DJ Biggs from retro 88.9. Before I get started with today's playlist. I just want to wish a good year to all the kids going back to school today! I hope everyone enjoyed their summer because I sure as hell did. Let's not let this hot weather stop us from getting this work done!" The radio turns on by itself, as an alarm for Hakeem. It was 6:40 in the morning.

The family dog jumps on his bed and licks his face. "It's too early for this Blacky!" He rolls over and pushes the Yorke aside. He looks for his phone to see if there were any missed calls, but there wasn't. Only a text from Andrew, asking if he was down for a wake and bake.

Along with Taryn, Andrew is Hakeem's other best friend. Andrew is a little bit more privileged then both him and Taryn. He comes from a high end middle class family.

As Hakeem walks to the bathroom he gives Andrew a call. The phone rings, but there was no answer, so he ends the call without leaving a voicemail. Brushing his teeth in the bathroom, he hears his mother walk in and say, "good morning Mr. Senior! I hope you have a good first day of school, I'm running off to work and I left your breakfast on the table."

"Thanks mom." He lifts his head from the sink and looks at her reflection in the mirror. "Still no word from dad yet?" He asks with a mouth full of toothpaste.

"No, but I'm sure he's fine." She shrugs. "He is an Exalus." She smiles, then rubs the back of his head gently. "I have to go honey, talk to you later."

He spits the toothpaste in the sink and replies, "later mom."

After he takes a shower and gets dressed. He walks downstairs to the kitchen, eyes glued to his phone. For some reason, he couldn't shake the weird feeling he went to sleep with. He starts eating his scrambled eggs and pancakes when Andrew finally calls him back.

"What's good nigga?"

"How many times do I have to tell you to stop calling me that?" Hakeem shakes his head. "You're lucky you're my favorite white boy!"

Andrew laughs. "You call me that all the time! Anyways, I'm on your side of town, are you down to smoke?"

"Yea, I would have been mad if you forgot about me."

"I'm going to be outside in five minutes, keep an eye out for me."

"No doubt." Hakeem ends the call.

He puts on his sneakers then texts Amber, "good morning beautiful." Within seconds, he opens another text message, also texting Taryn "good morning."

Taryn returns the text with a phone call, before he could close his screen. "So, did you score last night! Or did she let you down easy?"

"She let me down easy." He snickers.

Taryn laughs uncontrollably. "I don't know what to tell you man." She paused. "No girl in a relationship decides she just wants to stop having sex for no reason. She's probably dealing with someone on the side. Do you want me to do so some research?"

"Shut up, she's not seeing no one on the side! She told me she wants to grow a stronger bond between us. She doesn't want our relationship to revolve around sex."

"Mm, I guess we'll see when school starts." She stops laughing. "What time are you heading there?"

"After this wake and bake session I'm getting into with Andrew."

He could hear Taryn shaking her head on the other side of the line. "Dude it's the first day of school and you're coming late and high?"

"We're finally seniors Taryn, who cares about coming to school on time!"

"You guys are losers! I still care about my attendance and education. Don't forget you still have to finish this school year! Who gets high before class anyways?"

"Seniors." He snickers. Andrew drives into Hakeem's driveway and honks his car horn. "I got to go, talk to you at school." He looks out of the window, then ends the call and goes back to the kitchen for some matches.

While he locks the front door, Andrew pulls down his car window, rubs his hands and shouts, "you ready for some new freshman booty?"

Hakeem walks to the car laughing. "You need to leave those little girls alone bro!"

"As I sat back and observed your relationship for the last month." He paused. "I'd rather not take your advice." He shrugs.

"Fuck you! What's that supposed to mean?" Hakeem replies approaching the passenger side of the car.

Andrew unlocks the door for him. "Bro, this our senior year! We're suppose to be the alpha males, but instead, your walking around being Ambers lap dog."

"You're just mad I finally hooked up with her and Emira still isn't showing you love." Hakeem sits down and shuts the door. "Amber looks better than any of the other seniors in school."

"Don't say that!" Andrew snickers. "I could have been had Emira! It's just, I always had bad timing." He paused to take out a cigar. "And Amber may be cute bro, but she's not the best-looking girl in school."

"She still looks better than any of your girls." Hakeem shrugs.

"So, my girls know to suck dick just fine, I'm not complaining." He replies breaking weed into the cigar.

Hakeem takes out his cellphone and records himself saying, "there's a word for people like him. It's called thirsty!"

CHAPTER 7

Isaiah

Ruben walks outside of his apartment complex with his bookbag on his back and a garbage bag in his hand. As he throws the garbage out, four cop cars drive past him and park in front of the apartments. He stops to be nosey for a couple of seconds then continues to walk to his car. He opens the car door and tosses his bookbag in the back seat.

"What the fuck! You don't see me sleeping!" Isaiah shouts after the bag falls on his head and onto the floor.

"What the fuck are you doing in my car!" Ruben looks at him puzzled.

Isaiah sits up, then ducks back down when he sees the cops. "I'm hot bro, we have to get off this block now!" Ruben shakes his head and starts the car. As they drive off, Ruben could see the cops running inside Isaiah's building. A couple of blocks down the street Isaiah finally lifts his head.

"Zay, on some real shit! You better fill me in on what's going on! It's the first day of school and you got cop's looking for you and you got me driving around like a fucking test dummy!"

Isaiah points to a parking spot on the side of the road in front of a bodega. "Park over there."

In the parked car, he tells him everything that happened the night before. "Wow, so you really ate out Leos girlfriend." Ruben laughs.

"Seriously? Out of everything I just said that's the only part you heard?"

Ruben shakes his head and turns toward him. "You know you're my dog, right? I don't want to sound like I'm ditching you, but I hope you don't think I'm getting involved in this. I told you to leave her alone!"

"Of course, I'm your dog after you heard what I did to him." He paused. "Truthfully, I wasn't expecting anything from you. I just needed to get away." Isaiah tries to put his dreads in a ponytail, but a cop car drives passes them, causing him to duck.

Watching Isaiah's movements, Ruben asks, "please don't tell me you still have the gun on you?"

He hesitates to answer. "I won't then. Just drop me across the street from that laundry spot we drove by yesterday."

Ruben gives him an unsure look then starts his car. Shaking his head, he replies, "you're really trying to go back to juvey or die trying."

CHAPTER 8

Hakeem

As Hakeem and Andrew get to school, they make their way through campus, when Amber texts him, "where are you? It's been two periods and I still haven't seen you!"

"Meet me by the café." He replies.

Andrew leans over to read the text and shakes his head. "Damn homie, we didn't pass three classrooms yet and she's already pulling your leash."

Hakeem laughs as he pushes his shoulder. "Don't you have some young pussy to find?"

"Please, I don't find them, they find me! It all comes with being the alpha male."

Amber was standing in front of the cafeteria with her best friend Emira. The two were wearing identical clothes. A white tee shirt with tight spandex that emphasis the girl's legs and booties. Amber and Emira are the popular girls in school, and Emira alone is known to be the head of the fashion police.

"There goes hubby." Emira says to Amber pointing at Hakeem.

Andrew jumps in front of him "here I am Emira! Even sexier up close!"

"You wish!" She replies, curling her hair with her finger, ignoring his advances.

"Emira you know Drew is the coolest white boy you know!" Hakeem responds for him.

"Not with that Tony the tiger t-shirt he's wearing!" She replies covering her mouth. Both Emira and Amber started laughing. Hakeem couldn't help but laugh too.

"Fuck all three of ya'll." Andrew says brushing his shoulder.

"Whoa I know what you guys had for breakfast." Amber says as they got closer.

"I got crumbs on me?" Hakeem replies, smelling his breath then wiping his lips.

"No, you know what I mean. Don't be silly." She replies with her hand on her hips rolling her eyes. Hakeem shakes his head, then gives her a kiss. "How many times do I have to tell you to stop smoking!" She pokes him. "You're better than that."

"You tell him girl!" Emira cheers her on. "You don't want to be like these smoked out college kids."

"Walk me to class," Amber puts her arms around Hakeem's.

"Let's go." He replies.

As they turned and left Andrew with Emira, Amber says to him, "this is our last year of high school, I don't want to sound like a bitch, but you really can't be doing stuff like this. We're this close to being free. Let's not mess it up by doing dumb shit."

"You know I only smoke on occasions, this is our last first day of school, that's kind of an occasion for me babe."

She takes out a folder with several pieces of paper and shows it to him. He looks at the papers and her with a puzzled expression. "These are the schools we will be applying for." She smiles.

As he shuffles through the papers he feels his phone vibrate. He takes his phone out to see who's calling and it's his mom. He puts his phone on silent then back in his pocket. "Damn these are a lot of schools." He looks back at her.

"You think that's a lot?"

He holds all the papers in the air. "I'm not going to answer that question. Not to mention three of these schools are mainly for fashion." She takes the papers back and puts them in her bag.

As they approach her classroom, she faces him and says, "we'll talk about this later." They peck lips and she walks inside her class.

He takes out his phone again and sees three missed calls from his mom. "Why is she tripping?" He thinks to himself. Instead of calling her back, he texts her saying, "I fed the dog before I left to school." Which he has no memory of doing. He continues to walk down the hallway toward his classroom.

"Look who finally showed up to school." Taryn walks up from behind him.

"Did I miss anything special?"

"No." She smiles.

Two of the school's toughest jocks, Chris and Samson walk by the two in the hallway. Chris is Taryn's ex-boyfriend. They've kept an on again off again relationship through their sophomore and junior years of high school.

"Taryn come to the locker room with me, I need some good luck for tonight's game!" Chris says as he grabs her by the arm.

"Get lost you pig!" She struggles pulling her arm back.

Hakeem turns around and pushes him, "she said leave her alone Chris!"

"Oh, aren't you the perfect gentleman." Chris replies sarcastically walking up to him.

Despite how muscular Chris is, Hakeem doesn't back down. "Why don't you try pulling my arm and see what happens?"

"Look who became Mr. Tough guy over the summer." Chris smirks at him then nods his head at Samson. Samson walks over to him and pulls his arm. As Hakeem turns to face Samson, Chris lands a left hook to his eye, picks him up and slams him on the floor.

As they begin to jump him, Taryn tries her hardest to break it up, but her presence at the moment means nothing. Finally, after several seconds' security guards come to separate them. The security guards seat the students on opposite sides of the dean's office. Hakeem looks in the mirror that was on the wall next to him, and notices his shiny new black eye. "I can't believe this," He sighs.

He looks in the other room and sees teachers laughing with the jocks writing them hall passes to get back to class. When he takes out his phone, he sees four messages from Amber saying, "I'm going to kill you," and seven more missed calls from his mom. As he goes to call his mother, she coincidentally runs inside of the dean's office crying.

"Mom?" He looks at her puzzled. "What are you doing here?

What's wrong? Why are you crying?"

The whole office gets quiet, even the jocks and the teachers in the other room couldn't help, but look. She grabs him and hugs him tight. "It's your dad." She sobs. "He died baby!"

"What?" he asks, looking at her in disbelief. The room is so quiet you could hear the clock on the wall click.

"He and uncle Jason got into an accident!" She continued.

Tears begin rolling down his face. "Let's go home." He says as he hugs her.

As they get in the car, he stares at his phone. He decides to call Isaiah, but there is no answer.

CHAPTER 9

Isaiah

Ruben drives around the neighborhood where the laundromat is, three times. "Are you sure you really want to do this?"

Isaiah bites his thumb nail, as he looks out of the window. "I got to get this money and leave town."

"Where will you go though?" Ruben looks at him in the rear-view mirror, puzzled. "What should I tell your pops when he comes back?"

"I'm not sure yet and nothing, tell him nothing." He puts his hand down. "As a matter of fact." He lifts his head back up. "Just pull over, I'm going to holla at you later."

Ruben pulls over to the corner Isaiah points to, and lets him out. "Good luck bro." The two exchange fist pumps.

Isaiah gets out of the car and walks up the street. As he gets closer to the laundromat, his heart starts beating faster. When he approaches the door, he takes a deep breath and walks inside, then continues to the backroom. The first half of the store is a laundry mat, and the backroom held illegal lottery.

Two other people were in the back with the owner Vinny. Vinny looks like your typical jailbird. Tattoos on his hand, neck and face. He was six feet tall, with jail weight still on his body. Vinny recognizes Isaiah immediately from the streets, and calls him over.

"What's good?" Isaiah asks, walking up to him.

"You got some balls roaming the streets after what happened last night."

His knowledge of last night shocks Isaiah. "What happened last night? I don't know what you're talking about." He replies in denial.

"The streets talk, and I'm usually the first to hear." Vinny snickers.

He looks Vinny in the eyes and shakes his head. "Give me change for a hundred, I got a couple of numbers I want to play."

"Anything for our hoods most wanted."

That comment makes Isaiah give him a doubtful look. Vinny smirks, then turns around to open the safe, that was in the cabinet against the wall behind the desk. As soon as he turns around, Isaiah wastes no time pulling out his jammed gun. "I hope I won't have to pull the trigger, I'm fucked if I do." He thinks to himself.

"The bruises on your face tells a story." Vinny continues. "Now I don't mind putting money in my pockets, so don't take this the wrong way but being here may not be the brightest choice, you shouldn't let your destiny be left up for grabs." He finally opens the safe and there were stacks of hundred dollar bills in rubber bands inside large zip lock bags with additional fifties, twenties and tens placed loosely.

Isaiah walks up to him and puts the gun to the back of his head. "You're right, I'm taking my destiny in my own hands!"

"Oh shit, you really are a dumb mother fucker!" The other two people in the room pull out shotguns behind him and aim them at his back.

"Fuck!" He says to himself. "I want everything! It's either the money or your life and if it's my life, your life is coming with me!" He shouts, applying pressure to the back of his head.

"Alright." Vinny replies, nodding his head.

"Hurry the fuck up! And you guys behind me put your shit down!"

"Lower your shit! You got it, you got it." Vinny replies, trying to remain calm.

Isaiah saw a blue book bag next to the table and picks it up. He throws it at him and yells, "fill that shit!"

"You know your days are numbered, right?" Vinny bends down holding the money, and starts to fill the book bag.

"Worry about your days, not mine." He grabs the bag out of his hands. "Now walk me to the front of the laundromat." The bag was so full, it could barely close. He looks over his shoulder and sees the men still grilling him. "He'll be back fellas." He smirks at them, as they make their way to the door. The two walk through the laundromat as everyone turns their head to watch.

Everybody that uses that laundry mat knows about the illegal activities. When the two get to the exit, Isaiah tells him to stop walking. He walks around him then says, "holla at you later," and backs out of the door, with the gun still aimed at his head.

Vinny stares at him with a look of vengeance as he walks out. As soon as Isaiah gets outside, he turns the corner and runs down the street, cutting through a back alley behind another bodega. "Fuck! I'm going to kill that little boy!" Vinny shouts with rage.

Isaiah keeps running through allies trying to avoid main roads, until he spots a Chinese store. He calls a cab to meet him there and orders food in the mean time.

He walks to a booth and sits down. He takes the bookbag off and puts it under the table. When he opens it, he tries to estimate how much money he has stolen. He rips one zip lock bag and takes a hundred-dollar bill out of the stack, but as soon as he closes the bag, two officers walk through the door. He silently panics.

They walk pass the booth without looking at him, and suddenly the reality of his crime sets in. As they placed their order, the cab shows up in front of the store and honks. Without hesitation he runs out and jumps in the cab.

With nowhere to go he assumes the cops had to have left his house by now, so he decides to go home to pack a few things. As they approach the apartment buildings, he looks around to make sure the neighborhood was clear of cops and his enemies, then pays the driver and gets out the cab.

Isaiah runs upstairs to his apartment and notices the door knob to his front door is broken. When he goes inside, he is shocked to see the whole apartment trashed. He shakes his head as he grabs a carryon bag hanging from the closet.

He lays it out on the floor and dumps the money from one bag into the other, then runs into his bedroom and changes into random clothes he sees lying around. He puts the jammed gun back in his pants and grabs three pairs of shirts and jeans to cover the money.

He takes a stack of hundreds out then closes his bag. He goes to his father's room and places it under his bed. When he gets on his knees to put it under the bed, he notices a wooden stake laying in the middle of the floor.

"What the fuck?" He thinks to himself. He shakes his head and leaves the money next to it.

As he walks back to the living room for his bag, he notices a red light blinking on the answering machine. "You have two new messages." The automatic machine voice says.

"Isaiah baby, it's grandma." He could hear the sadness and unlevel pattern in her voice. "Your dad and uncle William died in an accident this morning." She paused. "I'm going to be heading over to Peekskill tonight. That's where the funeral will be held. Pack your things, I'm sending someone to pick you up tomorrow. You're going to be staying with me. Call me when you get this message baby. I love you."

"End of first message." He stands over the machine stunned, then slowly walks to the sofa and sits on the edge.

"What the fuck?" He says to himself staring at the floor.

"Yo Zay, its Keem, I know it's been a minute since we've talked. I tried calling you on your cell, but I guess you have a new number. I just found out about our dads, I don't know if anybody reached out to you yet but feel free to call me. I know nobody's down there with you, but if you could find your way up here, our door is open. Hit me cuz."

He looks at the machine for a couple of seconds then walks back to it and deletes both messages. He grabs his bag and walks out. Still on alert, he looks both ways before exiting the building. "If the cops find out I have family in Peekskill they might follow me up there." He thinks to himself. "Shit I wouldn't mind seeing Keem, but no way I'm living with that old dirt bag. I don't even know why she would even suggest that. She must have been around people."

In no time, he was in front of the fence in the back-parking lot. He throws his bag over the fence, then jumps on the garbage can to hop over. When he lands, the dogs were already on guard ready to chase him. With seconds to spare before being dog lunch, he grabs his bag and runs.

He walks up to Tyriek's house and pounds on the door. "Why are you knocking like the cops? What did I tell you about calling before coming!" Tyriek opens the door disturbed.

"Let me in man!" He brushes into him and enters the house. Tyriek shuts the door as he walks passed him. "Roll up some weed, I need your help." He drops his bag on the sofa and sits next to it, then takes out the jammed gun and rests it on the counter.

Tyriek gives him a crazy look. "You still have that! I already heard what happened to Leo, you're hot in the streets! Why would you bring that gun back here?"

He scratches his head. "I thought you could fix it or something. I don't know, why would you give me a gun that doesn't work?"

"You can't be serious. Go outside and stash that somewhere!" Isaiah walks outside just in time to miss a cop car drive by. He is too paranoid to walk anywhere, so he just tosses the gun in the bushes in front of the house. He walks back inside the house as Tyriek lights his joint. "There's only so much I could do for you." He continued.

"This is my last favor. I need a ride out of town."

CHAPTER 10

Hakeem

A week later.

"I can't believe today is the funeral." Taryn says staring out the window, as Andrew parks his car in the church parking lot.

"I know, I can't believe it's been a week already. I feel bad for his family, losing both like that. You know, I lost my uncle once. I cried for weeks, still do." She looks at him and shakes her head as she unbuckles her seatbelt. "Has anyone heard from Isaiah yet?" He asks, unbuckling his seatbelt.

"Hakeem said, when his grandma's friends went to pick him up he was gone. His apartment was trashed too. I think there's a rumor that's he's on the run from the cops." She says looking at herself in the mirror.

"Really? I guess that would explain the cops by the entrance." He replies getting out the car to fix his attire. "Damn Isaiah really became a badass." He smirks, then closes the door.

"I don't think he's that bad." She replies getting out of the car. "He used to pretend to be gangster, but I could see right through him. He must have gotten up with the wrong crowd or something." She walks around the car to meet him on the other side.

"I don't remember the last time Hakeem even mentioned Isaiah. Are they still cool?" He asks as they make their way to the funeral.

"He has his reasons, you know they used to be like brothers when we were younger. I guess they just grew apart." She fixes his collar at the door then follows him in.

"Do you want any water?" Amber whispers to Hakeem as she places her hands on his.

"No, I'm fine." He replies, staring at the two closed coffins. He was sitting in the front row with Amber, Camille and his grandmother. He turns his head just in time to see Taryn and Andrew enter the Church. They both wave at him as they grab a seat in the back row. He nods back at them and takes another look around the room for Isaiah, but he was still nowhere to be found.

When the pastor calls people up for eulogies, Camille is too emotional to stand in front of the congregation, so his grandmother goes first. As she makes her way to the podium, someone's cell phone began ringing. The volume on the phone, grabbed everyone's attention.

The gentleman stands up embarrassed, and tries to slide in between people's legs to get out of the row. Hakeem takes a good look at him, but doesn't recognize him. He stares at him, from his head down to the cell phone he was holding. The man was wearing a ring that resembles the ring his father wears and for a second, he thought it belonged to him. It was a gold band with a pyramid in the middle and Egyptian scriptures written around it.

As the man gets to the end of the row, the last person sitting, stands up to let him out. The two exchange a handshake that exposes his ring, and he notices that they are identical. Suspicious, Hakeem quickly looks at another person sitting on the opposite side of them, and sees he is sporting the same ring. "Who are these people?" He thinks to himself.

When Hakeem looks away from the man's hand, he notices the man was looking back at him. Not only him, but every other person that seems to be friends of his father. Hakeem turns his attention back to his grandmother, trying not to make anything of it. As she was thanking everyone that came, he notices a chain hanging from her neck. A ruby pendant stuck out of her shirt collar. It was nothing special, but resembled something you would catch a witch wearing in a Salem movie.

She puts on a fake smile as she looks around the room, then starts telling a story about both Jason and William's childhood. She spoke about the many ways they became closer once their older sister Grace died in a fire. While his grandmother was talking, he looks down at her hand and notices she was wearing the same ring. When she finishes, she sits back down next to Camille.

The pastor calls Hakeem up next to share a few words. When he gets to the podium, he observes everyone that was sitting before him, and realizes the only people that didn't have the ring were his mother, his friends and himself.

He looks down and begins his eulogy. "My father was a great man." He pauses then looks up. "So, was my uncle Jason. I don't have much family so I appreciate the ones I do have and cherish the moments we shared together. Growing up, my father gave me a lot of speeches, and encouraged any silly dream I had telling me there's nothing a Exalus can't do!" The congregation laughs. "I told him I wanted to travel the world after high school, to write poetry and short stories about how beautiful and ugly the world is. His response was, the world is yours and there better not be one story I don't send back home for him to read."

He looks at his father casket and continues, "you were my biggest fan and I thank you for that. I wouldn't be who I am today if it wasn't for you." As the congregation applauds, he thanks everyone for coming, then sits back down next to Amber and his mother, and watches his father's friends go next to give their eulogies. The rings still have Hakeem feeling suspicious, so he pays close attention to every word they have to say.

He knew his uncle and grandmother had the same ring as his father, and always figured it was a family heirloom, but with everyone in the room wearing it, he wasn't sure if these people were coworkers or gang members.

What made him even more suspicious, is that everyone who had something to say couldn't thank both his father and uncle enough for saving their lives. They never got into details with their stories, but still managed to get their appreciation out. As much as Hakeem thought he knew his father, it wasn't until this moment that he realized he didn't know him at all.

The pastor went back to the podium to dismiss the church. "We will be bringing the Exalus brothers to the cemetery now. That's where the second part of the funeral will be held. Will everyone rise and let the family go first. The following rows may follow. The reception will be held at Camille Exalus house, the wife of William Exalus. The address is at the bottom of your pamphlet."

As Hakeem walks down the aisle to leave, he taps Taryn who is sitting at the end of her row. "Ride with me and Amber." He says, she nods her head and gets behind Amber. He greets Andrew as the three walk out behind his mother and grandmother. Once outside, they head towards Amber's car which isn't parked far. Amber holds his hand as they walk "Thank you for coming Taryn, I really appreciate it." He keeps his head faced down, until they reach the car door.

"You know I'm always here for you. I'm going to miss your father too." Taryn replies, but can't help seeing the two holding hands.

The two let go of each other to get in the car. Once seated, Amber looks at him and asks, "do you see how many love ones your father and uncle have. There's nothing better than leaving this world loved."

He looks at her and smiles a little. "You're right."

As Amber starts following the hearse, Taryn looks out of the window and gets lost in her thoughts.

CHAPTER 11

Vinny

"It's been a week and not one of you have seen Isaiah yet? Vinny asks, as he exhales smoke from his cigar.

"No, we got guys on every corner too! I think he got out of town faster than we thought he would."

Vinny grins at his henchmen. "Let's go pay a visit to this kid Leo."

Four cars park at Leo's house within the hour. Three men get out of each car including Vinny. Dimitri and three other guys are standing outside the house. When he and his crew walk on Leo's property, the guys around Dimitri grab their bats and wait.

"We have a mutual problem!" Vinny announces.

"We do?" Dimitri replies, puzzled.

"The dread head."

Dimitri looks him up and down along with the guys he was with. "Follow me."

When they enter the house, Leo is sitting on the couch watching T.V. He has a cast on his leg and is wearing a shoulder brace. Dimitri walks up to him and says, "homie right here wants Zay's head too. By the looks of it, he got goons."

Vinny walks up to Leo after and says, "let's talk business."

"I've been trying for two days! Dude really is nowhere to be found." Leo tries to fix himself on the couch.

"Who does he hang out with?"

"I've been told he chills with this fake drug dealer named Tyriek, but nobody has seen him in the streets lately either." Dimitri adds, crossing his arm.

"Show me where he lives!"

Vinny and his crew follows Dimitri along with his crew to Tyriek's house. The house looks like no one has been home for a while, with all the mail stuffed in the mailbox. They walk up the driveway and ring the doorbell, but there is no answer. Some of the men circle the house to see if there is a window or a side door open, but no such luck. After ten minutes of waiting, Vinny tells his men to get back in the car because they have money to make. As he walks away from the door, he notices the muzzle of a gun sticking out the bottom of the bushes. He kneels and picks it up. It is the same gun Isaiah used to rob him. When he shows Dimitri, Dimitri confirms that it is the same gun that was used on Leo.

CHAPTER 12

Hakeem

"I'm happy all these strangers are finally leaving the house." Hakeem says to his mom as she stands over the sink in the kitchen.

She looks up surprised she wasn't the only one in the kitchen. "Tell me about it, I'm grateful and all, but if you ask me, I would have thought your father and uncle Jason were a part of a secret society, the way their friends carry themselves."

He shakes his head with a smirk on his face and he sits down. "You know what's crazy, I feel the same way."

"Mrs. Exalus! I insist you let me wash these dishes for you, you should be with the rest of your family and friends." Amber says, interrupting the two as she enters the kitchen.

Camille turns around and smiles. "Amber you're too sweet. Thank you, but its fine."

"Please, let me help!" She begs again.

Camille looks at her for a few seconds, then nods her head. She dries her hands and thanks her as she walks out of the kitchen. Amber opens the draw in front of the sink and takes out a pair of rubber gloves to wash the dishes.

Hakeem walks up behind her and kisses her on the cheek. "Thank you for being here for me through this, you really showed me your true colors."

"I've always showed you my true colors. Always!" She kisses him on the lips.

"I probably won't be going to school tomorrow. I need another day to really grasp onto reality."

"I was kind of hoping you weren't going to school tomorrow." She leans against his chest.

"Mm, sounds like you have something planned up your sleeve."

"Well we are seniors, so missing one day shouldn't be that bad. I was thinking about ditching, and spending my day here with you." She gives him an adorable puppy face.

He laughs. "What time would you like to come over tomorrow?"

"I was thinking about spending the night upstairs with you to be honest."

A warm feeling fills his gut as he kisses her. Smirking, he whispers "I sleep naked."

She burst out laughing, until his grandmother walks in. The two separate.

"Hey grandma, how are you holding up?" Hakeem asks trying not to look suspicious.

"I'm at peace." She replies, then approaches Amber. "Where's your manners Keem? You must be my grandson's girlfriend!" She extends her hand out.

"It's a pleasure to meet you, my name is Amber." She shakes her hand.

"Likewise. Hakeem's father mentioned you to me. I hope you've been keeping him out of trouble, he's too good looking to be walking around with bruises on his face."

"I've been trying my best, and I agree, he is." Amber smiles looking at Hakeem.

Grandma smiles too, then faces him. "May I have a word with you in private for a second?"

"Yea, of course." The two walk out of the kitchen and into the hallway. On the way to the front door, Hakeem is greeted by one of his father's friends, a tall skinny Asian man with big glasses sitting on top of his nose, with a military haircut.

"Hey, your Hakeem, right? My name is Aaron, I was a close friend of your fathers, my condolence." He reaches his hand out for a handshake. Hakeem gives him a half smile then shakes his hand. He glances down at his hand and sees him wearing the same ring as everyone else.

"Tell me something." He pauses. "What's up with the ring? Is it supposed to mean something, or was there a sale at sears? I can't help but notice everyone has this same exact style, including my dad."

Aaron smiles as he turns over his hand, and looks at the ring. "This old thing? It's just something given to hero's."

"Hero's?" Hakeem repeats sarcastically. He looks back at his grandma then gives him a perplexed look. "Thank you again for coming." He then continues to walk outside, alongside his grandma.

She sits down on the bench in front of the house. She pats the seat next to her, as Hakeem stands looking at her. When he does sit, she clears her throat and begins speaking. "There's a lot of things you don't know about our family. Things we've kept sheltered from you, until we thought the time would be right."

"Are you a drug lord grandma?" He raises his eyebrow at her.

She laughs and shakes her head. "No. I'm actually something much bigger than that, and so are you. I've noticed how suspicious you've become. And I want to tell you everything, but I shouldn't until we find Isaiah. He's just as special as you are, but unfortunately a little more fragile than you. His home has officially been broken. It's important that we find him before the cops do! I need you and your friends to go out and look for him tomorrow."

"What makes you think he'll be up here?" He looks at her puzzled.

"Your father wasn't the only one who was buried today." She pats his knee, then walks back inside. After a couple of seconds, he gets up and walks inside too. Little did they know, Isaiah was in a parked car up the street, watching them.

"When are you going to man up and go see your fam bro? The cops didn't even follow them home. We been on the road for a week now!" Tyriek says as he inhales the joint.

"Can you stop crying. You're going home with fifteen thousand. And you don't have to spend anything until we go our separate ways. Just do me a favor and stick around until I figure out where I want to settle. You act like you have something special waiting for you back home. You don't have any girl's bro!" Isaiah grabs the joint out of his hand.

"Speak for yourself."

"Let's go back to the hotel before we get spotted." He inhales the joint. Tyriek starts the car and drives away.

"There you are!" Taryn grabs Hakeem by his arm. "I got something for you." She whispers in his ear. She slips a bag of weed into his pocket and gives him a kiss on the cheek. "Thank me later. I have to bring Justina home, she has an exam in the

47

morning." He gives her a hug then greets her sister Justina who is standing beside her. "I wish I could stay with you and the family."

"It's cool, Amber is spending the night."

"Check you out." She snickers, with a surprised facial expression.

He nods his head not noticing the jealousy in her tone. "Can I ask you for a favor?"

"Anything."

"My grandma thinks Isaiah is going to make his way up here. Tomorrow can you keep an eye out for him, and call me if by any chance you see him."

"Yea, I wasn't planning on going to school anyways. After I drop my sister off tomorrow, I'll pick up Andrew and roam the streets."

"Thank you." He gives her another hug and a kiss on the cheek, then walks away.

A couple of hours pass until the house is completely empty of all guests. "Amber are you sure your parents are ok with you staying?" Camille asks, standing in front of Hakeem's bedroom door.

"Yea, they're ok with it." She replies, walking out of the bathroom wearing his t-shirt and basketball shorts.

"Ok then, if you need anything I'm down the hall."

"I should be the one saying that." Amber places her hand on her arm. Camille grabs her hand and smiles.

"Ok mom, can I have my girlfriend back?" Hakeem interrupts sarcastically as he walks out of his room.

They both look at him and laugh. "You kids be safe. I don't want

Amber's parents coming here with lawsuits and drama." Camille lets go of Amber and points her finger at him.

Hakeem grabs Amber closer and replies, "nothing bad is going to happen mom, cut it out."

"Make sure of it! I'm going to bed now, goodnight kids." She turns around and heads to her room.

"Good night." Both Hakeem and Amber reply. The two go back inside of his room and sit on his bed. He pulls out the bag of weed from his pocket, before sliding his jeans off.

"You're seriously about to smoke now?" She looks at him puzzled.

"Yea, Taryn gave this to me as a gift. It's going to help me sleep easier." He opens the bag and sniffs it, then grabs some white paper out of the draw next to his bed and sits back next to her. As he tries to unravel the white paper, she puts her hands over his, and gives him a kiss.

"You won't need that to help you sleep tonight." She kisses him again and takes his shirt off. He drops everything on the floor and gets comfortable on his bed. "Do you think your mom will hear us?" She whispers in his ear.

He reaches for his remote and turns the volume on the T.V a little louder, then whispers back, "no."

CHAPTER 13

The alarm goes off, and the radio seems louder than usual. Hakeem rolls over and turns it off. As soon as he leans back over, Amber is already awake, kissing his neck. She starts rubbing on his body and they waste no time going for a morning round. After they finish, she gives him a kiss and rests on his chest.

"I don't ever want to leave your arms," She looks into his eyes.

"I don't ever want to let you go." He replies.

There is a sudden knock on the room door, panicking, him and Amber starts looking for their clothes on the floor.

"Hakeem, me and your grandma have some errands to take care of. I don't know what time we'll be back, there should be left over food in the refrigerator." Camille says, on the other side of the door.

"Ok mom, you and grandma be safe!" Hakeem replies, looking at the door waiting patiently.

"You too, love you."

"Love you too mom." Both Hakeem and Amber wait until they hear her footsteps going downstairs, before they jump back into bed.

CHAPTER 14

Isaiah

"Yo Zay, you do know I'm not on the run with you, right? I don't want to sound grimy, but today I'm going back home with or without you." Tyriek says, as he walks into Isaiah's half of the hotel. The two stay in a double room hotel on the other side of town.

"Whatever, I don't want to hear your bitching voice anyways."

"I can't lie, your fam lives in a nice town. Its quiet up here."

"I know. It's different here then back in the hood. Let's go to a food spot for some breakfast than check the mall out. I need to go shopping." Isaiah says as he gets out of bed.

CHAPTER 15

Taryn

"Taryn if you don't wake up, I'm going to dump water on your face!" Justina screams.

"Are you serious? Its morning already?" She cries.

"Yea its morning. I told you to be up 20 minutes ago, hurry up and get dressed so you can drop me at school." Taryn wipes her eyes and crawls out of bed. She walks to the bathroom to wash her face. As she puts the toothpaste on her toothbrush, Justina walks in on her. "I'm actually surprised you remembered to be home to bring me to school."

"What's that supposed to mean?" She looks at her, then starts brushing her teeth.

"I'm just saying, yesterday was Hakeem's dad funeral. I know how close you two are, I figured you would have forgotten about me and went back."

She rinses her mouth, then continues to brush her teeth. "Well I didn't forget, and his girlfriend stayed over."

Justina laughs a little. "So, he kicked you to the curb basically?" She tilts her head to the side.

Taryn gives her a dirty look. "He didn't kick me to the curb. That's my best friend and nobody's going to change that!" She rinses her mouth again then puts her toothbrush down. She walks pass her out of the bathroom and goes back to her room.

"You two are just weird, I thought best friends were always supposed to make the best couples." Justina continues to follow her.

"You're about three words away from taking the bus Justina. You know we're just friends. Now let me get dressed in peace, I want to stop at The Shack to pick up breakfast before I drop you off."

CHAPTER 16

Isaiah

"You see that ass?" Tyriek asks, as they get out the car to head toward The Shack. "Goddamn, these girls up here are healthy." The two walk inside, and it is full of teens hanging out. The line to order food isn't long though and the two join the line, while admiring how cool it is the kids up here have a real hang out spot.

Tyriek notices a cute girl in front of them on line. He taps Isaiah's arm and says, "watch this." "Hey, what's good beautiful, can I holla at you?"

The girl turns around, it is Emira. She looks both him and Isaiah up and down. "I never seen you here before. Ew, are you a freshman? Hell no, you can't holla at me! You need to take care of yourself, before you even think about talking to me!"

Isaiah starts laughing when he sees the frustration on his face. Tyriek loses his cool. "Your ass is too flat to be acting bougie with me!"

Her face turns red, causing Isaiah to laugh harder than before. "Not as flat as your pockets, you broke bum! I don't ever want to see you again!" She turns around with her arms crossed.

After Isaiah finishes laughing, he taps Tyriek's shoulder and whispers, "watch this." "Hey, I think we got off on the wrong foot, my friend doesn't deal with rejection very well. Let me buy you breakfast." He pulls out a stack of hundreds from his pocket and taunts it.

Her eyes light up with joy when she sees his money. She looks back at him and gives him a smile. "What's your name again?"

"You can call me Zay. Now let's get some food."

Tyriek shakes his head at the sight of them turning their back to

54

him. The two speak the whole time the food is being made and even after the food is ready. As they walk out of The Shack, he gives her his phone so she can put her number in it. "Hit me up, I might have some time in my schedule for you." She smiles, showing off her dimples.

Isaiah walks over to the car where Tyriek is waiting, and laughs. "What's the point of having money if you don't know how to talk to bitches?" He shakes his head.

Taryn

"Why must you drive like an old lady?" Justina complains, as Taryn drives into The Shack parking lot.

"You're going to make it to class, just hurry up and get our food. I already ordered it." Taryn stops her car on the side of The Shack, as she hands Justina money for the food, the side of her eyes catches Isaiah opening the passenger side door to a car parked ahead of her. Her mouth drops, she quickly jumps out the car, mistakenly putting it in neutral instead of park.

"Are you trying to kill me!" Justina screams, as the car keeps rolling. Taryn jumps back into the car and presses on the break to put the car in park. By the time she looks back up, the car Isaiah was in had already left.

"Fuck! Where is he going?" She asks herself.

"Stop being thirsty, whoever that was, was just talking to Emira. There goes another man that left you for a prettier girl."

She looks at Justina and replies, "I really fucking hate you. Go get our stupid food!" As Justina walks inside The Shack, Taryn walks up to Emira who is still standing by the entrance. "Emira, I know this is random, but I need that boy's number you were just talking to."

"Are you serious? Do you hear yourself right now?" Emira snaps her neck back.

"I know him, it's not like that. He's in trouble right now and I need to speak to him."

"Oh, he's a bad boy too." Emira smirks after hearing that and walks away. "I'm not Amber sweetie, you won't be best friends with my potential husband."

"No way, you're outside arguing with Emira for a random guy's number." Justina interrupts, walking out of The Shack. "How embarrassing! I can't believe you're my sister." She shakes her head and walks back to the car.

Taryn sighs as she looks to the sky, then follows her back to her car. Once seated, she calls Hakeem on her phone.

"Since when do you know how to cook?" Hakeem asks Amber as he finishes the scramble eggs on her plate.

"It's not every day we wake up together, but I'm going to cook for you more often." His phone interrupts the two. Amber looks at his screen before he gets a chance to. "It's your friend Taryn. Why is she calling you so early?"

Scratching his head, he suddenly remembers about Isaiah. "I had her do me a favor." He picks up his phone and answers, "hey, what's the word?"

"I just missed your juvenile cousin literally by ten seconds." Taryn replies, after she swallows a gulp of juice.

"What? Seriously? Where?" He replies, with his back erect.

"At The Shack. I saw him leaving when I arrived. If I wasn't with my sister I would have chased him down."

"Damn, any idea where he might of went?"

"I don't know, but Emira might. I think they exchanged numbers. I tried getting it out of her, but she was being a bitch about it and left."

Hakeem looks at Amber, who seems to be eavesdropping on the conversation. "Stay close to your phone, I might have a solution. Thank you again." He ends the call.

When Taryn finally gets to school, Justina gets out the car and says, "if I fail because I'm late, mom is going to kill you." Then slams the door.

"Whatever." Taryn rolls her eyes, then takes out her phone and texts Andrew, "be ready in five minutes, I'm kidnapping you."

Hakeem

"Why are you looking at me like that?" Amber asks wiping her mouth.

He rubs her shoulder gently and replies "I need a favor."

"Oh, now you need my help, after your best friend failed you." She replies sarcastically.

"Not even babe." His hand drops from her shoulder down to her hand. "It just a long story."

"Make it short then." She looks him in his eyes.

"My grandma wants me to find my cousin Isaiah, and Taryn is helping me."

"I wish you would've told me from the beginning." She shakes her head and takes her hand back. "I would have helped find him too."

"I know you would have, that's why I didn't say anything." He replies then kisses her cheek. "Well it's actually not too late for you to help. Taryn says she saw him and Emira talking before he left The Shack."

"Emira is hooking up with a killer?" She interrupts him to ask.

"He's not a killer! He never killed anybody!"

"But he shot someone?"

He doesn't respond. She picks up her phone and calls Emira. "What's up girl, you didn't see my text last night?" Emira asks, answering the phone.

"I didn't, but listen. Tell me where Isaiah told you he was going." Amber cuts her off and gets straight to the point.

"Oh man, you want him too?" Emiras voice sounds offended. "I understood Taryn's thirsty ass, but you? You have a man."

"Can you calm down Emira, that boy is Hakeem's cousin. We need to find him."

Emira sighs. "I'm about to meet him at the Larimar mall in 20 minutes."

"Me and Hakeem are going there now. Don't tell him we're coming!" She ends the call and looks at him. "He's going to the mall."

"Yes!" He gets up from the table. "Let's grab some clothes and go." He grabs his phone on the way out the kitchen, and texts Taryn, "Larimar mall."

Isaiah

"How long do you think I'll be wanted for until the cops stop caring about me?" Isaiah asks Tyriek as they try on sneakers at

Foot Station.

"Truthfully, I don't know. I figured your dad's funeral would have been the best place to catch you and the fact they didn't means you might actually be safe in this town. They have no real reason to look for you up here anymore."

Isaiah nods his head and tells the employee he wants size 9.5 in the whole row.

"Bro, how is all of that plus my sneakers going to fit in my car?" Tyriek looks at him puzzled.

"Your leaving when we get to the hotel anyways. You could come back here on your way out of town." Isaiah had so many sneakers the store had to give him a pushing cart to put everything into, to walk out the mall. "Shorty from earlier said she's on her way to the mall." He says as he pushes the cart outside the store.

"So now I have to chaperone the two of you? The price of this job just went up!" The two sit down at the food court to rest for a little. Tyriek looks at him and asks, "do you even know how your dad died?"

Isaiah looks back at him and replies, "he and my uncle got in some kind of accident."

"It doesn't bother you that you don't know the real story yet?"

Isaiah raises his eyebrows at him, then looks away. A couple of minutes pass without them speaking, until Isaiah stands up and says, "let's put my stuff in the car."

The two take the elevator to the first floor. As they walk pass a couple of stores and make it to the middle of the first floor, they coincidently walk straight into Taryn and Andrew. The four look at each other for a couple of seconds in silence.

"So, the first thing you do when you come up here is rob Foot Station?" Taryn asks, with her hands on her hips.

"Check the receipts. Don't be mad because you can't afford a shopping spree." Isaiah replies with a smirk.

Tyriek looks at both of them, and asks him, "you know her?"

"Unfortunately," Isaiah looks Andrew up and down then back at her. "I'm disappointed in you. I always thought you would have end up with Hakeem, but here you are with Malibu's most wanted."

"Shut up, I'm not with him!" She barks back.

"Fuck you, I'm not Malibu's most wanted either. It's me Andrew."

"Andrew? Andrew?" Isaiah examines him. "Oh snap, check how you turned out." He nods his head.

"You should talk, Americas most wanted. You're coming with us." She whispers.

"Whoa, you're turning me in Taryn?" He gives her a stank face.

"Yea, to your grandma. She's been looking all over for you. She wants you to come back to Hakeem house."

"Why couldn't Hakeem get me himself, how did you even know I was here?" He asks, with a puzzled facial expression.

"I have my ways." Taryn smirks.

"That still doesn't answer my first question."

"I did come here to get you myself." Hakeem interrupts, as he and Amber walks toward them. There was a moment of silence as the two examined each other. "It's been a while Zay."

"Yea, it's been a while. What happened to your face?" Isaiah asks, continuing to look him up and down.

"Don't worry about it." Hakeem shrugs. "It still looks better than yours."

Isaiah smirks then faces Tyriek. "Grab my stuff from the hotel and bring it to Hakeem's house. I'm going to ride with them back."

"Finally!" He replies in joy.

"Check you out cuz, you upgraded to a higher class of pussy." Isaiah says to Hakeem examining Amber. Both Amber and Taryn look at him disgusted, while Andrew can't resist laughing.

"Zay if you're going to stay here or be around my friends and my girl, keep those ignorant comments to yourself!"

"Come on cuz. I at least said what Malibu over there was thinking too."

Everyone heads to the exit, but before they get to the door, they are confronted by some unwanted friends. "Can you believe this?" Chris says to Samson as they approach everyone.

"I almost felt sorry for beating you up the day you found out about your father's death, but it hasn't even been a week yet, and your using his insurance money on sneakers. You deserved that ass whooping. And another!" Samson says to Hakeem.

Isaiah examines both Chris and Samson. "Are you serious Keem? These are the little bitches that been giving you problems?" He let's go of his cart and posts up next to Hakeem.

"Who are you supposed to be? Whoopi Goldberg?" Chris asks, then starts laughing.

"No, he thinks he's Booker T!" Samson replies, laughing even harder.

"You know what, just hand those sneakers over and we won't give you a hard time today." Chris says to the both of them and smiles.

Amber tries to stop Hakeem, but it's too late. "If you could take on the two of us, you could take the shoes off our feet's too." He steps forward.

"Is that so?" Chris rubs his hands.

Isaiah looks behind him at Taryn and says, "make sure all of my sneakers are in the car by the time we're finished." She nods her head. As he turns his head, Samson charges at Hakeem, but he misses both punches. Hakeem picks him up in the air and slams him on the floor.

Chris runs up to Isaiah and throws a right jab. Isaiah dodges it and puts him in a headlock. After a couple of seconds of trying to break free from it, he falls asleep in his arm. Hakeem puts his knees on Samson chest and starts hitting him, but he blocks his face using his forearms.

"I don't know where you come off trying to disrespect me, but this ends now!" Hakeem stands up and kicks him in the stomach. Isaiah looks over at Taryn and Amber who are running to the car with the last of the bags, while Andrew and Tyriek watch them from the side and look out for security.

Isaiah stops Hakeem by grabbing his arm to leave. He nods his head then follow him as all four of them run out the mall.

Both Amber and Taryn's car arrive at Hakeem's house at the same time. "I still can't believe what I just saw! That shit was fucking crazy!" Andrew says as they walk up the stairs to Hakeem's house door.

"It wasn't that serious white boy." Isaiah replies then stops to admire Hakeem's house up close, while everyone is carrying his bags. Everyone carries between three to five bags each. "Are you sure your mom is cool with me being here?" He asks Hakeem with an unsure facial expression.

"Positive! Your family Zay, we even cleaned out a room for you." Hakeem leads everyone inside and shows him his new room. It is upstairs between his and his mother's room. Everyone drops Isaiah bags next to his bed.

"I think I should go home, you two have some catching up to do." Amber turns to Hakeem to say.

"You don't have too."

"I know, but I feel I should." She kisses him and waves to the rest.

"Now that she is gone, can we get high?" Andrew asks, breaking the silence.

Isaiah laughs. "Check you out slim shady! You guys smoke?"

"Do we smoke?" Andrew huffs sticking his thumb out.

"I still have your gift from last night too Taryn, let me go get that." Hakeem leads Andrew and Taryn out of Isaiah's room.

Not too long after, Tyriek drives up to the house honking. Isaiah walks outside to gather his remaining things. As he gets in the car he opens the bag which holds the rest of his money and asks, "everything is here right?"

"I'm mad you have to ask." Tyriek shakes his head.

"I met you in juvey bro, don't look at me like you're a saint. I have to ask." Isaiah continues to count his money, then hands him a handful of hundreds. "Make sure you break Ruben off some of this. Good looks on everything Ty!" The two share a handshake.

"No doubt, just be safe out here."

"When my name is off the radar, I'll be back in the hood." Isaiah replies, closing his bag.

Tyriek laughs and shakes his head, "you're probably coming back for Erica not me."

Isaiah laughs too. "You got jokes, I'm going to catch you though." He gets out the car and watches him drive away.

Hakeem meets Isaiah at the house door and pats him on the back. "Welcome home cuz." He tries reaching for his bag, but he tightens his grip on it.

"I got this."

The four sit in Hakeem's backyard, smoke joints and eat left over food from the reception, the day before.

"How did you get Emira's number so fast? I've been trying to get with her since elementary school, and you got further then me all in one morning" Andrew asks Isaiah curious.

"How did you... That's how you guys found me!" Isaiah's eyes widen. "Eh, she's an airhead." He shrugs. "If you want girls like that, you have to step your swag up. Don't worry I'll sleep with her for you." He smirks, then looks at Taryn. "What's your story? If you're not with Justin Bieber here or my cousin, what are you doing with your life?"

"I'm not dating right now, I'm just focusing on my school work. You actually just beat up my ex 45 minutes ago."

"Oh, how unfortunate we had to meet that way. We could have been friends." Isaiah replies sarcastically, but looks disappointed.

"How did you get the money to buy all those sneakers?" She leans forward on her seat.

"Why do you want to know?" He leans back.

"Because, that money is obviously the reason you're on the run! And I want to know what you did."

Hakeem looks over at the two, ready to hear his answer.

"MY MONEY IS NOT THE REASON WHY I'M ON THE RUN. AND HOW I GOT IT, IS NONE OF YOUR BUSINESS!" HE PASSES THE JOINT TO ANDREW. "YOU KNOW WHAT GUYS, I'M HIGH AND TIRED. I'M GOING TO GO TAKE A NAP. KEEM WAKE ME UP WHEN GRANDMA COMES HOME." HE STANDS UP AND WALKS INSIDE.

CHAPTER 17

Tyriek

4 hours later

When Tyriek enters his driveway, he notices a bunch of random thugs standing outside of his house. He opens the car door and approaches them. "Are yawl lost? Cause yawl surely aren't here for me!"

"You're right, we're not here for you, but we're not lost." Vinny replies, walking down the house steps. Dimitri walks up to Tyriek and blindsides him with the end of a shotgun.

"Search him!" Dimitri shouts at his henchmens. One of them takes his keychain off him and tosses it to Vinny to open the house door. Three men carry him inside, while another two grab his shopping bags out of his car. When they get inside the house, they empty his pockets. One of the men empty the bag that contained all of his money.

"This money looks familiar!" Vinny says to him holding the stack of money to his face.

"All money looks the same! I don't know what you're talking about!" Tyriek pleas.

Vinny nods his head then punches him in the face. "I'm not here to play games! Where did that fuck boy pay you to bring him?"

"I don't know what you're talking about!"

"Give me the hammer!" He shouts at his henchman with his hand extended out. When he receives it, he swings it at him and hits him in the stomach. Tyriek cries out as he tries to crawl away.

Dimitri steps in front of him and kneels, "You know what else looks familiar Ty? This gun!" He waves the jammed gun in his face.

"I never seen that gun before. He looks away. "Why the fuck are you bringing me into this?" He screams, still holding his stomach.

"You brought yourself into this. Hiding his gun at your house, accepting money you knew wasn't his. You could've just been honest and took the straightforward way out, but you wanted to make things difficult." Vinny replies walking besides Dimitri.

Dimitri stands back up and shouts "ok boys, burn him and the house down!"

Both Dimitri and Vinny's henchmen grab gas containers from outside and pour it all over the house and on top of him. Completely trashing the house, some of the men find his weed stash and take it too as well as his tablet, laptop, and pills. Vinny walks over to him and hits him in the stomach with the hammer one more time. Everyone steps on him on their way out. Vinny stands at the door with a lighter in his hand and a mean mug on his face.

"Stop don't do this!" Tyriek cries out.

"Tell me the truth!" He flickers the light. "Where is he?"

Tyriek looks down as he wipes gasoline off his face. Vinny holds the lit lighter close to the ground to intimidate him. When he looks back up, he shakes his head and replies, "he's in New York!"

"Where in New York?" Vinny barks.

Tyriek shakes his head again, then replies, "Peekskill."

CHAPTER 18

Hakeem

"Alright grandma, Zay is here. Are you going to tell us the truth about our family now?" Hakeem asks, following his grandma into the guest room.

"I told you he wouldn't be hard to find." She smirks. "Let me just change my clothes and I'll meet you boys out back."

He goes upstairs to Isaiah's room and wakes him up.

"Isaiah! Look at you, all grown up! It's so good to see you again." Camille says giving him a hug in the middle of the hallway.

"It's nice to see you too auntie. Thank you for giving me a place to crash." He rubs her back with one hand.

"Don't mention it. Our house is your house. That's what family is for." She replies, grabbing both his shoulders and looking him in the eyes.

He nods his head and turns away to look inside Hakeem's room, "your friends left?" He asks him.

"Yea, they left some time ago."

"Well I'm going to let you boys be, I'll be in my room if anything." She gives Isaiah another hug, then leaves them.

The two nod their heads at her then walk downstairs. When they reach, their grandma is already waiting and standing in front of the guest room.

"Isaiah you're here!" She smiles. "You've grown so much since the last time I seen you. I see you still have dreads." She sounds displeased.

"Thank you. Yea they became a part of me." He uses his right hand to caress his hair.

She walks up to him and gives him a hug. "Can you boys come outside with me?" The two nod their heads and follow her through the front door. Hakeem and Isaiah sit on the bench as she stands in front of them.

"Ok boys, what I'm going to tell you isn't easy to say, and it's going to sound absurd. But every word that comes out of my mouth is the truth. We were going to wait until the two of you were twenty-one to tell you about our ancestors, but everything changed with the death of your fathers. It's important that you two are aware of the world that we live in." She pauses. "You both are descendants of an ancient tribe that fought against evil, the same evil that lives today! The same evil that killed my son's!"

"Evil? Really?" Isaiah looks at Hakeem, then back at her. He stands up and replies, "save your story, I heard enough!"

"What?" She looks at him puzzled.

"You're not going to stand here and tell me my father died fighting evil like I'm some kind of gullible punk!" He points at her. "The fact that you would even say that, makes me doubt you even know him. There's not one bible back home, so if you think you're going to seduce me into some church convention I'm going to have to pass."

"Isaiah sit down! I knew your father better than you ever did. I'm not talking about no man-made religion. I'm talking about real creatures that terrorize the night! You are different than other people, the both of you." She pauses. "Centuries ago there was a war on this earth, and it wasn't man against man. It was man against beast, demons. Man was enslaved by demons all over the world. Our great father was one of the strongest hunters that was punished extremely for being captured killing vampires. While he was imprisoned, he fell in love with a powerful witch who transformed him into a metahuman, the world's savor. She had him drink a potion one night before making love to him. When they both came, they created something bigger than them both. Our great father became stronger, smarter, quicker than your average men. He gathered a small team of men and revolted against the

70

demons. After a couple of years and a couple of alliances they were able to lock most of the demons in a hell dimension, we call purgatory. The witch he fell in love with, our great mother gave birth to three kids. Two boys and one witch. The boys gain their hunter abilities at the age of twenty-one and the girl becomes aware of magic at an earlier age. This is how our family have been formed for generations."

"So, we came from a family of witches, hunters, vampires and demons? There's only one problem with this fairy tale, me and Isaiah don't have any brothers or sisters." Hakeem stands up. Isaiah smirks at him and shakes his head pleased with his question.

"Your father didn't want to bring in any more children into the world until he knew it was absolutely safe. There was nothing more William ever wanted then to see his family live a normal life, and well for you Isaiah, unfortunately your mother died too young. With both of your father's death, there's no easy way of convincing the both of you, how much we need you."

"We?" Isaiah replies unconvinced.

"The world. You two are the last men in our family. The last of the Exalus bloodline. The faith of the world literally rests in your hands."

"So, what was this trip our fathers went on? How did they die? And what are you expecting from us if they couldn't accomplish it?" Hakeem folds his arms.

"This last trip they went on was the first step to our final mission. We planned on putting an end to all supernatural creatures. Legend has it if an Exalus warrior digest vampire blood, after 24 hours they will be capable of seeing ancient weapons formed centuries ago, that will bring complete destruction among demons. Tools that were hidden from the public eye in fear of what they can do.

There's a specific weapon we are on the hunt for. It's called the Hell Atomizer. The theory is this tool is a direct link to purgatory. And once opened, it will rain for seven days and seven nights across the globe. And any demon caught in this rain will burn instantly, cleansing the earth." She pauses. "Needless to say, we went to see if the legend was true. There was a tip stating that vampire were seen near the mountains in South America. They tracked down the nest and killed everything, but one. They were killed by a demon retreating back with this." She pulls out two vacutainers full of blood. "Your fathers didn't have a chance to drink out of it. Thank god, they would have become vampires if they died with any of this in their system. But what I'm trying to say is, that they didn't die in vain, not if you let them. They did the hard part of the mission, all we need you to do, is drink this!" She extends the vacutainers out.

"Ok, I think we need to bring you to the loony bin. No way you're expecting us to drink blood!" Isaiah replies. As he stands back up to leave, she stops him from moving with her mind. She turns slightly toward the driveway and waves her right hand toward the parked cars, causing them to float off the floor. Hakeem and Isaiah are shocked. When she sees her point has been proven, she put the cars back down gently and lets Isaiah go free. The two stand speechless.

"Everything I said is true, you two are our last hope!" She faces them.

"Does my mom know about this?" Hakeem asks still confused.

"No, your father didn't want to involve her. But Isaiah's mom knew." She pauses. "Despite how dangerous some missions were, Jason still brought her along. It was his foolish decision that got her killed. I urge you two to not repeat any of this!" Isaiah looks appalled. "Have faith in me and drink this."

The two look at each other than back at her. "I don't know. This all sound crazy. What if it doesn't work?" Hakeem asks, still suspicious.

"It will work." She puts the vacutainers in both of their hands. "I know you don't understand yet, but I promise in 24 hours you will."

After a moment to think, Hakeem replies, "ok, I believe in you." He closes his eyes and downs the vacutainer. Isaiah and his grandma both look at him as he drinks the last drop. When he finishes it, he makes a face of disgust and waves it back at her. "Top five on my never to drink again list!"

"Do you really need the both of us to drink it?" Isaiah looks back at her. "Can't Hakeem drink this for me?"

"No, I need the both of you."

He shakes his head then closes his eyes and drinks it.

"Thank you, boys." She smiles. "Now I want the both of you to stay in tonight. We must make sure you're safe. We can't afford any more trouble. It's only a matter of time until you two really see the world for what it really is!' She takes the empty vacutainers from the boys and walks back inside leaving them outside.

Isaiah looks at Hakeem and says, "tell your white boy to come back with some weed. I need to get high." He taps him on the chest then walks inside, leaving him outside by himself.

CHAPTER 19

The next morning.

The doorbell rings. Camille answers the door with pins in her mouth and one hand on her hair, rushing to get ready to leave for work. "Good morning ma." Taryn kisses her on the cheek entering the home.

"Good morning Taryn." She replies, taking the pins out of her mouth and placing it in her hair.

"I'm not sure if we were able to talk the other night at the reception. But I just want you to know I'm here for you, the both of you, you two mean a lot to me and so did William. If there's anything you need don't hesitate to call me." Taryn grabs her hand.

"Thank you baby, the only favor I'm going to need from you though, is to keep an eye on Hakeem. Being in school the next couple of days won't be easy, but having genuine people like you around makes life easier sometimes." She takes her hand back and put her shoes on. Standing in front of the door, she looks at Taryn and gives her another kiss on the cheek. "Hakeem is still sleeping, feel free to wake him up and make some breakfast. Just don't wake grandma or Isaiah up."

"You got it ma." Taryn nods her head, then looks at her with curiosity. "I know it's none of my business, but how long are they going to stay up here?"

"Well grandma is going home at the end of this week and Isaiah will be staying here with us. Grandma got a hold of the police department down there, supposedly the person who got shot had them stop the search."

"Really?" Taryn replies, shocked.

"Yea, that boy got some luck on his side." She shakes her head. "Well I have to go, oh yea, can you feed the dog for me before you kids go to school? See you later."

Taryn nods her head and closes the door behind her as she leaves. She tries not to trip over the dog who is barking next to her feet. "Shh! I'm going to feed you." She picks the dog up and brings it into the kitchen. She puts the dog on the counter and reaches up top for the cupboards, to get some dog food.

"Mm, let me find out you matured early." Isaiah says, admiring her slim body.

"Are you checking me out Zay?" She turns her attention to him. "Ew, why are you walking around the house in your boxers?" She turns away, grossed out.

"Well if I knew your sexy ass was coming, I would have been walking around the house naked." He enters the kitchen and gets closer to her.

"Gross. Here, she's a perfect match for you." She picks up the dog and hands it to him than pours the food into the bowl.

"I'm going to the bathroom then back to bed." He places the dog on the floor. "Do me a favor, brush your teeth before you take my big little cousin to school." He snickers as he walks out the kitchen.

She gives him a dirty look and leaves the kitchen too. "Brush your teeth before you take my big little cousin to school." She mimics him. "I hope your stupid hair falls out!" She walks upstairs and goes to Hakeem's room. She walks in without knocking. As she reaches her hand over to turn on the light, she takes a second to think to herself, then turns around and locks the door.

She then walks to his bed side and sits on the end of the bed, placing her hand under the covers to play with his penis. "Wake up punk." She whispers in his ear as she gently strokes him.

He smiles, opening his eyes, hoping to see Amber, but is quickly disappointed when he sees Taryn. He grabs her hand to stop. "Chill, what if I got some on my sheets."

With a suspicious look on her face, she replies "not like it would be the first time, but ok." She removes her hand from him and goes to turn on the lights. He adjusts himself on the bed, as he tells her

76

to have a seat next to him. She walks back over and tries to hide the little anger of rejection she is feeling. "Can you just go take a shower already?" she asks, standing over him.

"What's wrong?" He replies, looking at her puzzled.

"You tell me, you're the one laying there with blue balls!" She replies, trying to avoid eye contact.

"Don't do that, I wanted to talk to you before we got into an awkward situation like this." He gets out of bed and stands in front of her as she pouts her lips. "Me and Amber have been getting close again, I just feel like we should give this a break. You will always be my best friend, but with everything that's been going on in my life, I just feel wrong cheating on her. The both of you have been here for me throughout everything and I should be fair to the both of you."

"You mean you feel bad now because she's actually fucking you again!" She replies sarcastically.

"Taryn!"

"I'm just saying what you're thinking. Like you said, I'll always be your best friend." She gives a stale half smile, then walks toward the door.

"I'll be downstairs in a few." He replies, watching her walk out.

"Alright." The door shuts behind her and her fake smile quickly turns into a frown as she let's go of the doorknob to head back downstairs.

When the two get to school, they meet up with Andrew in the parking lot. "Did you guys hear about the party the twins are throwing tonight?" Andrew asks both Hakeem and Taryn as they walk up the stairs to enter school.

"Yea, I heard about it. They invited me but I wasn't sure if you guys were in a partying mood." Taryn replies, walking in between the two.

"You guys could go, don't let me stop you from having fun"

"You're not coming?" Andrew asks Hakeem, speaking over Taryn.

"I don't know, I feel anti-social." As Hakeem and his friends enter the hallways, a group of people walk up to him and give him their condolences.

When they walk away, Andrew continues, "it's cool, I wouldn't want to ride with your cousin anyways. Dude basically smoked my whole pack yesterday. Does everyone from Philadelphia have a high tolerance for weed?"

Taryn laughs. "I don't think he has any brain cells left to lose." Hakeem laughs along with her.

The three walk to Taryn's classroom first. When she walks inside, Amber walks up from behind him and surprises him. "There you are babe." She gives him a hug and a kiss. "There's a party at the twins tonight, can you come show face with me for a couple of minutes?" She pouts at him.

"Really, you want me to go to a party? I'm not in the mood." Hakeem looks away.

"I'm not either, I just want to be with you today, but I already promised I'd go since last week." She replies in a baby voice. "I'm only stopping by for ten minutes, then I'm yours for the night."

Hakeem looks back at her for a few seconds then folds. "Fine, you win I'll go. Only for ten minutes."

The two kiss, "I'll see you in two periods. Bye Andrew." She waves as she walks away.

"Sucker!" Andrew laughs.

"Shut up!" He laughs and pushes him away.

Isaiah

Isaiah walks into the kitchen and sees his grandma sitting down eating breakfast. He walks over and steals a bacon off her plate. "So how many demons have you seen your whole life?" He asks.

"More than you can imagine." She replies, looking at him going through her plate. She shakes her head and just hands him her leftovers.

"Where's your battle scars? The buck fifties, the collection of dead zombie heads as trophies?" He sarcastically asks.

"I'm not a hunter baby, just a powerful witch. Even though we are on the same team, we play distinct roles."

He nods his head, then looks down at the plate. "Where did my mom fit in, in all of this?"

"She didn't. Her only role was to be your mother," she pauses. "Joining your father on missions were strictly their ideas."

"How did she really die?" He lifts his head up to ask. His question catches her off guard. Just as she begins to stutter, a car pulls into the driveway and honks.

"Save this conversation for later." She kisses him on the cheek and stands up.

"Where are you going?" He asks, puzzled.

"I'm going to see some friends about your situation. See if we could get you into school up here."

"Don't waste your time." He mumbles, stuffing his face again. She shakes her head pretending not to hear him and leaves the kitchen. The horn honks again as she walks outside the house.

"We don't have all day Adeline!" Aaron shouts from his car window. As she gets in the car, Isaiah peeks through the window, to see who she's leaving with. "So, what's the verdict?" Aaron asks, before she gets a chance to put her seatbelt on.

"In 15 hours, we will finally be able to track down the tool that will kill all demons." She smirks.

"Did you tell Jason's son the truth about his mother yet?"

"Not yet, you just saved me some more time." Her smirk slightly fades.

"How do you think he'll react when he finds out you killed her?" Aaron asks, with a curious facial expression.

"Honestly, I'm afraid to find out." She frowns. He nods his head then fixes his rearview mirror and reverses.

Hakeem

The day goes by as the sun begins to set and the twin's party start. "Whose idea was it to put gummy bears in vodka?" Andrew asks Taryn as they are drinking on the back patio of the house party.

"Some old guy who probably never grew up."

The notification on Andrew's phone makes a noise, as Hakeem's texts comes through. "Just arrived."

"Your best friend is here." He says to Taryn checking his phone.

"Let's go find him." She replies, looking down at his phone too.

The two walk through the crowd of teenagers in the living room.

80

Half way through, he taps her shoulder and points, "check the corner on the left!" When she looks over, she notices Isaiah and Emira talking in the kitchen. "He might actually sleep with her for me." He smiles.

Taryn gives him a confused facial expression and continues walking toward the front door. As the two get to the entrance, they walk right into Hakeem and Amber. "Hey guys." She says to both.

"Hey Taryn, hey Andrew." Amber waves.

"How's the party going?" Hakeem asks, looking around.

"It's alright, we haven't been here for long, but I see potential." Andrew replies, after sipping his cup.

"Have you guys seen the twins?" Amber asks.

"No, but we saw your best friend feeling up on Hakeem's cousin." Taryn smirks.

"What!"

"Isaiah is here?" Hakeem asks.

"Yea over there." Andrew points at the two in the kitchen. All four of them watch Isaiah making out with Emira, caressing her ass. Amber breaks the circle by walking to the kitchen, the other three follow.

"Really Emira, your making out with this random thug at a house party? Don't you know better?" She slams her hand on the counter.

Emira backs up from Isaiah and wipes her mouth softly. She looks at her confused and shouts, "don't talk to me like I'm a little girl, you're not my mom!"

"I'm not your mom, I'm your best friend. I won't allow you to do hoe shit!" Amber points at her.

"Yo, what's good with your girl Keem? Control her before I do." Isaiah says to Hakeem, but is looking at Amber.

"What?" Amber replies, insulted, tilting her head at him.

"Yes! I finished my cup. I get to eat the gummy bears at the best time." Andrew taps Taryn's arm to say.

"Shut up!" Taryn replies, unbothered.

"Chill Zay." Hakeem replies, with his hand extended out.

"You heard me bitch!" Isaiah barks at her. He looks at Hakeem and replies, "you going to come here and tell me to chill? When your girl is the one making a scene?"

"Don't call my girl a bitch!" Hakeem steps in front of her and into his face, furious.

"Oh, my god! You're a bitch! Picking bitches over family, no wonder why I stopped fucking with you!" Isaiah tightens his fist.

As the argument gets heated, Chris and Samson walk into the kitchen with a few friends and make everything worst. "Ha, ha, ha, look at the two monkeys arguing Sam." Chris smirks.

Isaiah and Hakeem get out of each other's face and turn around to face Chris and Samson who have brought eight other jocks with them. "Can't you guys take an ass whooping like men, and get over it?" Isaiah asks with a crooked face.

"Every dog has its day." Samson replies, with his arms crossed.

"But today isn't yours." Chris ended his sentence still smiling.

"Leave us alone!" Amber shouts.

"You'll get smacked too if you don't shut your mouth." One of the jocks replies.

"If you lay a finger on her!" Hakeem shouts stepping forward tightening his fist.

"You'll what? Get fucked up faster?" Chris laughs.

"Let's take them outside." Samson rubbed his hands.

Isaiah shoves Emira out the way and tries to open the kitchen draw to grab a knife. Four jocks rush him, and one of them closes the draw on him before he gets a chance to take it out. Two of the jocks grab his arms and the other two grab his legs. Chris and Samson along with another jock grab Hakeem.

"You're coming outside with us! Boys make sure the friends don't follow!" Chris says to the other three jocks. The whole party pauses as they watch the jocks carry the cousins outside. As soon as the door closes behind them, the music starts playing again.

"Andrew do something, you going to just let them take Hakeem like that?" Amber shouts.

"What do you want me to do, put on a batman suit? I'm out numbered." He replies, looking at the jocks.

"Bring them to the alley around the corner!" Samson shouts to everyone. The gang carries the two down the street. With all the commotion going on, no one notices three cars creeping up behind them.

"There he is." Said one of the men in the all black car.

The jocks throw the two into the alley. Hakeem helps Isaiah off the floor, as the jocks circle them. "You guys don't look so tough now!" Chris shouts in excitement.

"You talk a lot of shit for someone whose only strong in numbers." Isaiah replies, looking around with his fist in the air. Samson smirks and pulls out a pocket knife. Hakeem and Isaiah stand side to side as the team of jocks close in on them.

When things look like it can't get any worse, a bullet flies out of one of the jocks eye socket. The gun shot shocks everyone as they watch him fall. "What the fuck?" Chris shouts confused, as blood splatters on his face and clothes. Suddenly, there are gunshots being fired at everyone. A bullet goes straight through Chris's forehead, blowing his brains out. Everyone ducks as his body falls, and tries to run toward the fence in the back, but only Samson and one other jock is successful in hoping it in time.

Gunshots continue to go off, as Hakeem and Isaiah try crawling to the fence. When the two finally lift their arms, they see dead bodies laid out in front of them. Five men wearing all black are standing in front of the alley. All five of them reload their guns as they stare at the two.

"Are they friends of yours?" Hakeem whispers to Isaiah, scared.

He squints his eyes at them. "Nope, I'm guessing they're not yours either."

"You got some unfinished business Zay!" One of the men announces.

"Uh, do I know you?" Isaiah asks, confused.

All the thugs laugh. "Oh, I'm pretty sure know you me." A deep voice replies, as he walks in between the men. It is Vinny accompanied by Dimitri.

"I'm pretty sure you know me too." Dimitri smirks.

Isaiah's eyes shoot open. "Shit!" He mumbles.

Raising his right hand over his shoulder, Hakeem interrupts, "I don't know what problems you have with my cousin, but let's work something out."

"Ok, do you have the rest of my thirty-five thousand dollars?" Vinny asks, taking out his gun.

"What!" Hakeem replies, in a high-pitched voice.

Dimitri lifts his gun in the air and doesn't hesitate to shoot him in the forehead. "I think he meant to say no." He smiles.

Isaiah stares at his dead cousin on the floor in shock. "You killed him…" He stutters.

"Where's my money boy!" Vinny shouts. Everyone aims their guns at him.

He reaches in his pocket and takes out five dollars. "Fuck you and your money!" He crumples it and throws it at his feet. "You better kill me, because you're not leaving here with it!" Tears of rage, fall down his face.

Vinny becomes furious and shoots him in the leg. He screams as he grabs his wound. "It's cool, your little friend Tyriek agreed to help make my money back, since he helped you spent it. Your life really doesn't mean much at this point!"

"Tyriek?" He cries in pain.

"Yeah, didn't take much for him to give you up either. Just a few bruises, a lot of gasoline and a little fire. If your dad was ever around to raise you, he would have told you watch the company you keep!" Vinny puts the gun away, turns around and walks behind everyone else. Before he leaves he continues to say, "this is a nice small town you fled to. You were this close to having a new life." He pinched his thumb and index finger together. "Boys, I never want to see him again!"

Dimitri steps up and shoots him in the shoulder, and as he yells in pain, the rest of the thugs continue to empty their clips in him, leaving him lifeless.

CHAPTER 20

Grandma

"Oh god!" Grandma says, standing up, grabbing her chest. She and Aaron are sitting on the bench outside of the Exalus house.

"What's wrong?" He stands up, concerned.

She looks up to the sky with a horrible look on her face. "Something terrible just happened."

Samson

A couple of minutes after the gunshots, Samson and his friend climbs out of a dumpster, which is around the corner from the fence they hopped.

"You think they left?"

"Yea, it's been a couple of minutes since the last shots were fired." Samson replies, dusting himself off.

"Who the fuck were they?" The jock asks, puzzled.

"I don't know!" The two take caution as they walk around the corner. When they see that the coast is clear, they hop back over the fence. They both land in a pool of blood, standing over the corpse of their friends, including Hakeem and Isaiah. Samson walks over the bodies, then stops to look at his best friend Chris. He sheds a tear at the sight of half his skull missing.

"Let's go get the rest!" The jock grabs his arm. "We need to call the cops!"

"Let's go." Samson replies in a gentle voice, his face shows no emotion. Before he follows his friend, he takes another look at Hakeem and Isaiah, then tries to snap out of it. The two sprint back to the house.

CHAPTER 21

Nether world/ Purgatory.

Isaiah

"Ah!" Isaiah shouts, sitting up from the floor. He looks around and sees corpses everywhere, then looks over at Hakeem, who is standing over his own body. Puzzled, he shouts, "What the fuck? There's two of you!" He jumps to his feet, and looks down. The sight of his own body leaves him paralyzed.

"You really got me killed." Hakeem wipes a tear falling on the left side of his cheek.

Isaiah stood speechless struggling to find words to say. "I'm really dead…" He stutters to himself in disbelief. Hakeem walks over to him as he bent over to touch his own dead body, and yolks him up to punch him in the face. As Isaiah falls, the ground begins to shake. Hakeem's knees buckles, as the earth feels like it is about to crumble, and all the corpses sink into the ground.

When the ground stops shaking, Isaiah stands back up and mumbles "what the fuck?" The two look at each other worried. The sound of thunder strikes the air, followed by little rain drops of blood. It rains blood for about forty-five seconds, then stopped.

"You can't be serious!" Hakeem shouts, soaked. They stand next to each other, covered in blood, as the world they are in turns into a grey abyss. All the buildings, houses, street lights, cars and trees sink to the ground. "Fuck this! I'm finding the road to heaven!" Hakeem shouts, running straight, which seems like nowhere. The land is empty with no objects in sight.

"So, you going to just leave me here in the middle of nowhere?" Isaiah shouts after him. Hakeem runs for five minutes, until he runs into a portal that brings him right back to where he started. Isaiah is surprised to see him approach from behind. "Heaven didn't want you huh?" He asks, sarcastically.

"This can't be happening!" Hakeem shouts, trying to run away again. Frustrated, he runs into an invisible wall. The two are shocked. Isaiah turns around and feels a wall behind him too. The cousins discover they are locked inside an invisible box. The two start screaming and knocking on the walls simultaneously. The ground begins shaking again, but this time more viciously. The two fall onto the floor as this goes on for several minutes. When the ground stops shaking, the sun rises from the floor afar, blinding them. As they cover their eyes, the moon rises as well and constantly rotates with the sun, causing day and night.

The grey shade that was covering the land loses its color when it starts to rain, and after the 16th day, the grass and trees start growing from the floor fast. They grow to a certain length then shrink back to the ground. On the 21st sunrise, water floods the entire land. The cousins stand in the invisible box amazed and horrified as the world around them transforms through these different seasons. It is as if they are standing in a virtual slideshow.

One day the area is flooded with water and then the next day it is as dry as a dessert. Another day they are surrounded by a jungle then the next, they are surrounded by mountains. One day they are surrounded by a lake of fire then the next, they are surrounded by pyramids. In every location that changes outside of the box, they see gold talismans that stand out, apart from everything else in the locations.

Finally, the sun and the moon stop rotating, and the full moon stands high above the two. They are surrounded by a destroyed village. They notice there is another moon in the sky opposite the other and become completely freaked out. It is completely quiet, until they hear footsteps.

"What the fuck is that?" Hakeem whispers.

"You heard that too?"

As the footsteps get louder, they begin to hear roars. Roars that don't sound like animals or humans. The two try punching the invisible wall again, but still have no luck breaking through. Isaiah takes a breather and looks into the sky. The sky is lit up with stars that look like they are on fire.

"Keem look up." Isaiah says under his breath. Hakeem looks to the sky and drops his arms to the side, as he back pedals in disbelief.

The footsteps and roars become louder. "We're fucked." Hakeem

90

says, looking at him. Suddenly the streets are covered with blood and corpses. Creatures begin jumping off the broken roofs and landing in the streets. The cousins are frozen in fear as their mouth's drop wide open. These creatures are tall, pale, eyes are cold blue, with sharp nails and a long sharp tail that wave in the air behind their wings. Saliva drips from their fangs.

Other creatures run out from the woods. Some are green, red, some have two heads, others have horns on their foreheads. A few are faceless. The street is flooded with all types of demons in a matter of seconds surrounding the cousins.

"Is it me or are they looking at us?" He whispers to Hakeem.

Hakeem nods his head then whispers back, "I think they see us too." Hakeem walks away from him and walks to the other side of the box. Most of the creature's heads turn along with him as he walks.

One of the demons steps out in front of the rest. This specific creature looks different though and there is no doubt about it that he is the leader. There are no horns on his head, but his whole body is pitch black with orange veins and orange eyes. It is naked and stands taller than any of the other creatures. It has a serious look on its face, as if it is the strongest out of the pack.

"Oh shit." Isaiah mumbles under his breath. The creature lets out a loud roar, that gets all the other creatures riled up. In the mist of the roaring, a woman makes her way to the front of all the creatures. Isaiah notices her instantly, and his eyes shoot open.

"Mom!" He shouts, running to the front of the box. Hakeem looks over at him, then over to the section of creatures he is facing. His mouth drops at the sight of his aunt.

The demon that is standing in front of all the creatures, points at the two cousins. Creatures from all corners of the village charge at them with more hoping off the roofs and landing on top of the invisible box the cousins are standing in. In a matter of seconds all they see are demons covering the box completely, trying their hardest to get inside.

The two stand in the middle and look around them. A couple of demons with hammers as hands start hitting the walls with extraordinary strength. Three of them are on top of the box, four more are at both the front and back of the box, and the last two are on both sides of the box. After a combination of a couple of blows, the cousins start seeing cracks begin to form in between them and the demons.

They are stunned at the sight of the cracks spreading all over the box. The two stand with their backs against each other, as they watch all the demons try even harder to get through. To Hakeem's surprise a path clears ahead of him. Before he can make sense of what is going on, the demon that told the creatures to get them, is standing at the end of the path. It charges down and breaks through the wall using its shoulders. The box shatters on the cousins, as the rest of the creatures fall on top of them.

CHAPTER 22

Hakeem

About three minutes after the jocks walked away. Both Hakeem and Isaiah's eyes open. They scream and gasp for air, as they squirm around the floor. Hakeem sits up and grabs his forehead. When he looks around him, he realizes that he is back in the alley where he was just shot a few minutes ago. The other bodies are still on the floor. He puts his index finger in the hole in his forehead and realizes he is numb to the feeling, and continues to dig for the bullet. When he finds it, he pulls it out and looks at it. The wound heals instantly.

When Isaiah sees him take the bullet out of his head, he begins picking at the wounds on his own leg. When he takes out a bullet, and sees himself heal, he quickly starts taking out the rest.

"Let's go, before those monsters come back!" Hakeem stands up and looks at him.

Isaiah stands up and looks to the sky. He takes a deep breath then looks back at him, "I think we're back cuz."

Hakeem takes a deep breath as well and relaxes his shoulders. "The air smells fresh, but I feel different."

"There was a bullet in your brain, of course you're going to feel different."

"Exactly, I just took a bullet out of my head!" Hakeem faces him and points. "You just took three out of your leg, and another two out of your skull! You still have eight more in your chest!" He pauses. "How is this real?"

"I don't know what's real anymore." The two look down at the corpses, when the scent of blood catches their attention. "Do you feel that temptation?" Isaiah asks, as his nose twitches.

"Yes, we need to find grandma now!"

Samson

"Call the cops! Somebody, call the cops!" Samson and his friend scream, as they run through the party. The music stops, as everyone stares at them and their bloody sneakers.

"What happened? Where is everyone else?" One jock asks, holding Andrew in a headlock.

"Their dead." Samson pauses. "They're all dead! Call the cops now!"

"What!" Taryn screams.

"What do you mean they're all dead? Where's Hakeem?" Amber asks worried, finally pushing her way out the kitchen.

"He's dead too." Samson looks down.

"What!" Amber cries, running towards him. She hits him on his chest as tears race down her cheeks.

"You're lying!" Emira shouts, running after Amber to hold her back and keep her calm. "Is Isaiah dead too?"

Samson nods his head in shame, "We had nothing to do with anyone's death, some thugs came right before we were going to fight and literally shot everyone. We were the only ones who got out in time!"

The jock finally lets Andrew go and looks at Samson, puzzled. "Dude are you serious? Chris too?"

"Everybody!" He screams. "Now will somebody please call the fucking cops!" Everyone races to dial the cops at the same time, as Taryn and Andrew run toward him.

"I hope you know you're going to jail with whoever you claim killed them!" Andrew shouts in his face.

"Listen punk, you're not the only one who lost a friend tonight, it wasn't our intention to kill anybody!"

Taryn shoves Samson's shoulders storming out of the house. "Don't just stand there, take us to him!" She demands.

"I don't think you want to see their bodies." He mumbles.

"If you don't show me his body, the cops will be picking up another one." Taryn threatens, as she makes her hand into a fist. Half of the party follow him as he leaves and leads Hakeem's friends to the alley. "Walk faster Samson!" She urges, walking behind him. When he gets to the alley and sees everybody in the same position except Hakeem and Isaiah, he freezes, as the girls scream at the sight of the corpses. Taryn covers her mouth when she notices Chris's brains hanging out of his skull. "I don't see Hakeem or Isaiah, Samson." She says in a faint voice.

"Where are they!" Amber barks, getting in front of him. He shakes his head, pointing to the area he saw them last. The only thing everyone saw were bullet shells scattered across the floor.

"They were there. I saw them, I swear I saw them." He stutters. Amber takes out her phone and calls Hakeem, but the call goes to voicemail, as if the phone were powered off.

Hakeem

"I never thought in my life, it was possible to move that fast!" Isaiah says to Hakeem filled with excitement, as they walk up his driveway.

"I didn't think a lot of things were possible before tonight." When Hakeem gets to the house door, he unlocks it and tries to walk in. "What the fuck?" He shouts, confused, scanning the inside of his house.

"Are you retarded? Move out the way!" Isaiah shoves him, and attempts to enter the home, but fails.

"It's like there's an invisible wall here. Why can't I get inside of my own house! Do you think this is another trick?" Hakeem asks, puzzled.

"I don't know." Isaiah replies, touching the invisible barrier. Angry, Hakeem punches the wall by the side of the door and leaves a big hole on the house. "Whoa." Isaiah says, stunned at the size of the hole. Hakeem takes his hand out and blows the dust off his knuckles with no sign of pain. "I wonder if I could do the same

96

thing." Isaiah says to himself as he folds his right hand into a fist.

"No! Don't punch my wall." He stops him. "We're not breaking down my house to get in. Just in case we really are back, we still need a place to live. We need to find grandma!"

"Whatever." Isaiah puts his fist down then walks toward the bench. "Hold up, Keem come over here! I don't know if I'm bugging, but I think I could smell her." He sniffs the air. "I smell that perfume she always wears."

Hakeem walks over and takes a sniff. "I smell her too." His eyes open in surprise. The two close their eyes and meditate on the scent for a few seconds.

"I could trace it, her scent, it's still fresh. She went that way." Isaiah points down the street.

CHAPTER 23

In a ware house 5 miles away.

Grandma

"This is all my fault!" Grandma cries to Aaron, who is handing stakes out to his henchmens.

"It's not your fault, you did what was instructed. No one could've seen this happening."

"They were too young!" She pinches the bridge on her nose.

"Go home, your daughter in law comes home from work soon, you need to come up with something to tell her. She needs to know her son and nephew won't be coming home." He puts his hands on her shoulders in a sensitive matter to comfort her. "You're a strong woman, but you shouldn't have to see your grandchildren possessed by these demons. Let the rest of us take it from here."

She shrugs his hand away and puts her head down, shaking both her fists agressively. "What if we're wrong?" She asks, looking back up.

"Wrong about what?"

"Everything. What if we could still save them?"

"You know we can't. This situation is no different than Jason's a couple of years ago, whatever is walking around in their body isn't them! And you will only hurt yourself, if you continue to hold on to this false hope. Please just go home, we will truly mourn them when this is over."

She nods her head then turns around. As she reaches her hand out for her jacket, she senses them. Her head turns to the door just as it is kicked down. The door goes flying to the middle of the room. Everybody grabs their weapons and positions themselves behind Aaron.

"See I told you she was there." Isaiah walks in with Hakeem following. Isaiah's smirk quickly fades at the sight of all the weapons, leaving him with a puzzled facial expression.

Hakeem looks around at all the armed men standing behind Aaron. Puzzled, he asks, "what's going on?"

One of the men shoots an arrow through his arm, as everyone spreads themselves out. "Ah!" Hakeem screams in agony. He looks down at his arm and pulls the arrow out. When he lifts his head back up, his face is different. Fangs come down the side of his mouth, as his eyes become bloodshot red, with veins showing underneath his eye sockets. He lets out a big roar and lunges himself at the men who shot him.

Isaiah looks at him like he sees a ghost. As another man loads his crossbow, Isaiah jumps in front of him and punches him to the floor. Hakeem knees the men and throws him across the room. When Isaiah sees that Hakeem could do that, he grabs the man in front of him and tosses him too.

Another man runs up to Isaiah and cuts him in the arm with a sword. His face goes through the same transformation as Hakeem. The second time the man swings, he dodges it. He tries again, but misses, Isaiah grabs him by the wrist and twists it, until he loses his grip of it. He then continues to grab him by the neck and tosses him across the room next to his last victim.

"We need to leave now!" Aaron runs to grandma, catching Hakeem's attention. Hakeem faces both of them and walks toward their direction. Another man jumps in between them, and charges toward him.

"Have you noticed they haven't bitten any of our men yet?" Grandma asks Aaron.

"We need to leave before one of them do get bitten, especially you!" He grabs her hand.

"These men aren't warriors. If Hakeem and Isaiah were 100% demons, they would have killed someone by now."

He looks at her confused as she takes her hand back. The man tries to stake Hakeem but fails, causing him to break his arm. Hakeem picks him up and is able to make eye contact with Isaiah.

He tosses the guy to him, and Isaiah jumps in the air and kicks him in the chest. The impact sends the man flying across the room into some boxes. The two cousins look at each other then to their grandma and Aaron. Once the tension dies down, their faces turn back to normal.

"You guys were really trying to kill us?" Isaiah asks.

"Grandma! Enough games, what the hell is going on?"

She looks at her grandchildren as if they are strangers. Cautious to reply, she stutters, "Hakeem? Isaiah? Is it really you?"

"It's a trick! Be careful." Aaron says, holding her arm trying to prevent her from walking toward them.

"A trick? Do we look like a pair of clowns? If anybody is playing a trick it's you!" Isaiah points at him, while Hakeem eyes are glued onto his grandma. "You're the reason we're like this! Don't look at us like you don't know us!"

She looks them in the eyes and shakes Aaron's hand off. She takes caution as she walks toward them. When she stands face to face with Hakeem, she carefully touches the side of his face and looks him in the eyes. She turns her head to Isaiah and does the same. "Oh, my god." She mumbles. "I can't believe this. I thought you two were dead."

"Did you not just see us walk through the door? Get attacked by your friends!" Isaiah replies, sarcastically with a confused facial expression.

"The both of you are vampires." She pauses. "You weren't supposed to die within 24 hours with the blood in your system." Tears stream down her face fast and she wipes them off with her sleeves and continues, "I'm sorry, but we never seen a vampire with humanity. We didn't know it was possible. The two of you just changed everything!"

Aaron slowly approaches behind her to get a closer look at Hakeem and Isaiah. "This is extraordinary!"

"Ok, how are you going to turn us back to humans?" Hakeem asks, folding his arms.

"There is no cure for this, only immortality or death." Aaron replies, squinting his eyes through his glasses at them.

"I'll take immortality!" Isaiah faces Hakeem. "You should to."

"I don't know what you guys do down there in Philadelphia, but I'm not biting people's necks when I'm hungry!"

"We'll find a way around that." Isaiah faces his grandma and asks, "is there any substitute food for vampires when they don't have an appetite for blood?"

"No." She replies. All the men slowly circle them. "We have to get you guys home." She looks at both of them.

Aaron taps her shoulder and interrupts her. "Can I have a word with you?" As the two walk away, he tells his men to put their guard down. When they reach the other side of the room, he continues, "are you sure you want to bring them home? I think we need to inform the Power Circle before making hasty calls like this. We don't want to upset them."

Isaiah and Hakeem look toward them and listen to their conversations. Despite the distance, they can hear every word.

"These are my grandchildren Aaron! I don't need advice on where to go from here. I'll call them in the morning, when we all settle down."

"All I'm saying is, you don't know if they'll still be themselves in the morning. When the craving for blood kicks in, you'll be placing Camille in danger."

Hakeem steps forward and interrupts. "Nobody's touching my mom! I don't know you Aaron" He points at him. "And you're really pissing me off. My family doesn't need your advice!"

Aaron turns his head toward him with his mouth open, speechless.

"I'll call you in the morning." She taps him on the chest and walks toward her grandchildren.

"I still need to drive you guys home." He clears his throat then follows.

Hakeem

It was 12 o'clock in the morning, when Camille got home from work. When she enters her driveway, she sees about 15 teenagers on her front lawn standing around. As she parks her car and gets out, Andrew, Taryn and Amber all run to her. "What's going on?" She asks with a worried expression.

"It's Hakeem and Isaiah! We can't find them, something bad happened!" Taryn replies, crying.

"What do you mean?" She looks over at all the other teenagers on the lawn, then at the big hole on the side of her house door. "What the hell has been going on!" She shouts, demanding answers. Before anyone could speak, a car enters the driveway and parks behind them. Everybody outside turns their attention to this mysterious car. When grandma, Isaiah and Hakeem get out, Taryn and Amber race toward Hakeem and give him a bear hug.

"Where have you been! We called you! We thought you were dead!" They shouted holding him tight.

"It's been a long night girls," He replies, hugging them back. Isaiah walks pass them and goes to the front of the house.

"Is someone going to explain the hole on the side of my house?" Camille asks, puzzled.

"Let's go inside," Grandma says to her.

As everyone walks with Hakeem to the front door, Amber says to him, "I'm not leaving your side tonight."

"I'm sorry you can't stay. I'm going to call you in the morning babe, I promise."

As they reach the top of the house, another car pulls into the driveway. Samson and the other jock that was from the alley jumps out the car. "No fucking way!" Samson points to them. "I saw you dead! The two of you!" He screams in disbelief, as he makes his way up the driveway.

Isaiah and Hakeem look at him with an unexpected reaction. "I don't know what you're talking about." Hakeem replies, with a confused facial expression. Samson makes his way pass everyone and walks up the three steps to stare them down.

"How are you guys alive?" He asks, with his eyes glued to Hakeem's forehead.

"Will you boys come in already!" Camille says, standing at the doorway. Before Hakeem can reply to him, his grandma grabs both of their wrist and pulls them inside.

CHAPTER 24

"It's been days since I seen you, I'm worried and I miss you!" Amber says to Hakeem over the phone.

"I miss you too, I wish I could be with you right now, but my family has been real strict about me leaving or having people over this week. I promise when everything blows over, not even God himself could separate us." He replies, turning over to his back on his bed.

"Well God is going to need to send all of his people if he thinks I'm not coming to see you tonight."

Hakeem laughs, "I'm going to let you know if God will need his angels or not later. Love you."

"I love you too. Talk to you later." The two end the call.

"You really grew up with no balls." Isaiah says, eavesdropping on the conversation from the doorway.

"What now, I'm not supposed to miss my girlfriend?"

"Just sneak her over, you're not a tad bit interested in finding out what tricks you could do as a vampire? We probably don't even cum anymore." He replies, walking into the room.

Hakeem laughs and shakes his head. "I'm not going to put her at risk until I know she's safe around me."

"And what makes you think she's not safe with you? We been home for three days living off packaged blood. I don't know about you, but I'm in complete control of myself, unless I have to spend another day inside."

"I know how you feel, but grandma knows best. We should just play it safe and listen to what she says for now."

"She might have advice for us on how to live our life, but she's not us. She wouldn't understand how we feel or how we think. Less than a week ago, she was ready to let us die. Since we didn't live up to her evil expectation, we were lucky to become lab rats."

"Don't think of it that way. We saw firsthand how dangerous these other creatures are. You can't be too quick to judge her."

Isaiah looks down, then back up to him. "Don't tell her we saw my mom when we died. I don't want to spend another day family bonding, no offense."

"What if she knows why she's there?"

"To be honest, I'm pretty sure that was hell. I don't know why she's there or if it even means anything that we saw her. But I want to leave this conversation alone."

"Alright."

Just as the two finish talking, Grandma and Aaron knock on Hakeem's room door then enter. "Ok boys, Camille went to work.

We closed all the blinds, come downstairs to the living room." She says with a smile on her face.

"Here we go." Isaiah sighs.

The two follow them downstairs and stand in the middle of the living room for further instructions. She takes a deep breath and speaks first. "Ok boys have a seat. I know these last couple of days haven't been easy, I can't promise the upcoming days will be either, but I do promise you I'm working on a way to make everything work. If there was any time we needed to be in each other's lives, it's right now!"

"So why haven't we told mom the truth yet? You don't think she's going to find it strange, 10 years from now I'll look the same while she grows old?" Hakeem asks as he sits down. Her eyes look to Aaron for answers.

"Your mom is so gullible, she still believes that hole in the wall is from firecrackers." Isaiah says to him laughing under his breath.

"And what are you going to say when she wants us to go out during the day?"

"I don't want to be seen with ugly people." Isaiah replies, laughing harder.

"Calm down boys." She interrupts. "Hakeem you're right, your mother is family. I don't enjoy lying to her, but I do it for her safety, I need you boys to understand and do the same." The cousins nod their heads, as Aaron opens the bag on the side of the sofa and takes out his laptop.

Taryn

The sound of the high school bell, alerts everyone that class is over. Taryn closes her notebook and places it in her bookbag, as she walks out the classroom, a fellow classmate walks up to her and asks how she is doing. She keeps her head down trying to avoid conversation, but still tells him she's fine. Everybody in school is depressed that week on behalf of the recent deaths. There are pictures of students posted all over the hallways and lockers. She gives the student a fake smile then thanks him for asking. As she walks away, Andrew walks into her.

"Look who finally came back to school."

"Hey Andrew." She replies giving him a hug. "I didn't want too, but my father is back home, I couldn't stand being under the same roof as him for another minute."

"Your mom let him back in the house? Is she crazy?"

"They were talking the whole time he was away. She promised him he could return home once he finished his half way home program. Didn't really take much for her to forgive him." She replies looking the other way.

"Did you?"

She looks at him and changes the topic. "Have you heard from Hakeem?"

"We haven't had a real solid conversation, I checked up on him two days ago, but he wasn't trying to let me inside the house. He told me he was going to call me when he's ready to talk. I guess he's not ready yet."

"It's weird how he's been brushing us off."

Andrew looks down at his shoes then back at her. "Do you think what Samson is saying is true?"

"That he saw Hakeem and Isaiah dead in the alley?"

"Yea."

"No! We saw them at the house that same night. There was not a scratch on their face!"

"I know." He pauses. "I don't know why I got this feeling they're keeping something from us."

"What do you mean?" The two walk around the corner and into the cafeteria. The first thing they notice, is a big crowd surrounding the table where Amber and Emira usually sit. They end their conversation and walk over to see what is going on. Samson and the jock from the other night are standing on opposite sides of the table of Amber and Emira.

"Your boyfriend is a freak!" Samson shouts.

"No, he's not!" Amber argues back.

"So how do you explain him being the only survivor?"

"Are you not a survivor too?" Emira backs her up.

"I escaped while the gunshots were still firing, we both did, and we both know for a fact Hakeem and his cousin were dead when we went back to the alley." He pounds his fist on the lunch table.

"You girls don't find it weird that he hasn't been to school all week?" The jock folds his arms, as Taryn looks at Andrew.

"I think it's weird that instead of mourning your best friends, you're still trying to come up with ways to pick on Hakeem." Amber slams her hands on the table.

Taryn taps Andrew to let him know she's about to walk away. As she turns around, Samson takes a glimpse at her, and shouts, "Don't leave so fast Taryn!"

She rolls her eyes back and turns back around. "I don't have time for your immature games or theories!"

"Immature Taryn? Chris died three nights ago, and you still haven't been to his house to pay respects to his parents!" All the students standing by the table, turn their heads and stare at her.

"Whether I go to his house or not it's none of your business!"

"Now would the reason you haven't been there yet, is because you've been with Hakeem this whole time?" He points at her. Amber couldn't resist looking her in the eyes for an answer. Taryn looks around the cafeteria at everyone anticipating a response.

"No, I wasn't. I haven't seen him since the night of the shooting." She replies weakly, avoiding eye contact with anyone.

"You see! Not even his so called best friend knows what's going on. And something weird is going on! I'm going to get to the bottom of this!" Samson makes sure the whole cafeteria can hear him.

"How about you help the cops find the shooter?" One of the students asks. Taryn slips out the crowd as everyone starts gossiping.

As she makes it down the hallway she hears, "Hey! Wait up!" To her surprise it is Amber. When she catches up, she continues to say, "don't listen to Samson. He's an asshole."

"I know." Taryn replies awkwardly.

"How are you holding up?" Amber asks, taking a step closer to her.

"I've been better. How are you?"

"I've been better too. Let me walk you to class?" She suggests.

"Uh ok." The two walk down the hallway and make a right.

As Amber holds her textbook in her hands, she looks over at Taryn and says, "I didn't mean to make this awkward, but you're my boyfriend's best friend. I don't know much about you or your relationship with Chris, but I feel obligated to be here for you. Is there anything you want to talk about?"

Taryn closes her eyes and folds her fist slightly, feeling offended. As she opens them and lets her fist free, she looks back at her and replies, "if you want to know if I saw Hakeem just ask. You don't have to pretend like you care."

"I…" Amber began to say then gets cuts off.

"I haven't seen him. Sorry you walked me to class for no reason." She turns around to walk inside, but Amber grabs her arm before she can get a foot in.

"Taryn, I really mean what I said." Amber looks her in the eyes. She pulls her arm back and continues to walk into the classroom.

Grandma

"Ok boys. Thank you for your cooperation, you can go to your rooms now. I'll talk to you later." Grandma says to the cousins. The two get up and walk back to Hakeem's room. When Aaron hears the door shut, he looks at her in relief.

"We got a lot of information today." He closes the laptop and places it back in his bag.

"We did. We're really going to pull this off." She smirks.

"I can't believe it, I'm going to bring all this information back to the Power Circle personally!"

"How long do you think they are going to give us, before we have to make a move?"

"Who knows, most likely a couple of days. You should savor your time with them." He replies placing the bag strap around his shoulder.

She walks him to the door and gives him a hug. "We'll talk later." She says, holding the door open for him.

"Don't hesitate to call if you need me." He replies, comforting her arm then finally leaving. When she shuts the door, she takes a deep breath and thinks to herself.

Hakeem

"Tell Amber to come through with Emira after school. I have to find out what this new body can do!" Isaiah says to Hakeem as they sit down on his bed.

"I told you, I don't want her anywhere near us until I know we're safe."

"Safe? You sound like Aaron and grandma. There's nothing wrong with us!"

"So, go outside. If there's nothing wrong with us, you should be able to go get my mail for me."

He stands up and replies, "there has to be a trick to this." He walks over to the window, which is covered by curtains and slowly moves it to the side. A beam of sunlight shoots through the room, missing him and touches Hakeem's hand. At first, little black particles begin to float around his hand, then in a matter of seconds, his hand is in flames. "Whoa." Isaiah says under his breath, as Hakeem shouts at the top of his lungs, screaming in pain. When their grandma rushes into the room, her eyes shoot open in shock, as she witnesses Isaiah trying to put out the fire on

Hakeem's hand, using the bed comforters.

"What did I tell you boys about sunlight!" She panics as the dog runs in the room, barking. When the cousins finally put the fire out, she stands at the door furious. "You boys don't listen!"

"Give us a break gramps, we've stayed inside for you for a couple of days now with no problems." Isaiah replies, throwing the comforter on the floor. Hakeem holds his hand up high and watches his burnt marks recover.

"Maybe, or maybe it's because of the spell I put on all the entrances that's preventing you two from leaving!" Isaiah smirks as he shakes his head. As Hakeem lifts his comforter off the floor to examine what's left of it, she walks toward the bed and snatches it from his hands, aggressively. "I can't afford to lose you two again! You boys need to grow up and listen!"

"Technically…" Isaiah started saying.

"Shut up and sit down!" She cuts him off. They walk over to the bed and sit down. "Aaron is reporting the information we received from you both to the Power Circle. Most likely by the end of the week we will have to leave here and travel to where this artifact is."

"Travel?" Hakeem interrupts to ask.

"Yes, we will be traveling."

Isaiah rolls his eyes and mumbles, "great. A family trip after death."

"Hush!" She walks closer to the two, "this is more than a family trip. To be honest once we leave you won't be coming back here."

"What!" Hakeem barks, standing up then tries to correct himself.

"Pardon me grandma, but what do you mean we won't be coming back here? I have a life here. I have a girlfriend, best friends, high school, a social life."

"I know you do. That's why it's important to leave now. Before people become suspicious of what you really are. You can't forget, you won't age with none of your loved ones."

"So, what are we supposed to do for the rest of eternity, not talk to people? This isn't fair! You're telling me to let go of the only life I know by Saturday?" Hakeem paces, then sits back down.

"The life you had is dead." She pauses. "It sounds cruel, but it's true. You don't belong here. I love the both of you and I don't ever want you boys to think different, but we have to live in reality."

"Ok, let's start living in reality!" Hakeem cuts her off. "This whole predicament is your fault. I didn't ask to drink no fucking vampire blood!" He points at her. "All I wanted was the truth about my family and now my life is a freak show!"

She nods her head. "You're right this is partially my fault. But, if it wasn't for me, your mother and your girlfriend along with your friends would be mourning you today." She places her hand on the side of his face, "look me in my eyes, I didn't ask for this life either, but unfortunately God took special interest with us." Hakeem turns his face, and folds his arms again. She positions herself to face both him and Isaiah, who are still sitting on the bed. "I've been working on a spell that will most likely, well, most definitely get me in trouble, when the Power Circle finds out, but I owe it to the both of you."

"What kind of spell?" Isaiah stands curious.

"Follow me." She walks out the room and leads the cousins into the guest room downstairs. "Have a seat on the bed." As they take

114

their seats, she walks to the corner of the room where all her bags are and spends 30 seconds searching for an old talisman. She picks up a little purple bag and sprinkles dust onto it, then turns around. "Ok boys, thank me later." She closes her eyes and takes a deep breath. When she exhales, she starts humming a little sound that quickly turns into a chant, that she mumbles very low. After a few seconds, her body begin to shake. When she opens her eyes, they are pitch black.

The cousins become worried and somewhat fearful of what may happen next. As her chants become louder, a long black cloud of smoke come out of the talisman and cover the ceiling inside the room. The cousins slowly get off the bed, looking astonished at what they are witnessing. The dark cloud splits in two and engulfs the cousin's bodies. It enters through their mouths, noses, ears and eyes. They try to resist, but the force is too strong. The thick dark smoke lifts them off their feet by a few inches and holds them for a few seconds. When it stops, they fall on all fours. As their head rises, their face transitions into vampires then turns back to normal.

"What was that?" Hakeem pants. She walks to the window and opens the blinds, causing the cousins to cover their face and scream for their lives. Realizing they're not burning, they peek through their hands, cautiously, then drop their arms completely.

SHE SMILES AT THEM BOTH. "YOUR FREEDOM."

CHAPTER 25

The cousins touch their chest and start to laugh as they jump to their feet. They race each other out the room and to the front door of the house. When she breaks the spell that prevents them from leaving, the cousins feel the barrier drop and runs straight to the front lawn.

She walks to the front door and stands by the side, to watch her grandchildren embrace the sunlight and take in the fresh air as if they just served a life sentence. "Not that it matters, but you two will notice a small tattoo on your body. That tattoo is permanent. That is what's protecting you two from the sunlight."

"What kind of tat?" Isaiah asks her, puzzled. Hakeem waste no time taking off his shirt to look. When Isaiah looks over at him, he finds it before he does. "Hold up. Its right there on the back of your shoulder." He grabs his triceps. He looks carefully, but can't make out what kind of symbol it is, so he takes his shirt off as well. Hakeem points his tattoo out and it is in the same spot as his. He looks carefully too, but can't make the tattoo out either.

"What does this mean?" Hakeem faces his grandma.

"It means you're free."

The cousins shake their heads and laugh, as they put their shirts back on. "I have to go see Amber!"

Still laughing, Isaiah turns to Hakeem and says, "damn brush your teeth first!"

"Wait just one second boys. I don't think I have to tell you how important it is that no one finds out that you're vampires. It is extremely stupid if you two flaunt these new abilities you have! You boys have an abbreviated time to spend with your friends and Camille, until we have to go." Hakeem nods his head and runs back inside leaving the two outside to look at each other. "Don't do anything stupid Isaiah." She points at him.

He nods his head with a devious smile and walks back inside.

Taryn

The short hand on the clock seemed to be stuck on the same number for what seemed like the whole class period. "How many of you started reading chapter nine?" The teacher asks everyone. Taryn's eyes keep drifting from the clock to the window, until a flock of birds flying by caught her attention. "Earth to Taryn!" The teacher says out loud.

She snaps out of her trance and looks around the class, while everyone looks back at her. "I'm sorry, may I go to the bathroom?" She grabs the hall pass and leaves. As she walks through the hallway, two students approach her mourning Chris. Avoiding conversation, she just walks past them and enters the bathroom. Inside, she walks back and forth in front of the mirror's thinking to herself. It's been a long time since she's been this depressed, dealing with the loss of her ex-boyfriend and the return of her abusive father, she feels like she has no one to talk too. Especially since Hakeem hasn't been retuning any of her messages. She takes out her phone and texts him "I need to see you." Then puts her phone back in her pocket. Before storming out the bathroom, she looks at herself in the mirror and gently touches the scar on the side of her face that barely shows because of her make up.

When she leaves the bathroom, she walks outside of school toward her car not returning the hall pass, and leaves the school property.

Amber

20 minutes pass before the bell rings, but as soon as it does Amber grabs her stuff and walks out her classroom. She doesn't get far before getting harassed by Samson. "Next time you talk to your boyfriend, tell him to stop hiding!" She brushes him off and continues to her next class. She grabs a seat by the window, while the rest of the students still enter. Before she opens her book, she glances out the window and sees Hakeem walking in the parking lot. Her eyes shoot open in disbelief. Jumping out of her seat, she quickly runs out of the classroom.

Taryn

Taryn's car pulls into Hakeem's driveway. As she steps out the car and takes a deep breath, Isaiah opens the house door and stares her down.

"Where's your cousin?"

"He went for a walk, but I'm here. I could scratch that itch for you." He smirks.

"Gross, can you stop!" He looks away from her and observes her car. "Do you know when he's coming back?" She continues.

Still looking at her car, he walks out the house and approaches it. "He'll be back later. How does this car treat you?" He begins rubbing the hood of the car.

"Good." She replies, looking at him sketchy.

He takes two thousand dollars out of his pockets and tosses it in her hands. "Let me borrow your car while you wait here for him!"

"Wait, what?" She looks down at the money then back at him. "Can you even drive?"

"Are you serious? I was hotwiring cars before you even got your permit!" He maneuvers behind her and gets in the driver seat to adjust the seat and feel on the steering wheel.

She takes a second to think about it, then puts the money in her pockets. "I'd rather come with you instead of letting you leave with my car."

"What are you waiting for then? Let's go!" He shuts the door on her.

She walks around the car and gets in the passenger seat. "I'm still keeping the money." She puts on her seatbelt. "Where are we going?"

He starts the car and adjusts the mirrors. Looking her in the eyes he replies, "I have to see some old friends." He then reverses her car out the driveway.

Amber

Amber runs outside the school and looks both ways. "I know I saw him." She says under her breath. She takes out her cell phone and walks down the stairs.

"Hey!" Hakeem says, standing behind her at the entrance of the school. She turns around flummoxed at the sight of him.

"Where did you come from?"

"I was around the corner, I was trying to call you."

"I thought you weren't allowed to leave the house today?" She looks at him puzzled.

"God didn't try hard enough to keep me away from you." He began walking toward her as she met him halfway on the steps. She gives him a hug, and as he holds her tight, he whispers "I miss you."

"I miss you too!"

He lets her go and asks, "can we talk?"

"Of course, I should be saying that to you!"

"I mean, can we talk somewhere else?"

"Where do you want to go?"

"Anywhere but here."

She looks at the school and bites her lips. "You know I'm going to get in trouble, right?" He smirks and grabs her hands. "Fine, only this once!" She folds.

As the two begin to walk down the stairs, the front door of the school opens and to their surprise, Samson runs outside screaming. "I knew you would show your face eventually!"

"Go back inside Sam!" She replies, tugging Hakeem's arm to ignore him, and continue to follow her downstairs, which he does.

Once ignored, Samson becomes aggravated and continues running after them, screaming, "you hear me talking to you!" Hakeem removes his arm from her possession and turns around. "What are you freak?" Samson shouts in his face.

"I'm not going to tell you again, leave me alone!" As she tries to hold Hakeem back, Samson grabs him by the collar. With no second to think, he grabs Samson's neck and throws him up the flight of stairs. Shocking himself and Amber. When he realizes what he has done, he quickly looks at Amber and sees that she is terrified.

"What are you?" She stutters, slowly back pedaling down the stairs.

"Something happened to me Amber." He drops his defense. "Come with me so I can explain." He takes a step toward her. She turns around and sprints down the stairs in fear. Once she reaches the parking lot, she runs in between busses and parked cars, until she sees hers. She looks over her shoulder and is relieved to see no one. Then her heart sinks at the sight of him standing by the hood of her car.

"This can't be real!"

"I'm not going to hurt you!" Hakeem raises his hands slowly and walks to her. She backs up and tries to run again, but once she turns around, he cuts her off and grabs her by the shoulders. He looks her in the eyes and continues, "have I ever gave you a reason to not trust me?"

She looks him back in the eyes and drops her defense. "How is this possible?"

"Can we please go somewhere more private so I can explain?" She bites her bottom lip then nods her head. He lets go of her shoulders, then follows her to her car.

Isaiah

"You really kidnapped me." Taryn says to Isaiah as they stop at a stoplight.

"You volunteered to come." He shrugs. "I didn't force you."

"Where are we? We been on the road forever!" She looks out of the window with her feet on the dashboard. The light turns green and he makes a left turn.

"This right here, is the hood sweetheart." He parks the car outside of the laundromat. "Wait right here. I have some business to handle." He gets out of the car and leaves the keys in the ignition.

"Like I'd get caught walking in streets like this." She replies under her breath. When he walks through the entrance, everyone stops what they're doing and look at him, as if they have just seen a ghost. He continues to walk toward the backroom door, unbothered. As soon as he opens the door, everyone sprints out the laundromat.

Taryn is confused when she sees the laundromat clear out in front of her.

"Who won the game last night?" One of Vinny's henchman asks the other.

"I didn't watch it, my baby mother was watching a movie on lifetime."

"You're pathetic." Vinny interrupts the conversation. "The Knick's won, cough up my bread!" As the men count their money to give to him, the door swings open. The room grows silent when Isaiah walks through the door. "What the fuck?" Vinny looks at him puzzled. Isaiah smirks, as he looks around the room. "You can't be alive... What the fuck is going on?" The two men slowly surround the table where Vinny is. Not saying a word, Isaiah slowly walks toward them. "What the fuck are you niggas waiting for?" Vinny takes out his gun. "Shoot this mother fucker!" He aims at Isaiah's head and shoots.

Isaiah catches the bullet before it can hit him. When he looks in his hand, he sees a hole in the middle of his palm with smoke airing from it. He grins his teeth, as he digs for the bullet and drops it on the floor. Vinny and his henchmen look stunned.

When Isaiah looks back up, everyone loads their guns and start shooting. Taryn hears the gunshots outside of the laundromat and starts to panic. She hops in the driver's seat and thinks to herself for a couple of seconds, then hears another gunshot. "Fuck this!" She puts the car in drive and speeds off. When she gets to the stop light, she puts her address in the gps.

As the last bullet hits him, his face transitions into a vampire. He gets in front of one of the men and snaps his neck. He then jumps in front of the other who is reloading his gun and shoves his hand through his chest. He pulls the man's heart out and throws it at Vinny's face to scare him. Vinny back pedals nervously. As he walks towards him, a sudden urge for blood runs through his veins. He licks the blood off each of his fingers as he smiles at him.

"You got it!" Tears fall down his bloody face. "You could have all the money that's here! Just let me live please!"

"You were this close to dying with a little bit of dignity." Isaiah flexes his fingers then yokes him by his throat.

"What are you?" He struggles to ask.

"The grim reaper." Isaiah tilts his head to the side and bites through his neck. When he finishes, he goes through Vinny's pockets and takes out his cell phone. He scrolls down his contacts to Tyriek's name and texts him, "where you at?"

Hakeem

The sun begins to set over the park. Hakeem is sitting on a boulder under the trees staring at Amber, who is finishing her ice cream by the garbage can. When she finishes it, she throw's her container away and walks back to him. She licks her fingers as she approaches him. He stands up and gives her a hug. As he holds her tight, he closes his eyes and sniffs her hair. "I love you."

"I know you do. I love you too. This whole situation is still unreal to me. One day you're my sweet little boyfriend and the next day you're a vampire." She looks him in the eyes. "I won't lie, it'll take some time for me to adjust, but for the most part I'm happy you're still you."

"I'm happy I'm still me to." The two let each other go and hold hands and stare at the sunset.

"I want to come with you."

"It's not safe, and I refuse to put your life in jeopardy."

"Just like you have no control over your life, you have no control over mine either!" He bites his lips and shakes his head. "Let's go." She pulls his hand. The two walk down the hill from the tree and head toward the exit. As they approach her car, his senses start to tingle. Not knowing why, he hesitates to get in the car. She starts her car and looks at him standing by the passenger door, staring up at the sky. "What's wrong?"

"Go to my house, I'll meet you there."

"Are you sure?"

An owl flies over the car heading toward the park leaving a scent Hakeem can't ignore. It lands on the entrance of the park and turns its head towards him. Hakeem looks it in the eyes and at once knows something is different about this creature.

"Yea go." He taps the top of the car and shuts the door. The owl doesn't move its eyes, as she drives off leaving him in the parking lot. When he approaches the entrance, the owl flies into the park and lands on the floor. It faces him as if it were waiting. He hesitates again, then keeps walking. He looks around the park to see if anyone is looking, but the park is empty. The stare the owl gives, makes him uncomfortable.

"What are you? You're not an owl!" He shouts as he stops walking.

The owl tilts his head sideways, but doesn't take its eyes off him. Instead, it jumps off the ground and transforms into a man, wearing casual clothes. This mystery man is skinny and about two inches taller than him, with a brown-skinned complexion. His left pupil is all black. When the man's feet touch the ground, he brushes feathers off his shoulders and smirks at him. "So, you're the vampire Purgatory has been raving about!"

CHAPTER 26

Isaiah

"Hey this is Taryn, clearly I can't answer the phone right now, leave a message and I'll call you back if you're important." The voicemail makes a beeping sound.

"You fucking bitch! I'm going to fucking strangle you when I see you! How the fuck you leave me out here! Ooooh you better hope I don't see your ass when I get back!" Isaiah says, then ends the phone call. He puts his phone down and looks at Tyriek's house, and sees his car in the driveway along with another two cars parked on the side of the road. He walks to the side of the house and puts his ear to the wall to listen in.

"You still pushing this nasty ass weed!" He could hear Dimitri's voice, followed by a group of laugher.

"It's all I could get for now." Tyriek replies.

"Give me that shit! When did Vinny say he's coming?"

"He'll be here in a few."

"Who has the number to the pizza spot?" Another voice asks. Isaiah moves his head from the wall and walks toward the cars on the street. Observing one of the cars, he puts his palm on the window then punches it. When the glass breaks, the car alarm goes off.

"What the fuck is going on?" One of the men shouts, followed by another loud sound of glass breaking. More car alarms go off at the same time. Dimitri jumps off the couch and rushes outside with everyone behind him.

"No way," His mouth drops. The steering wheel was taken out of one car and tossed into the windshield behind it.

"My car!" One of the man cries. Everyone except Tyriek runs toward the cars with their hands on their heads, shocked.

"Who did this shit?!" Dimitri screams. Tyriek looks around his street from his stoop and is just as confused as everyone else. There wasn't a soul in sight. Dimitri sticks his head in the car and sees a cell phone. When he reaches for it, he realizes the phone belongs to Vinny. Everyone stands around him, puzzled. Not taking his eyes off the phone, he pats down his waist and notices his gun isn't on him. He puts the phone down and leads everyone back down the driveway. When the group makes it halfway to the house, one of the guys walking in the back makes an unusual squeaking sound.

When everyone looks back, he is gone. "Ed? Where the fuck did you go? Stop playing games!" Dimitri says, hesitating to keep moving, as if his feet are glued to the floor.

"I don't think he's playing games…" The other guy stutters, looking around the street. Suddenly, Ed's body falls lifeless in between Tyriek and Dimitri. Everyone stares at the body for a few seconds in complete shock, then looks up toward the sky. After seeing nothing but stars and jet fumes, they all slowly begin to walk toward the body.

"Is that a bite mark on his neck?" Tyriek asks unsure, examining the body. "I'm getting the hell out of here!" As everyone prepares to run back inside, to their surprise, Isaiah is standing on the stoop preventing them from going any further. "Holy shit." Tyriek says in disbelief. Dimitris mouth hangs open, as he looks at Isaiah with a blank stare. He tries to find words to say, but nothing but gibberish comes out. Blood still dripping from Isaiah's chin, as he wipes what's left off and grins at Dimitri.

"Who is this guy? Where did he come from?" Dimitris friend asks, cracking his knuckles.

As Isaiah smirks, Dimitris friend waste no time charging him. He throws a punch, but Isaiah grabs his forearm and pops his elbow bone out of his arm socket. Causing him to scream for his life. Isaiah then places his hand over his mouth and snaps his neck.

Dimitri and Tyriek stand erect, as they watch him fall onto the ground, still in disbelief. Isaiah looks down at the body then back up to lock eyes with Dimitri.

"This can't be real…" Dimitri stutters under his breath, back pedaling. His knees buckle once his back touches the front of Tyriek's car.

"Are your friend's dead bodies not real enough for you?" Isaiah asks, walking toward him.

Dimitri trips over his feet in a poor attempt to run around the car. Panicking, he quickly turns over to his back and sticks his hand out toward Isaiah. Still stuttering, he says, "I killed you… I watched you die…"

"I'm not the same person that died that night." Isaiah leans in closer, then transforms into a vampire. Tyriek is stunned at his face transformation. Isaiah charges him and bites his neck viciously. While Isaiah is feasting, Tyriek quickly runs back to his stoop. Isaiah throws Dimitri's corpse on the floor as if he were a dummy, and stares Tyriek down.

Hakeem

"Who are you?" Hakeem asks anxious for an answer.

The man steps forward, observing Hakeem's height before giving him a response. "Right question, but you should be asking yourself this."

"You're not a psychologist! So, cut the shit. Who are you? I'm not going to ask again!"

"I'm no different than you, just stronger, so watch your tone." Hakeem hesitates as he continues, "you're on the wrong side."

"What?"

"You heard me. You're not human, what are you still doing with that old witch?"

"I may not be human, but that's still my family. Be careful with your next set of words are or you'll regret it!"

He smirks. "I don't know who you're fooling with this tough talk. I know all about you Hakeem. You are not built for the war that is approaching. Now be a smart little boy and tell me what you told your grandma."

Hakeem grins back at him. "I don't know what you're talking about, but do me a favor, keep your opinions and your theories to yourself. I don't want to see you again." He tightens his fist then turns around to walk away.

The man cracks his knuckles and shouts, "I'm happy you didn't make this easy!"

"What?" Hakeem replies, turning back around. The man punches him in the face, causing him to stumble, then punches him again in the chest. Hakeem falls into the bushes then gets yoked back out and slammed on to the floor. He shakes his head trying to get back on his feet, then the guy attempts to throw another punch but misses. Hakeem is able to counter it and hit him back in the face.

The man back pedals a little, then rubs his chin. Smirking, he says, "you still hit like a human." Placing his hand over his stomach he begins to laugh uncontrollably. As he laughs, his right eyeball becomes pitch black. The man grows a couple of inches taller and becomes muscular. His laughter turns into a growl, as his teeth and jaw grow larger. Hakeem grins his teeth, frightened at this new transformation. As he charges toward Hakeem, his whole body completely changes into a yeti. Hakeem's eyes widen, as the beast yokes him by the neck and pounds him in the chest.

He picks Hakeem up then drops him on top of his knees. Hakeem lets out a cry of pain as the beast grips his head and tosses him further inside the park. Before he could get off the floor, the beast charges at him and kicks him in the face. He rolls over and tries to keep conscious, but his eyes become blurry. He sees double as the beast walks toward him, transforming back into an average height man.

"I understand you're new to being a demon, so I'm only going to tell you once. Rule number one, it's us over humans, always! Now considering your ancestors blood line, you've had a death wish from birth." He kneels in front of him. "Lucky for you we all will look pass that, if you simply accept what side you belong on." Hakeem shakes his head to regain proper vision, and when he does, he doesn't say a word. "This spell that witch did on you. That makes you a day walker, it's cute, but it doesn't make you special. You won't be special until you realize your role in the new world order. You have until the end of the week to cut that witch off. When we speak again I will be looking forward to hearing where that Hell Atomizer is." He pats him on the shoulder then stands up and looks to the sky, "the name is Zechariah by the way. And if you disappoint me the next time we meet, your house will be a graveyard for all the people you love. Mark my words."

He looks back down at Hakeem and gives him a smirk and a wink, then jumps in the air and turns into a bird. Hakeem lays his head back on to the floor with his arms stretched out and his eyelids get heavier the further Zechariah flies away.

Isaiah

Tyriek waves his hands surrendering to Isaiah, as he slowly back pedals into his house. "Zay, uh I'm not sure if you remember me. But it's Ty, your homeboy. You don't want to hurt me."

Isaiah wipes his blood off his mouth, as he walks toward him. "I really don't know what I want to do with you!"

"Huh, what did I do?"

"You know what you did! You sold me out!" Isaiah punches the barrier wall preventing him from walking inside. "I trusted you! And you threw me under the bus! You thought I wouldn't find out?" He points at him.

Tyriek puts his head down and sheds a tear. "I'm sorry bro, I really am. I swear I didn't want to snitch, but when I got back home they were waiting for me." He wipes his eyes. "I didn't even have a chance to run or hide. They whipped my ass as soon as I pulled into my driveway, then threatened to burn me alive when they found the money on me. They poured gasoline all over me and the house."

Isaiah grins his teeth and shakes his head. "I could still smell it. Your motor mouth got me killed Ty!" He places his hands on his hips and turns around to take a deep breath. "I guess I should have known better than to let you come back home."

"If they killed you, how are you here? Are you a zombie?" Tyriek asks, hesitating to walk toward the door.

"Do I look like a mother fucking zombie?"

"I mean, you just bit a chunk out of Dimitris neck, and you admitted to dying." He replies, confused.

"It's a long story. Just know I'm stronger then you could ever imagine. Faster and smarter, it's like I've been reborn."

"Are you going to kill me?"

Isaiah turns around and looks him in the eyes. "No." Tyriek takes a breather and slowly walks outside. The two sit down on the stoop as he continues to apologize. "It's ok, I forgive you, I'm sorry for putting you in this circumstance in the first place." Isaiah doesn't sit for long, he gets back up and asks Tyriek to borrow his car.

"Let me just ride with you. Give me a chance to redeem myself. I want to be strong like you…" He stutters.

"I have no set destination. If you come with me I don't know where this road will take us."

"It doesn't matter, I owe you. I'm in your debt."

Isaiah nods his head. "To be honest, I'm not 100% sure if this will work, but just do what I say." He nods his head, as Isaiah instructs him to go inside for an empty shot glass.

"I don't understand what you're going to do with this, but here." He hands Isaiah the shot glass.

"Don't ask questions, just have faith in me." Isaiah slits his wrist with his index fingernail and let's blood drip inside of the cup. "Drink this." He hands Tyriek the cup. Tyriek looks at the shot glass of blood, then back at Isaiah. He takes the shot glass, then pinch his nose and downs it. When he finishes, he sticks his tongue out, as if he were going to vomit.

"Here, what now?" He hands back the shot glass.

Isaiah observes it to make sure he drank it all, then tosses it to the floor. "Death."

"What?"

Isaiah grabs his neck and snaps it.

Amber

"Where is he?" Amber says to herself biting her fingernails. She was sitting in her car waiting for Hakeem in his driveway. Grandma walks downstairs of the house and sees a bright light shining through the window curtains. When Amber see's Hakeem's grandma looking through the window, she notices her headlights are still on and quickly turns it off. Grandma opens the front door of the house and walks outside. Unsure who is in the car, she approaches it anyways and looks through the window cautiously. "Hey grandma, its me." Amber lowers her car window.

"Oh, thank god, I forgot what kind of car you drive." Grandma looks into the passenger seat and notices she is alone. "Where's Hakeem?"

"Oh, uh, I was just with him a couple of minutes ago at the park. He told me he was going to meet me here."

She nods her head. "Ok. Come inside, you shouldn't be waiting outside in the dark."

Hesitating to answer, Amber takes another look down the street in hopes of seeing Hakeem. When she sees he's still nowhere in sight, she nods her head and turns her car off. She gets out the car and follows her inside.

"How's school? Do you know what college you're going to next year yet?" Grandma asks, leading her to the kitchen.

"School is ok. I have scholarships to a couple of schools. I just haven't made up my mind on what I want to do yet." She replies, grabbing a seat by the table. She looks down for a moment then says, "to be honest, it depends on where Hakeem goes."

Grandma squints her eyes and bites the bottom of her lip in anger and frustration, as she tilts her head sideways toward her. "Did you speak to Hakeem yet? Like really have a conversation?" Just as Amber readies herself to reply, the front door opens.

"Grandma! Amber!" Hakeem shouts interrupting the two. Grandma backs off her and walks out the kitchen with her following. Both of them look him up and down, as he stood in front of the doorway. Before they get a chance to say anything, he declares there is a problem.

"What happened to you?" Amber asks, worried.

"What's going on Hakeem?" Grandma asks, worried too.

He closes the door behind him and replies, "I just fought some type of creature at the park. It's still roaming the streets right now!"

Grandma's eyes shoot open at his response. She turns to Amber and points to the door, "you should go home."

"What? No!" She looks back at her, then runs toward Hakeem to give him a hug. He held his right arm over her as he raises his eyebrows at his grandma.

"Hakeem send her home now!" She redirected her finger at the door.

Amber looks Hakeem in the eyes for a couple of seconds and then back to her. She steps away from him and replies, "I know the truth. I know he's a vampire. I know you're a witch too."

"Amber!" He tries to say to cut her off, but is too late.

Grandma drops her hand and shakes her head. "Why does she know this?" She asks Hakeem.

"It's ok, I'm not running away. I love Hakeem no matter what!" Amber answers for herself.

Hakeem scratches the back of his head, as he tries to laugh the pressure off. "It's a long story grandma."

"Let me have a word with you in private!" She stares him down. The two walk to the kitchen, leaving Amber in the living room. She slams her hands on the table trying to intimidate him. "I expected this from Isaiah! I told you to keep this confidential!"

"It doesn't have to be as difficult as you make it." He replies taking a seat.

"You're going to regret this!" She points at him then shakes her head. "What attacked you at the park?"

"I don't know. One minute it was an owl, the next a man, then it turned it a yeti, then flew away as a bird. I feel like I'm in an episode of The X Files."

She grins her teeth. "It was a shapeshifter. Damn! What is one doing in New York? They don't usually come up to this side of the coast."

"It wanted to know what me and Isaiah told you about the Hell Atomizer. It called itself Zechariah."

She looks surprised when she hears this information. "Zechariah?

The name doesn't ring a bell, I'm going to call Aaron to see if we have any information on him in our archives. Listen, nobody else can know about this. I don't care if it's your mom! You hear me? Look at me!"

He looks her in the eyes and replies, "Ok."

"Where's your cousin Isaiah? We need to find him before that demon does!" He takes out his phone and realizes he missed 15 calls from Taryn. As he calls her back, loud music blasting from the outside of the house catches both of their attention. The two look at each other, then walk out the kitchen.

Amber is looking out the window, then turns around when she hears their footsteps. "It's Taryn." She says to Hakeem.

Grandma grabs his arm and says, "remember what I just told you!" He ends the phone call and nods his head.

"You're not going to tell Taryn? That's your best friend!" Amber steps away from the window and crosses her arms.

"Amber stop! This isn't a social club or a fraternity. You are not safe with us, neither is she! Hakeem shouldn't have told you about this, it doesn't concern you!" Grandma then faces Hakeem and continues, "if you're really Taryn's friend you will leave her out of this!"

The doorbell rings followed by multiple knocks. Amber standing between the door and the two replies, "pardon me Mrs. Exalus, but we all live in this world too. We deserve to be aware of the unknown. I love Hakeem and I have the right to live my life how I want too." The knocks gets louder as they start to hear Taryn's voice screaming for someone to answer. Grandma doesn't respond, but instead stares Amber in her eyes. In a matter of seconds, they are in a trance. When Hakeem notices how stiff Amber's body has become, he gets worried.

"Grandma what are you doing?" He faces her and yells.

She blinks twice and ends the trance. When Amber awakes up from it, she wipes her face, then sees faceless demons surrounding her, crawling on the ceiling and walls of the house. Supernatural bugs appear to be crawling out of every crack in the floor and are marching toward her. She screams at the top of her lungs and sprints out the door. As Hakeem prepare to chase her, his grandma grabs his arm and whispers, "I gave her a peak of a few unknown's that exist on earth. She'll be fine."

As Amber sprint's outside, she runs past Taryn who is standing at the door frustrated. She runs straight to her car and wastes no time starting it and reversing out the driveway. She is so determined to leave, she doesn't turn her headlights on until she makes it down the street.

Taryn

Taryn watches her leave then gather her thoughts and charges in. "I can't stand you! Do you have any idea how many times I called you! Your delinquent cousin just brought me to a shootout in the projects!" She pokes him in his shoulder.

"What? Where did he take you?" He replies, looking puzzled.

"Philadelphia, I'm assuming his old neighborhood. He had me wait for him outside of a laundromat while he had to handle what he called business."

"Where is he now?" Grandma interrupts the story.

"I don't know." She looks at her then back at Hakeem. "I waited a couple of minutes after the gun shots, but I was scared when he didn't come out. So, I left. I called the cops and told them the location, but my phone died on the highway while I was trying to get in touch with you."

"I'm sorry Taryn, I just saw your calls. I was actually in the middle of calling you back." He shows her his call log.

"I've been calling you way before I even left here with Isaiah." She ignores it.

"Taryn, I know you must be tired. Go home and rest, thank you for coming straight to us after this. We'll take it from here." Grandma interrupts again.

"I don't mind going back there with you guys." Taryn faces her.

Grandma smiles, "you did enough sweetheart. Just go home to your family. We'll keep in touch."

"Let me walk you to your car." Hakeem says, grabbing her hand. She nods her head at grandma and follows him out the door.

"Honestly Hakeem, I really didn't want to go home." She takes her hand back and rubs her shoulder. "My dad is back. He's been here for two days. It's just awkward and I'm not ready."

"Your mom really let him come back?" He looks at her puzzled, then shakes his head. "Damn, I know how serious this is, but you can't stay tonight, not with my grandma here and Isaiah being MIA."

"Wow, you really changed." She scrunches her face at him.

"What are you talking about?"

"Never mind! I hope you guys find Isaiah." She replies, marching toward her car.

He grabs the car door as she opens it and replies, "no tell me! How did I change? You know right now isn't the right time. It's complicated."

"Whatever! Ever since Amber started giving you pussy again, you've been acting Hollywood toward me! Then you shut me out of your life completely since the night of Chris's death! My dad is back and you don't even care!" She paused. "You know what, just forget it. I'm just going to go home. I'll see you when I see you."

"Listen." His voice got soft, letting go of the door. She quickly shuts the door on him and starts the car. "Taryn!" He shouts raising his hands. As she puts her car in reverse and leaves the driveway, his mother arrives at the house. He shakes his head and steps back. Angry, he takes his phone out of his pocket and scrolls down his contacts to Isaiah and calls him.

CHAPTER 27

Isaiah

A couple of minutes pass when Isaiah catches himself lost glaring into the stars. Tyriek's eyes shoot open, as he sits up grabbing his chest, gasping for air. He looks around him as if he were lost. "About time you woke up. I thought I really killed you." Isaiah says turning his attention to Tyriek. He grabs the side of his neck and cracks it back in place, then looks behind him at Isaiah, who was standing on the stoop. "You're going to lay down there all night or what? I have moves to make!"

Tyriek stands up and faces him. Still holding his neck with one hand, confused, he stutters, "did you just… Did you just kill me bro?"

"Yea" Isaiah replies, with no hesitation. "Your new life cost you your old one."

"I feel different." Tyriek looks at his hands. "My senses are heightened, it feels like I just snorted an entire brick of cocaine, but I'm still grounded."

Isaiah laughs. "Wait until you try some blood."

Tyriek put his hands down and gives him an unsure look. "I just drank yours, it's not that appealing."

"Don't worry, you're going to love the blood I spill at our next destination."

"Hold on, let me get my keys." Tyriek replies, patting himself down then going inside the house. Isaiah examines the damaged place, as Tyriek goes to the kitchen for his keys. He notices a black bag laying by the sofa filled with guns. When Tyriek comes back to the living room, he is kneeling over the bag with a pistol in his hand. "So, who's next?"

"Leo." He drops the gun back in the bag, then stands up. "Let's go."

"I don't think you're going to be able to find him."

"Why?" Isaiah looks at him puzzled.

"Word around town, him and Erica moved."

"Seriously?" He asks, disappointed.

"Yea, they left yesterday. They packed their shit and left without telling anyone. Not even Dimitri knew where they went."

It took a moment for this information to sink into Isaiah. "I'm still going to find him!" He replies, determined.

"How?" Tyriek looks at him puzzled. Isaiah walks out of the house and considers the stars as if they were going to guide him, but instead of receiving an answer he received a phone call. When he takes out his phone and looks at his screen, he shakes his head at the sight of Hakeem's name. He lets the phone ring several more times before finally answering.

"What do you want cuz?"

"Why the hell did you bring my best friend to a shootout? Are you fucking crazy?" Hakeem barks.

Isaiah tries not to laugh as he replies, "I don't know what you're talking about. Have you seen her though? Tell her she forgot to say bye before she left me out here."

"Don't ever get in a car with her again!"

Isaiah couldn't help but smirk as he shakes his head. "Is this the only reason you called me? Can I go now?"

"We need you to come home now! I just got attacked by a demon at the park. It might be coming for you next."

"What? Are you serious? What kind of demon was it?" His smirk quickly fades.

"Some type of shapeshifter." Hakeem paused. "I never seen anything like this. Come home we need to find out how to kill it together, before it finds you."

"Alright." He sighs then ends the phone call. He puts the phone back in his pocket then faces Tyriek who is standing at the door. "Change of plans, we'll find Leo another day."

The dark skies turned light blue as the sun prepared to rise. Isaiah parks Tyriek's car several houses away from Hakeem's. Before he gets out the car, he tells Tyriek to go back to the hotel they stayed at the last time.

"That's it for the night? I thought we was getting more blood?" Tyriek replies, disappointed.

"You didn't have enough? I'll bring you something fresh later, just make sure no sunlight enters that room."

"How long are we going to be staying here for?"

"Hopefully not long. The world is bigger than Philadelphia and Peekskill." Isaiah replies getting out of the driver seat. Tyriek gets out of the passenger seat and walks around the car to the driver's side. The two give each other a pound as he enters the car.

"I'll text you the room number." He replies as the two go their separate ways.

Hakeem

Camille opens Hakeem's window blinds, letting the sun shine through the room. "Wake up!"

"What time is it?" He grunts and covers his head with his pillow.

"Time for you to get ready for school."

"School?" He removes the pillow from his face.

"Yes, you need to catch up on your work." He lets out a groan as he shoves his face back into the pillow. She walks to his bedside and sits down. "How have you been holding up honey?" She places her hand on his leg.

He fixes himself so his back could lean against the headboard. "I'm alright mom. Do you think I could stay home one more day, please?"

"There's something different about you." She squints her eyes at him.

"What do you mean?" He squints back.

"I don't know. It must be because I miss being around you. I've picked up a lot of hours lately and haven't been home.

"I miss you too. I understand, the bills need to be paid. I should talk to my manager later today, maybe I could pick up some more hours to help."

She moves her hand from his leg to his arm and replies, "just worry about graduating. I'm doing all of this for you, you don't have to do anything for me."

143

"I love you mom." He smiles.

"I love you too." She smiles back. "I'll see you later, you can go back to school tomorrow." She stands up and walks to the door. "Sometime next week, I will stop at the board of education and get Isaiah registered."

"Don't waste your time." He replies under his breath. More time passed before he made his way to Isaiah's room, but to his surprise Isaiah wasn't there. He walks downstairs and looks in the living room and around the kitchen. When he sees, he was in neither place, he notices the door leading to the backyard is slightly open. He opens it further, and sees him sitting on the table smoking a joint. He walks outside and shuts the door behind him.

When Isaiah sees him walk out, he takes another puff and watches him grab a seat behind him. The two don't speak at first, until Isaiah breaks the silence. "Aren't you tired of getting beat up?"

Hakeem smirks and shakes his head. "I actually held my own. Let me see that joint." Isaiah passes it him. After he inhales it, he continues, "I can't believe you really brought Taryn to Philadelphia. What were you thinking?"

"Revenge." Isaiah replies, looking at the clouds.

"You brought her to the hood for revenge? Are you retarded?" Hakeem stands up and walks around the table.

Isaiah bites his lips and shakes his head. "She would've been safe with me. Unlike you I can actually hold my own."

"What! Being able to bite people is holding your own?" He looks at him puzzled. "What if she got shot as a casualty?"

"She didn't."

"So what, you're a killer now? You went back to settle the score?" Isaiah looks away and doesn't respond. Hakeem looks at him disgusted, then sits back down and inhales the joint again. He passes it back then continues, "the demon wanted to know about the Hell Atomizer."

Isaiah looks at the joint then back to him, "did you tell it?"

"No, we fought. It told me I have until the end of the week to drop grandma and give up the information or it's going to kill everyone around me."

Isaiah inhales the joint, stands up and throws it away. "Too be honest, I was thinking about ditching grandma anyways."

"What?" Hakeem shoots up from his seat, placing both arms on the table.

"Before you come at me, just hear me out." Isaiah puts his arms out. "Grandma wants us to find this artifact that's going to destroy all of the demons walking on Earth, last time I checked, I'm a demon and so are you." He points at him. "Whatever that demon wants with the Hell Atomizer, can't be any worse then why she wants it."

Hakeem puts his head down for a second, then looks back at him. "Finding this tool was the last thing our fathers wanted. I must find it. I have to find it, for my dad."

"I understand." Isaiah paused. "I wish I could say I feel the same way." He knocks on the table then walks pass him to go back inside.

"So that's it? You're just going to leave?"

Isaiah stops walking to reply, "you're welcome to join me, but I can see it in your eyes you don't want to leave."

There is a moment of silence between the two, then he continues to walk inside. After he changes his clothes he meets Hakeem in the living room. "I still don't like the idea of this. We're family we should stick together." Hakeem replies, with his arms crossed.

Isaiah laughs and shakes his head. "Family? I haven't been a part of this family since I was 10. You know when my mom died, grandma didn't call me, not one time. Not to ask how I'm feeling, not to ask how dad is treating me, not even to say happy birthday. Too hell with this family! I had to become a fucking vampire for her to show interest in my life." Hakeem remains silent. "At least you have something to fight for, I don't."

"Fine." Hakeem mumbles. Isaiah nods his head and walks toward the door. As he walks out, Hakeem asks, "what should I tell her when she comes home?"

"Anything, tell her I staked myself for all I care."

Hakeem nods his head. "Just be safe cuz. You might think this world is against you, but I'm not."

Isaiah nods his head again then closes the door behind him.

Amber

"Are you ok?" Emira asks Amber, as she stares off into space.

"Yea." She replies, snapping back to reality.

"Are you sure girl? There's something off about you. Not to mention you wore that shirt last Thursday." Amber looks down at her shirt and shrugs. The girls pay for their lunch and walk off the line toward their table.

Right before they sit at their normal lunch table, Amber notices Samson enter the cafeteria. With no time to think, she grabs

Emira's arm and says, "let's sit over there."

"What? Next to the losers?" Amber tightens her grip around her arm and gives her a funny stare. Emira lets out a sigh and replies, "ok." As the two walk to the back of the cafeteria, Samson notices Amber knocking people aside to find a seat. "What's going on? Why are you so hostile?" Emira places her tray on the table, which was on the far side of the cafeteria and sits.

Before she can reply, Samson walks up behind Emira and stares her down. "Where did you go yesterday? I know you saw what that freak did to me!"

Amber hesitates to answer, but was able to stutter out, "I don't know what you're talking about..."

"What?" He replies in disbelief.

Eating her French fries, Emira looks at both Amber and Samson and interrupts. "What is he talking about?"

"I don't know." Amber shakes her head. "I left while you two were talking."

"You're a liar! I saw you when he assaulted me!"

"Wait! You were with Hakeem yesterday and didn't tell me?" Emira drops her fry and tilts her head at her.

"I didn't see anything Samson! Leave me alone already!" Amber becomes aggravated.

He shakes his head and replies, "I didn't come here to give you a tough time, I could have easily made a scene in the middle of the cafeteria, but I came to speak to you individually." He points at her. "I'm going to expose him, you could either stay with him or go down with him!" He turns around and charges off. Amber stares at her plate, then stands up.

"Whoa! What's going on?" Emira asks, looking puzzled.

"Nothing, I'm going to the bathroom, I'll be back." As she walks out of the cafeteria, she takes out her phone and calls Hakeem.

CHAPTER 28

Isaiah

"My room is around the corner." Isaiah says to the two girls that were following him upstairs from the hotel lobby. The hotel wasn't fancy, but it was a private owned two flight floor lodge.

The girls whisper to each other and start laughing. "Is your friend cute?" One of them asks.

Isaiah smirks and shakes his head as he knocks on the door, "you're about to find out." The door opens and Tyriek smiles at the sight of the two girls behind him.

As the three walk inside, one of the girls ask, "why is it so dark in here?" Tyriek closes the door behind them and turns into a vampire. The girl's scream at the sight of Tyriek's new face. When they grab Isaiah for protection, Isaiah laughs and turns into a vampire too. Blood splatters on the cheap carpets and bed sheets as the two rip into the girls.

Isaiah sparks a joint as he watches Tyriek bite the limb's off the girl's neck trying to suck as much blood as he can. "You should've given me both of those bitches! I'm not going to have anything else to eat until the sun goes down," He stands up and licks his lips and fingers.

"Can you calm down? I'm hungry too. You'll survive until tonight." Isaiah replies, looking at the corpses and blood residue left all over the place. "What are we going to tell room service when they see this room?"

"Who cares, they'll get stuffed in the bathtub along with them." He replies, walking past Isaiah to sit on the bed.

"There's more to life than this. We are the strongest creatures walking the planet, Ty. Let's start making power moves!"

"Power moves? What do you mean?" Tyriek looks at him puzzled.

Isaiah passes him the joint. "You'll see for yourself. Tune into the local news channel." He grabs the hotel key off the counter and walks out the room.

Hakeem

A black Hyundai parks in Hakeem's driveway. His grandma and Aaron get out of the car and walk inside the house. "Hakeem! Isaiah!" She shouts as she shuts the door behind her. The two walk to the kitchen and wait for Hakeem to walk downstairs to meet them.

"Hey grandma." He sits down at the table and nods his head at Aaron.

"Where's Isaiah?" She asks.

He scratches the back of his head and replies, "he left."

"Again?" She looks at him puzzled.

"What?" Aaron interrupts, then walks to the window and looks through the blinds. "It's broad daylight outside, how did he leave?"

"I was waiting for the right time to tell you." She shakes her head, then pauses. "I turned the boys into day walkers."

Aaron squints his eyes at her then looks at Hakeem. He opens the blinds to let sun shine through the room and is shocked to see that the sunlight has no effect on Hakeem. "Are you crazy? Are you trying to get us on the shit list?"

"We got the information we needed from them. They're clearly cooperating with the mission, them being able to walk during the day will benefit us."

"Do you know what the Power Circle will do when they find out!" Aaron replies, pointing at Hakeem.

"Stop talking to my grandma in that tone!" Hakeem pounds on the table, standing up.

Aaron looks at Hakeem appalled, then turns to his grandma, "Adeline, may I have a word with you in private?"

She nods her head. Hakeem quickly grabs her hand and continues, "whatever you have to say to her, you can say in front of me."

She puts her other hand over his and say's "It's ok." The room grows quiet as Hakeem looks at the two of them, then let's go of her hand. When the two leave the kitchen, Hakeem closes his eyes, so he can focus on hearing the conversation the two are having.

"Those boys are abominations, no matter how you try to justify this situation. What happens if they come to realize the power they really have?" Aaron whispers in her ear in the hallway entering the living room.

"We wouldn't be so eager to join this suicide mission." Hakeem walks out of the kitchen and answers the question for his grandma.

Both Aaron and his grandma look at him. "Hakeem!" She tries to hush him.

"No, he wanted to know." He points at him. "So, I'm going to tell him. He's in my house calling us abominations, but depending on us to do his job for him!"

"Is that why Isaiah left?" Aaron asks.

"Yea." He nods his head.

Aaron shakes his head then looks at grandma. "This is on your head, not mine!"

"We'll get him back!" She crosses her arms.

"Honestly, I don't think you will." Hakeem replies.

"Call him now! I want to speak to him." She barks.

"I need some air." Aaron massages his forehead. He turns around and walks out the front door, angry that this is all happening. As Hakeem takes out his cell phone, he receives a call from Amber.

He turns around and answers the phone, "hey babe, right now really isn't an appropriate time. Are you ok?"

"Hey, I'm ok. I had a weird dream last night, but I'll tell you about it later. Listen, Samson just threatened me that he's going to expose you. Please be careful."

"Expose me? What's wrong with that guy? Thank you for the heads-up baby. I'm going to call you later. Love you."

"Love you too." Hakeem ends the call and turns back around.

"Who's going to expose you?" Grandma asks, puzzled, walking toward him.

"Don't worry about it." He replies, scrolling down to Isaiah's number to call him in front of her. When he calls the line goes straight to voicemail.

Isaiah

Isaiah parks Tyriek's car on the side of the road, outside of the towns bank. Dressed in all black, he looks at his reflection in the rear-view mirror. When he sees Hakeem's phone call he clicks ignore and he puts on a mask that resembles the president. He grabs two duffel bags and gets out of the car, leaving it running.

"Thank you for banking with us today, please come again." The teller says to a customer as they walk out. Isaiah walks in after the customer and wastes no time grabbing the teller by his neck. "Stop." He tries to say, gasping for air. Everybody in the room stops and stares at him holding the teller in the air by his throat.

Isaiah laughs at the sight of all the facial expressions in the room, then throws the duffle bags over the counter. "Fill the bag or I'll kill him!" Holding the bags, the teller looks at them then back at the bags, then at the register.

"Are you kidding me! You don't even have a gun!" One of the civilian's shouts. Two officers who are walking by notices the commotion going on and runs inside. They approach him with their guns drawn, ready to shoot. He turns around with the man still in the air fighting for freedom, until he finally passes out.

"Place him on the floor now! And keep your hands where we can see them!" One officer shouts. Isaiah looks up at the man who is passed-out and tosses him on top of him. Shocked, the other officer starts to shoot. Running through the bullets, Isaiah slams him on the floor and forces him to shoot himself in the face. Panicking, the teller presses a button under the table to set off an alarm.

When the other cop finally gets off the floor, Isaiah kicks him and breaks his leg. He screams as Isaiah holds him at gun point. "Fill the bag now! Or the pig is getting it, then you after!" He threatens the teller. Everyone in the bank drops to the floor in fear. The teller nods her head and starts filling the bags.

Isaiah shoots a bullet in the air to show he means business. The teller fills the bags as quickly as she can. As she hands the bags over, he shoots the cop in the head, splattering blood all over her clothes. He grabs the bags from her hands as she screams then shoots her in the face too. Everyone in the bank screams and cover their heads. When he turns around to leave, outside is flooded with cop cars. He doesn't hesitate to walk out despite all the guns that are aimed at him from every corner on the street.

"Stop right there!" "Freeze!" officers scream with their fingers on their triggers. He looks around them and begins to laugh. A news helicopter flies over everyone and tries recording what is going on. He places the duffle bags straps over his shoulders and runs toward them. The cops start shooting simultaneously while he jumps on the roof of a cop car, and leaps over officers to the ground and continues to run between back alleys until he gets away.

Camille

"Hey Camille" The doctor taps her on her shoulder and places his clipboard on his desk. "You've been working real hard this morning, you should take a break."

"Are you sure? I really don't mind checking in the next patient." She replies unbothered.

"Yes, take a break. Eat something, come back in 15 minutes. Betty will cover for you." She nods her head, washes her hands and walks out of the room. When she walks into the staff room, she greets her coworkers who are watching TV and heads straight to the coffee machine.

"Breaking news! Video of one man robbing a bank in Peekskill, New York, killing two officers and an employee," says the anchorman on the TV.

"Oh my, turn up the volume!" one coworker says. As the music from the news start to play, Camille finishes pouring herself a cup of coffee and turns around to watch.

"Good afternoon ladies and gentlemen. My name is Michael and this is channel 14 joining you with breaking news! Today at the local bank down in Peekskill, New York, a masked man showed supernatural strength as he killed two armed officers and fled the scene with unbelievable speed. Here's the footage." As the video plays, she notices the dreads hanging from the bottom of the mask and becomes suspicious.

"It can't be." She mumbles under her breath with the coffee mug under her chin.

"This guy is creepy!" a coworker shouts.

The Anchorman continues, "the criminal in the video is still on the loose. We don't know what his face looks like, but we know he is about 5'7, 5'8, African American with dreadlocks and is extremely dangerous. If anyone sees a man that fits this description, please call the police!" She holds the coffee mug to her chest in disbelief. She walks to her locker and takes out her phone to call Hakeem.

Hakeem

"You're fucked." Aaron says to grandma as he looks at the fuel being left behind by the jet soaring through the skies.

"You're exaggerating Aaron, nothing is preventing us from finding the Atomizer." He bites his lips to prevent himself from saying anything he'll regret.

Hakeem walks outside and looks at them both. "Still no word from him, he's probably long gone by now."

"Did he leave anything in his room? I'll put a locator spell on him." Grandma asks.

"I think so." As they walk back in the house, Hakeem's cell phone rings. When he sees it's his mom, he looks at his grandma and answers the phone.

"Are you with Isaiah?" Camille quickly asks when he answers.

The question catches him off guard. He hesitates to answer and decides to lie. "Yea, he's in his room, why?"

"Thank god. Turn on the news, they're talking about a robbery in town today at the bank, and the description fits Isaiah to the tee, but the things that man can do are unreal!"

"What?" He runs over to the sofa and looks for the television remote.

"I've never seen anything like this before," She continues.

When he finds the remote he tells his mom he'll call her back and ends the phone call. When he finds the news channel, everyone's mouth drop.

"We need to find him now!" Grandma scream.

Aaron looks at the both of them and replies, "you find him. I'm reporting back to the Power Circle before I get sent for!" Without saying bye, he storms out the door.

"What does he mean he'll get sent for?" Hakeem ask looking at his grandma.

"I'll fill you in later, we need to find Isaiah before he does anything else reckless." Hakeem nods his head, then leads her upstairs to Isaiah's room.

Isaiah

When Isaiah walks into the hotel room, he throws the duffel bags in the middle of the room. Tyriek stands up and applauds him. "That was some gangster shit Zay! You're all over the news right now!"

Isaiah laughs as he licks his thumbs then rubs his hands. "Help me count this money!" The TV is still on the news channel. When Isaiah sees himself on the screen he instantly regrets not taking more money. He opens the bag and takes out a handful of cash. Within seconds of holding it, the money bursts into green paint all over him, Tyriek and everything else in that area of the room. Shocked, the two open their eyes and stare at the open bag. Tyriek starts to laughing hard. Isaiah becomes aggravated and kicks the second duffel bag across the room.

"You did all of that for no reason."

Wiping his face, Isaiah replies, "the teller is lucky she's dead. I'd kill her again!" Tyriek stops laughing and walks to the sink and washes his face.

"If I was there with you, your plan would of went better. We would have at least been able to get some real money along with the counterfeit." He walks pass Tyriek to wash his face as well. "I hope me becoming a day walker is another part of your so-called power moves." Tyriek continues.

"My grandma would probably kill you before she turned you into one."

"Negotiate something with her!" Tyriek pleads.

"The only way she might do it is if we help find some dumb ass ancient tool for her. Which I remind you, will kill us!" He walks toward a seat by the wall.

"How about we play by her rules until we find it. Then we ditch her with it." Isaiah sits down as if a light bulb lights up in his mind. "How about you get your cousin to talk to her. She'd most likely listen to him." Tyriek continues as he follows him to the other side of the room. Isaiah takes out his phone and looks at all the missed calls from him.

"We should have tried negotiating before I robbed that bank."

"Who cares. Look how many times they called you! They clearly want you back." Isaiah shakes his head then calls him back.

"Zay, what the fuck are you thinking? Do you know how much attention you just brought to us?" Hakeem barks when he answers the phone.

"Nobody saw my face cuz, you're over reacting!"

"I'm standing next to grandma, she wants you back home now!" Hakeem puts the phone on speaker for her to talk.

"If you don't come home, we'll come find you and bring you home!" She adds.

"I'll come back under one condition. I turned one of my friends into a vampire by accident. Turn him into a day walker, then I'll come back."

"What! No. What are you doing Isaiah? This isn't a game! I'm not turning your friend into a day walker!" Grandma barks.

"I never said this was a game. If he was one of Hakeem's friends, you would do it."

"No I wouldn't. You boys shouldn't be turning anybody into vampires. Are you out of your mind?"

"Well it's done. Turn him into a day walker or I'm leaving town."

"I'm not turning him. I'm going to find you no matter where you go. You think you're strong? You have no idea what I'm capable of!"

Isaiah shakes his head. "It doesn't have to be difficult grandma. Just do what I say, we could get the atomizer together."

"I said no Isaiah. You're not in charge here. Your friend was never part of the plan. When Aaron finds out about him, there's nothing I can say that will save him."

"What?" Isaiah looks at his cell phone angry.

"What were you expecting me to say? I told you specifically not to do anything stupid! And the first day out the house, you take Taryn to a shootout, the second day you rob a bank, not to mention you killed people! You turned your friend into a vampire and now your demanding me to turn him into a day walker! This is not what our family is about!" She waits for a response from him, but he says nothing.

"Just come home and forget about your friend. Let him leave town before things get out of control." Hakeem interrupts.

"How about no. Fuck the both of you. Keem you're a coward for that suggestion. Let's see how strong your principles are when someone close to you becomes one of us." Isaiah ends the call.

"I'm guessing she's not down to turn me into a day walker?" Tyriek replies crossing his arms. Isaiah shakes his head then lets out a little laugh.

"You're ugly anyways, some faces shouldn't be seen in the day." Isaiah's phone rings again, but before it can ring a second time, he crushes it in his hands and lets the pieces fall onto the floor.

Hakeem

Hakeem tries to call him again but the call goes straight to voicemail. "Damn, he turned his phone off. Did he sound serious about turning one of my friends?" He asks his grandma.

"Yes, very serious." She replies taking one of Isaiah's shirt from the draw and storming out of his room. The two walk into the guest room and as she goes through her bags, Hakeem sits on the bed and looks at his phone. "Found it!" She shouts holding a small pouch in the air. He gets back on his feet as she lays Isaiah's t-shirt on the ground. He watches as she sprinkles black powder from the pouch over the shirt and waves her hands over it. She whispers a few words, then the shirt lights on fire. It burns for a few seconds and then evaporates into an image of Isaiah than into a small ball of green light. Once formed, the small ball of light bounces from wall to wall out of control. "This light will take you to him." She continues, admiring what she has created. The ball of light suddenly stops moving and holds steady, it slowly starts to levitate and move out the room.

"You don't think people in town will find this floating ball of light strange?" Hakeem asks as the ball passes him.

"Only those with supernatural abilities are able to see this. Now hurry up and don't lose it!"

"You're not coming?" He looks at her concerned.

"No, you can do this on your own. I need to get a hold of Aaron."

He nods his head then leaves the room.

Amber

"Whoa, did you get that alert on your phone?" A teenager asks the others in the back of the classroom.

"Yea, some dude with dreads went on a killing spree at the bank today." The others replied.

"Dreads? Did they identify who it was?" Emira turns around at her desk and asks.

"They didn't, the guy was wearing a mask. Here's a picture of him though." The teen holds out his phone. Emira studies the picture and snatches the phone out of his hand when she notices that the masked man resembles Isaiah. "You know him?" He asks observing her facial expression.

Before she can respond, the teacher yells at them to put their phones away. She quickly sends the link to herself then hands it back. She raises her hand and asks if she can use the bathroom. Pacing the hallway for a few minutes with her eyes glued to her phone, she eventually ends up in front of Amber's classroom. As Amber takes notes, a student behind her taps her shoulder and points to Emira standing outside the classroom door trying to get her attention.

"May I use the bathroom?" She asks her teacher. He nods his head and she quickly walks out of the classroom. When she closes the door behind her, Emira hands her the phone. She starts watching the video as they walk down the hallway. Once the video starts, Emira pays close attention to her face for her reaction. Amber stops walking and looks at the screen shocked when she notices the dreads on the masked man.

"That's Zay isn't it?" Emira wastes no time in questioning her. She looks at her and hesitates to give her an answer. "Samson was right the whole time. They are freaks and you didn't tell me!"

"You don't know if that's him." Amber shakes her head.

"Come on Amber, who else from here has dreads!" She points to the ground and continues, "don't lie to me, that's your boyfriend's cousin." She grabs her phone back. Before Amber can say anything, Isaiah walks out of the men's bathroom in front of them and looks at them with a smile.

Hakeem

The small ball of light brings Hakeem to Isaiah's hotel room door and the ball of light goes through the door. Before Hakeem can get a chance to knock, he hears Tyriek's reaction. "What the fuck!" Tyriek tries to run out of the room, but meets Hakeem face to face when he opens the door.

Hakeem looks over his shoulder and sees the green paint all over the dark room. When he doesn't see Isaiah, Hakeem grabs his collar and presses him against the wall. "Where's Zay?"

"I don't know. Let go of me!" Tyriek replies trying to break free. The small ball of light begins to make its way pass the two vampires and back into the hallway.

Hakeem applies more pressure and continues, "when the sun goes down, leave town! I don't ever want to see you again!" He let's go of him and follows the ball of light down the hall.

"Or what? What will you do?" Tyriek yells back while leaning on the wall.

"Zay won't be able to save you."

Tyriek fixes his collar. "It's like that? Too bad you won't be able to get to him in time to save your girlfriend." He laughs.

"What?" Hakeem stops walking. When he turns around, Tyriek slams the room door. Hakeem gets ready to charge toward the door, but realizes the ball of the light floating out of the hotel. Instead of going forward, he takes out his phone and calls Amber. The call goes straight to voicemail.

Amber

"What are you doing here?" Amber asks.

"I was looking for someone, but I think I found her." Isaiah steps

162

closer to the two. She steps back cautiously as she tries to keep a fake smile on her face. He looks Emira up and down as she steps back too. "You look beautiful today."

"Thank you." She replies nervously, quickly moving behind Amber.

"Seriously, who were you looking for? Is it Hakeem?" Amber stutters. Her cellphone starts to ring, and not taking her eyes off him, she pulls her phone out of her back pocket. She glimpses down and sees its Hakeem calling. Isaiah looks down at her phone and sees his name too. He takes another step toward her and snatches the phone from her.

"He doesn't need to know I'm here." He says as he breaks her phone. Emira lets out a little squeak then runs down the hallway, leaving Amber by herself.

"Why are you acting like this? What do you want?" She backs up into the locker.

"I'm going to do what Hakeem should have done days ago. Turn you into a queen." He bites the palm of his hand, before she gets a chance to react, he shoves his bloody hand into her mouth and on the side of her face. She quickly kicks him in the groin and runs down the hallway. Bent over laughing, he watches her run away. Panicking, she runs to a fire alarm and pulls it. The hallway is quickly flooded with students and teachers. She tries to blend in with the crowd as they make their way out to the closest exit. When the door opens, to her surprise Isaiah is standing there smiling. Shocked, she turns around and pushes her way through the crowd back inside. Bumping into students, she unintentionally runs into a teacher's arm.

"Whoa, where are you going young lady?" He asks. She quickly lifts her head up with fear all over her face. The teacher notices the blood on her lips and cheeks. "What happened? Are you ok? You need to see the nurse!" She turns her head around to see if Isaiah followed her inside, but he is nowhere in sight.

Taryn

"I don't think I'm going back to class." Taryn says to Andrew as they walk out of the school using a different exit, not too far away from the one Amber was near.

"What? ms. know it all isn't spending a full day at school?" She shakes her head as she looks in her bag for her keys. "What's up with you? You have been acting shady all day. Is it your dad?" Andrew looks at her worried.

"She is probably realizing how fake she is." Isaiah interrupts the conversation. The two look at him surprised.

"What are you doing here? Where's Keem?" Andrew asks.

"Probably at home wiping my grandma's ass. Taryn knows why I'm here."

"Isaiah, I'm sorry I left you there. I was going to return your calls."

"When? In another two days?" Isaiah replies sarcastically.

"What's going on?" Andrew asks confused.

"It doesn't concern you," Isaiah replies unbothered.

She shakes her head as she takes her keys out of her bag, "I apologized already Zay, what else do you want from me?" Isaiah shakes his head too and doesn't answer. She shrugs her shoulders and faces Andrew, "let's go." The two try walking away until Isaiah grabs her arm aggressively. "What the fuck Isaiah! Let me go!"

"Bro, what are you doing?" Andrew steps up to him. Isaiah smirks at him, as he lets Taryn pull her arm away.

"Fucking creep!" She shouts walking away. Andrew shakes his head at him and follows her.

When the two make their way to the parking lot, Andrew points to his car in the back and says, "I parked over there. Meet you at The Shack?" She nods her head in agreement then walks in the opposite direction toward her car. When she opens her car door, Isaiah approaches from behind and slams it shut.

"What's your problem?" She turns around and yells.

"Shut up!" He grabs her by the mouth and looks around for any witnesses and notices a sewer. He wraps his arms around her and drags her to it. Using one hand, he takes the top off the sewer. Struggling to break free, she bites his hands but inflicts no pain. Laughing, he slightly let's go of her mouth for a little.

"Help!" She tries to scream, but he quickly tightens his grip again.

"Nobody is going to save you, you piece of shit!" He bites the same palm he had bitten earlier, when she sees him do this, she tries to wrestle away. Right before he puts the bloody hand on her face, he notices a small ball of light floating in the air. "What the hell?" He says to himself, dropping his hand.

"Let her go Zay, now!" Hakeem shouts as he arrives.

"You being here won't change anything!" He replies.

"You don't need to do this, you made your point!"

When he lets go of her mouth, she shouts out for help from Hakeem. "No. I don't think I have!" He replies then shoves his palm down her mouth.

"Zay no!" Hakeem reaches his hand out, but Isaiah snaps her neck and drops her body in the sewer.

"Write about this bitch!" He looks at Hakeem then flees. Hakeem runs to the sewer and screams out her name in anger and fear.

CHAPTER 29

Taryn wakes up and with the sunlight shining from above it causes her to feel a burning sensation on her back. Screaming in pain, she jumps from the floor before she catches on fire and runs into the shadows. She grabs the side of her neck and gasps for air as she cools off. "Taryn!" Hakeem shouts again. She looks up but only sees a blur from the direction of the sunlight.

"Hakeem?" She asks in a faint voice. When he hears her voice, he instantly jumps into the sewer and lands on his feet. Acknowledging each other, the two run into each other's arms. "Hakeem what did Isaiah do to me?" She asks shaken up.

"I'll explain."

Grandma

The loud ringtone disturbed the silence within the house. Grandma picks up her phone to see whose calling. When she sees the unknown number, she hesitates to answer and lets the call go to voicemail. Within seconds the unknown number calls again. She takes a deep breath and answers. "Hello Adeline, how are you and the boys?" a deep voice ask. She instantly knows it is the Power Circle.

Still hesitating to speak, she replies, "everything is being dealt with."

"Aaron tells us you turned the boys into day walkers, is this true?"

"Yes, I did. They're not a threat! Turning them into day walkers will speed up the process."

"Adeline your impulsive behavior will not be tolerated!"

"I was going to tell you what happened." She replied.

"You were isn't the same as you did! We are extremely disappointed in you." He pauses for a second and the line is completely silent. "There was a meeting held and due your grandchildren's circumstance, we feel we can no longer trust your

167

judgement. You are hereby suspended from the mission until further notice."

"What? No, I haven't made any hasty decisions without thinking every moment through, you can't do this!" Her voice cracks.

"We want you to come back to the citadel to finish this discussion in person."

"What about the boys? The mission?" She pleads.

"Warriors are being sent to your town to kill them. We have all the information we need. We no longer need their services."

"We don't need to kill them! They're not as bad as you think!" She cries.

"We just watched a video of Isaiah killing and robbing people. Defending your grandchildren stop's now! If you continue it will not end well. Good bye Adeline." He ends the phone call, leaving her emotionless in the middle of living room unsure what to do next.

Isaiah

When Isaiah walks into the hotel room, Tyriek is standing in front of the TV feeding on the room service attendant. He quickly shuts the door behind him and yells, "you seriously couldn't wait? Now we to have to kill everyone who comes looking for him until the sun goes down!"

Tyriek takes a breather with his mouth covered with blood. "I told you I was hungry." Just as Isaiah locks the door, there is a knock on the opposite end. Tyriek drops the body and walks away from the TV. Isaiah looks through the peephole and sees a cop.

He looks back at Tyriek and says, "the fun just arrived." When he opens the door, a strange odor instantly hits him. He hesitates to speak.

The cop smiles and introduces himself, "Isaiah, right?"

He looks the cop up and down and into his eyes. He notices his left pupil is all black and replies, "you must be Zechariah?"

"Hakeem told you about me huh?" He walks pass Isaiah and into the hotel room. He studies Tyriek and looks around the room. When he sees the paint from the counterfeit money on the floor and walls, he begins to laugh, then nods his head with approval when he discovers the dead bodies they are hiding.

"Why are you dressed like a cop?" Isaiah asks.

"I wanted to see the show in person, but it was over by the time I arrived." He turns to face Isaiah as he shuts the door.

"Tell me why me and my boy shouldn't rip you apart and leave you next to these bodies." Isaiah points to the corpses.

"That would be the last dumb attempt you make today." He replies then looks behind him at Tyriek.

"Who is this guy?" Tyriek asks as he walks around him toward Isaiah.

"What do you want?" Isaiah crosses his arms.

"If Hakeem told you about me. You know what I want!"

Isaiah smirks. "I do know what you want. The real question is why should I tell you anything? What makes you any different than the old lady?"

"Unlike the witch, I won't keep secrets from you."

"Secrets? What secrets is she keeping from me?" Isaiah asks

dropping his arms and taking a step closer.

"I know she didn't tell you why you saw your mother in purgatory."

His comment catches him off guard. "We never spoke about me seeing her there."

Zechariah smiles as he shrugs his shoulder. "Well you should've asked. I'm quite curious to hear what story she would have thrown together."

"What do you know?"

"I know you believe you and your cousin are the first vampires in your family, but you weren't. Your mother was. And not only was she the first, your grandma was the one who killed her!"

"I don't believe you." He points at him.

"Ask her yourself!" Keeping his eyes on him, Isaiah taps Tyriek's arm and takes his phone from him. He looks down at the phone for a couple of seconds then looks up at Tyriek who looks even more confused than he is. He shakes his head and dials his grandma's number. When the line picks up, it is silent.

"Hello? Isaiah, is it you?" She asks.

He hesitates to answer. "Yea, its me."

"Isaiah, I'm not going to tell you again. Come home now!"

Still looking at Zechariah, he asks, "did you kill my mom?"

The line becomes quiet. "Isaiah listen." Her voice gets soft. He removes the phone from his ears and ends the call.

"You're right, she did kill her." He replies looking puzzled.

Zechariah nods his head. "I want you to join me to find this Atomizer."

"My word won't be good enough?"

"She failed to tell you another thing. Of course you know the Atomizer can be used to lock the rest of us in purgatory, but what you don't know, is it can be used to free the other side. Your mother can be freed again." Speechless, Isaiah nods his head agreeing to join. "Good, I'm going to set up some arrangements after I kill your grandma," He says as he walks toward the door.

Isaiah places his hand on his chest. "I want to be there, I want to see her die."

Zechariah looks him in the eyes and smiles. "It'll go a lot smoother if you aren't there." Isaiah removes his hand and doesn't respond.

When he opens the door to leave, Isaiah says "don't kill Hakeem." He smiles then closes the door behind him.

Grandma

After the phone call from Isaiah, grandma tries to recall but the call goes straight to voicemail. She sits down on the couch and runs her fingers through her hair as she bows her head down in frustration. After a couple of minutes, she gets up and starts making her way to the guest room when the doorbell rings. She pauses for a second to think who could be at the door, but after hearing the doorbell ring again, she quickly walks to open it.

Amber is standing there looking shaken up. Her face suddenly becomes worried. "Are you ok? Did Isaiah hurt you?" Amber looks her in the eyes and nods her head.

"He tried too, but I got away. Is Hakeem home?"

"No, but come inside, you'll be safe here." She moves to the side and lets her in. But Amber hesitates to walk in. She looks around the house cautiously before sticking her feet in, scared of the idea that a demon could pop out of the closet and grab her. Grandma notices her hesitation and says, "It's ok, Hakeem will be home soon."

Taryn

As the hours drag out, the sun begins to set.

"Taryn, it's safe for us to resurface, the sun is setting." Hakeem says, looking out of the entrance of the sewer. The two climb the ladder out of the sewer and back into the high school parking lot.

"Everything feels so weird, am I going to get used to this feeling?" She asks looking up to the stars.

"To be honest, I don't know. I'm not even used to this."

"I feel empty inside." She replies holding her stomach. He looks at her and doesn't respond. Instead he looks up at the stars too.

"We need to get home to my grandma."

She nods her head as she looks at him. "I'll drive." The two walks to her car, but when they get in, Hakeem stops her from opening the door.

"Wait. Let's run, we'll get there faster." He says.

"Run? I have a car." She looks at him puzzled.

He grabs her hand and says, "your car will be here tomorrow, trust me." She nods her head and locks her door. "Follow me." He slowly starts to jog away, as she catches up to him, within seconds they take off in full speed. Running through traffic, the two run all over town before they head back to his house.

"How is this possible?" She asks full of enthusiasm. The two stop in front of the water fountain on main street.

"I asked that question too many times this week." He smiles.

"Is it just me or does the stars look really bright tonight."

"It's just you." He laughs gently as she hits him softly on the shoulders. The two stare at each other and he proposes an idea. "I know where you could get a better look at them."

"Where?"

"You'll see." He leans back and starts running away. She smiles then chases after him feeling free and forgetting all the burden she has been dealing with. She follows him to a hill outside of town. When they get to the top they can see their entire town and more.

"Wow, this view is beautiful, I have never been here before!" She is amazed at the clear view of the stars. "This is unbelievable."

"I told you." He can't take his eyes off the stars either.

The two spend a couple of minutes in silence before she apologizes about last night. "It wasn't right of me to put you on the spot like that, especially with what you're dealing with. I'm sorry."

He looks at her and apologizes too, "It's ok. I'm sorry I couldn't be there for you yesterday. I'm even more sorry that my cousin got you involved into this. Are you ready?" She nods her head and the two race down the hill.

Amber

"I'm worried, Hakeem should have been here by now." Amber says to grandma as they sit on the sofa.

"I'm worried too, but I know Hakeem can handle Isaiah." She

replies.

Amber shakes her head. "What was he trying to prove by feeding me his blood?"

Grandma looks at her puzzled. "You didn't tell me he fed you his blood, I didn't know he got that far."

"I didn't? I thought I did. Does that mean anything? Am I going to become a vampire?" Amber panics.

"No, as long as you don't die within 24 hours you'll be ok." Amber sighs in relief. "But, the next upcoming days won't be pleasant for you!"

"What are you talking about?"

"Every human has their own experience when they digest vampire blood. We will have to wait and see what's yours."

"Experience? I'm confused." As grandma prepares to explain, Hakeem opens the front door and walks in. Taryn tries to walk in after, but a barrier wall prevents her. Amber jumps off the couch and runs into his arms. "You're safe!"

"Yea, I'm safe." He replies holding her.

"Ew, why do you smell like this?" She sniffs him then steps away.

"We spent the day in the sewers."

Grandma stands up from the couch and walks toward the door.

"Hakeem why can't I come in?" Taryn asks as she holds her hand against the invisible barrier wall. Grandma notices and shakes her head.

"I was too late, I couldn't get to Isaiah in time." Hakeem pleads to his grandma.

"She's a vampire too?" Amber ask looking over his shoulder at her. He nods his head.

"You're a vampire too?" Taryn asks.

"No, Hakeem filled me in on everything yesterday." Amber says relieved. He cuts her off to ask his grandma to invite Taryn inside.

"It won't work, I don't live here, only your mother can invite her in." She replies.

"Wait, you knew about all of this since yesterday?" Taryn asks Amber. Amber notices tension in her voice and doesn't respond. Taryn bites her lip and shakes her head slowly. "So, I was the only one left out huh?"

"I told you already, I was going to tell you at the right time." Hakeem pleads.

"So yesterday was the right time for Amber to know and not me?" Taryn looks at him puzzled.

"No, Taryn."

"You know what, it's ok. I'm going to just go home." She cuts him off and turns around and walks away.

"What! Why? No!" He charges out the house after her.

She turns around and replies, "It's not like I could come inside Hakeem! I'm tired, I stink and I'm not spending my night outside of your house waiting for your mom. I'm better off going home."

"No, you should be here with us."

"Stop pretending like you care now! If I wasn't this, you wouldn't care! Go back inside and keep Amber safe!" Before he can reply, she runs away in full speed.

Hakeem

The next morning before sunrise, there is a weak knock on Hakeem's door. Hakeem who is wide awake, unwraps his arms around Amber who is still sleeping and slowly creeps out of bed. Wearing nothing but his pajama pants, he cracks open his room door to his grandma. "Hakeem, let me have a word with you before everyone wakes up." When the two get downstairs, they walk straight into the kitchen. She turns on the lights and tells him to have a seat.

"I know. I'm going to find Isaiah once I know Amber is safe from becoming an animal." Hakeem says grabbing a seat at the table.

She nods her head emotionless and replies, "there's something I have to be honest with you about."

"What is it?"

She looks down for a second and shakes her head slowly. "I made a terrible mistake."

"What did you do grandma? Did you kill Zay?" He stands up. The room is quiet. "Grandma!" He shouts aggressively.

Tears fall down the side of her cheeks as she folds her fist. "No, I didn't kill him. I killed his mother." Shocked, he sat back down speechless as she continues. "I didn't know it was possible that, you could still be in tuned with your conscience as a vampire until you became one. Your father and I had no idea."

"No wonder." He sighs.

Wiping the tears from her face she looks at him puzzled, "no wonder what?"

He took a moment before giving her an answer. "We saw her in purgatory the night we died."

"You did? You guys didn't tell us that!"

"Isaiah didn't want me to tell you. Does he know?"

"Yes." She nods her head.

"When did you tell him?"

"I didn't."

"So how did he find out?"

"I don't know."

As the two look at each other puzzled, Amber walks into the kitchen and interrupts, "good morning."

"Good morning, did we wake you?" Hakeem looks at her.

"No, I woke up on my own. I came downstairs when I noticed you weren't in bed. I'm going to get some fresh air then go back upstairs."

Grandma smiles at her and says, "don't stay outside for too long." Amber nods her head and walks out the back door.

"I have something else to tell you." Grandma continues when the backdoor shuts. Hakeem gives her back his attention. "The Power Circle saw the news clip of Isaiah at the bank. They no longer want to work with us to find the Atomizer."

"What do you mean they no longer want to work with us?" Hakeem looks at her puzzled.

"I've been suspended from the mission, they want me to return back to citadel to speak with them in person."

"The citadel? So, where does this leave me?"

"I tried to plead with them, but they doubt my judgement. They have the same mindset your father and I had. They are sending warriors out here to kill the both of you, and once they find out about your friend Taryn and Isaiah's friend, they will kill them too."

Hakeem shakes his head. "Why do they need to kill me? They're going to find the Atomizer anyways! I'm the freaking reason why they even know where to look!"

"I know. I tried so hard for it not to be this way." Before he can reply, his mother walks into the kitchen with her puppy.

"Good morning guys, why are the two of you up so early?" He notices a weird but familiar scent coming from the dog. Before grandma can greet her, he cuts her off.

"That's not Blacky! Mom put that dog down now!"

"What are you talking about Hakeem?" She looks at him puzzled then down at her dog, "what is he saying little munchkin?" She continues. She suddenly notices the dog's left pupil is all black and becomes stunned. At that very moment, a loud groan comes from outside, which causes everyone to look at the door. When the backdoor opens, it is Amber carrying their dead dog inside. Grandma's eyes widen, as Camille's mouth drops.

"Drop that thing mom! And get out the kitchen!" Hakeem repeats himself. The dog starts laughing in a human voice then transforms back into a human. Still speechless, Camille backs up slowly into the wall. When Amber see's the dog transforming, she drops the dead dog and stands shocked.

After Zechariah finishes, Hakeem pushes Amber out the door with his elbow screaming "leave!" Zechariah turns around and smiles at Camille. As she stands there horrified, his right hand turns into a long black sharp blade. When she tries to leave, he impales her deep in the stomach. Hakeem's face transforms as he runs and jumps on his back, throwing him into the hallway. Camille grabs her wound and drops to the floor.

Zechariah swings back at him with his sharp hand, but misses. As his hand goes through the hallway wall, Hakeem uppercuts his face. His head snaps back and Hakeem grabs him and throws him against the opposite wall. Pulling the sharp hand out the wall causes the family pictures along with other paintings that were hanging on the wall to fall. Hakeem grabs his shoulders, then kicks him in the spine. Zechariah screams in pain as he drops to the floor.

Grandma runs over to Camille and holds her hands over hers to help stop the blood from coming out of the wound. "I'm here, don't panic."

Hakeem tosses Zechariah into the living room. As he rolls on the floor, he rolls behind the sofa and turns into a yeti. The beast stands up and charges back at him. Hakeem attempts to throw a punch, but the beast grabs his fist, pulls him closer and breaks his arm. As Hakeem screams in pain, the beast grabs him by the throat and throws him through the hallway ceiling. Hakeem lands inside of his mother's room.

Grandma bows her head over Camille's open wound and starts whispering. Camille lays on the floor in pain fighting for air. Blood is spilling out of her mouth and stomach. Amber runs back inside the house to stand over them. "Oh my god!" She repeats out loud.

"Stop! I'm taking care of this, get out of here! Get to safety, we'll find you after!" As grandma replies, large hairy fingers grab the side of the entrance to the kitchen.

"You won't live long enough to save anybody witch." The beast smiles at the three girls.

"Run!" Grandma screams. Amber looks at him and freezes. When he tries to force himself through the entrance, he realizes he is too big to fit and begins to transform again. Grandma stands up and pulls Camille's body away from the entrance, leaving a streak of blood that follows. She continues to chant her spell but it doesn't look as if it is working. As Zechariah is turning back into his human body, he lets out a loud roar that brings Amber back to reality. She quickly looks around and runs behind the counter. When he finishes changing into his human form, he charges into the kitchen.

Hakeem gets off the floor and screams as he pushes his arm back into its socket, he wastes no time jumping back through the hole in the floor. As Zechariah comes inches away from grandma, she stops him by stretching a hand out and placing the other on her temple. He suddenly can't move, frustrated, he spits in her face.

 Losing focus, she lets down her barrier and he grabs her by the throat. From behind the counter, Amber grabs two sharp knives and throws them at him. He screams in pain as both impale his back. He turns around and screams, "I swear you will die next!" then turns back around to face grandma. She places her hand by the side of his face and closes her eyes. Within seconds she is inflicting pain on him using nothing but her mind. Struggling to let go, he loosens his grip around her neck. She brushes his hand off her as he drops to his knees in pain, both of his hands covering his ears as if his head is going to explode. Hakeem runs into the kitchen and grabs him by the neck. Applying pressure, Zechariah lays down fighting for air. "This isn't over." He struggles, then begins to transform again. This time into something smaller, making Hakeem lose his grip on him.

He turns into a small mouse than runs out of the house. Hakeem tries chasing after him, but loses sight of it in the grass. When the two run out the house, grandma instantly focuses her attention back to Camille who is completely passed out on the floor. She gets back on her knees and put her hands over Camille's chest while Amber runs around the counter to watch. Tears fall down grandma's eyes as she realizes it's too late. Amber covers her mouth and cries at the sight of grandma's tears. When Hakeem walks in the kitchen, he see's everyone standing over his mother's body.

"She lost too much blood, I couldn't save her." Grandma says emotionless, keeping her face straight forward letting reality sink in. Hakeem drops to his knees over his mother's head and cries as he holds her tight. Grandma pats him on the back and stands up. Amber lets him grieve for a few, before walking over and patting his back too. He lifts Camille's body up and carries her to the living room. He places her on the carpet next to the broken sofa, as his grandma and Amber follows. The room is silent. He turns around to face the two, then turns back around to leave without saying a word.

"Where are you going?" Grandma asks.

He opens the front door and replies, "We need to kill Zechariah, I'm bringing Zay home."

"Wait I'm coming with you!" Amber shouts, then runs after him, but by the time she reaches the door, he is gone.

CHAPTER 30

Taryn

There is a knock at Taryn's room door. Peeking through her window, she tries to avoid sunlight from the sun rising. "Taryn, are you there?" Her mother asks as she knocks on the door again.

"Yes." She finally replies.

"Open the door, I want to speak to you."

She looks at the door with an unsure facial expression and puts on a fake sick voice. "I don't feel too good mom."

"Open the door so I can see you." Taryn walks to the door and opens it, her mother stands there and looks at her from head to toe. "What's wrong with you? You look perfectly fine." She continues. Before Taryn can reply, her father stumbles out of the other bedroom drunk.

"Can you explain why your car isn't in the driveway?" He asks.

"Not to you." She gives him an attitude.

"What!" Her father barks charging toward her room. She folds her arms and doesn't budge. "Listen little girl when I ask you a question politely, I expect a respectful answer!" He continues slurring his words.

"I left my car at school because I didn't feel good, I was brought home by a friend." She replies annoyed, avoiding eye contact.

"You lying little bitch! If you didn't feel good, why didn't you let your sister drive you home or leave her the keys to drive herself home?" He points to Justina's room and continues, "now how the fuck do you expect your sister to get to school?" Before she can answer, Justina walks out of the bathroom overhearing the argument.

"It's ok dad. It's not that serious, it's still early I'll catch the bus to school and just drive her car back." Justina tries to calm him down.

"I am not lying. I don't feel good. Mom talk to him!" Taryn pleas.

Her mother looks at her and replies, "I agree with your father. You look perfectly fine. We overheard you telling Justina to invite you in last night as if you were playing a game. It's hard to believe you were sick since you left school."

"I am sick, I don't care if you two don't believe me! I'm not going"

"Who the fuck do you think you're talking too?" Her father screams barging into the room.

"Honey calm down." Her mother says to him as she tries to hold him back.

He shoves her to into the wall and screams in Taryn's face. "Were not asking you to go to school!" He slaps her in the face then continues, "we're telling you!" She holds the side of her face as a tear falls down.

"Ok." She replies, putting her head down.

"Good." He replies, turning around.

"Dad that wasn't necessary." Justina says as he walks pass her.

He looks in her eyes and yells, "go to your room and get ready for school!"

Thirty minutes pass while Taryn stands in her room in the same clothes. Lost in thought, she is staring at the window blinds in a trance. There is a knock on her door that wakes her up. "Taryn, are you ready?" Justina asks.

"No, just go without me."

Justina shrugs her shoulders and walks downstairs. As she grabs Taryn's car keys and walk out the front door, her father sticks his head out the kitchen to see if both are leaving. When he notices Justina leaves by herself, he becomes furious. He storms up the stairs and barges into Taryn's room.

"Why are you still here!" He yells, charging at her then grabbing her by the arm. "I'll drag you to the bus stop myself, you little brat!" He tries to pull her, but she doesn't move. When he notices how strong her resistance is, he turns around to smack her but misses. She shoves him in the chest causing him to fly into the wall across the room, nearly breaking through the other side. The impact leaves a gigantic hole in the wall. Struggling to get off the floor, he stares at her puzzled. She has the same facial expression as she stares at her hands, trying to understand her new strength.

When he gets to his feet, her mother comes running into the room screaming, "What's going on?" He quickly charges back at her and tries to push her, but fails. She grabs him by both of his wrists and twists his arms until bones pop out of both of his biceps. He drops to his knees in tears, as she slowly backs into the wall shocked at what she has just done. Her mother cries as she runs towards the father's side.

"I didn't mean too." She says to her mom as she covers her mouth. Blood is gushing out of both her father arm's. When her mother sees the amount of blood he is losing, she gets up and runs to the bathroom for towels. The smell of blood has every nerve in Taryn's body craving to feast. She hesitates to step forward, but the veins underneath her eyes slowly start to show, then her fangs slowly start to come down. The urge to eat is too much for her to fight. She gets on her knees in front of him and grabs his left arm. When he looks up at her and sees her face, he screams louder. She closes her eyes and bites his arm hungrily.

Her mother runs back into the room when she hears her husband scream. Her mouth drops wide open as the towels she brought drops to the floor. Her father's head is leaning against the side of the bed for support, while his eyes is rolled to the back of his skull. Blood is splattered on his chest and chin as Taryn rips through his veins. Tears fall down her mother's face as she runs towards them. "Get off him you monster!" She screams grabbing Taryn's shoulder trying to pull her off. She pushes her mother back with one arm as she drains him to his last drop. Her mother falls on her back in front of the entrance of the room.

When Taryn is finished, her face becomes normal as the top of her father's dead body falls to the floor. Her eyes shoot open when she finally becomes conscious of what she did. Her mother sits up from the floor and cries louder at the sight of her dead husband. "No!" She screams reaching her arms out. Taryn turns around and sees her mother in tears, horrified.

"Mom." She says in a soft voice. She touches her lips then notices blood on her fingertips.

"Don't call me that you demon!" She replies getting off the floor and running out of the room. Taryn slowly gets off the floor too, keeping her eyes on her dead father's body and the blood that surrounds him.

Taryn's mother stumbles as she runs downstairs. She finds the house phone in the living room and tries to call the cops, but by the time she dials the number, Taryn grabs the phone from her.

"You can't call the cops on me mom. I'm not the monster, he is!" Her mother steps back in fear with tears still falling from her eyes.

"You're not my child! I don't know what you are!" She replies then turns around and runs to the front door. When she opens it, she lets a bright sunlight shine inside the room. Taryn closes the door on her before the door opens too wide. "Don't kill me please! Let me go!" She cries as she slides onto the floor still holding the door knob.

"Mom, I don't want to kill you."

"Stop calling me that!" She kicks her in the knee and runs to the kitchen. Taryn stumbles as her mother runs pass her. When she gets to the kitchen, she takes a butcher knife out from the sink. Taryn stands in front of the kitchen speechless as she waves the knife in her face.

"Mom, stop!" Taryn cries out as she dodges her mother's attempt to cut her.

"Die bitch!" She screams as she keeps swinging. Taryn is finally able to grab the wrist that is holding the knife, and the two look each other in the eyes, both tearing up.

"It doesn't have to be like this, just listen to me!" Taryn pleas. Her mother cocks back and spits in her face.

186

"You killed my husband, I don't want to hear anything that comes out of your mouth!" Taryn lets go of her wrist and steps back to wipe her face. Doing so, her mother rushes her and stabs her in the middle of her chest. Taryn screams as she backs into the wall. The room is silent when she doesn't drop to the floor. She looks at her mother then down at the knife that is sticking out her chest. She pulls it out and drops it on the floor.

Her mother's mouth drops as her eyes shoot open when she sees the wound on her chest heal. Taryn's face transforms as she takes a step toward her. Her mother screams at this new face and runs toward the door as fast as she can. When she gets to it, she turns the doorknob back and forth panicking. When she finally gets it open, Taryn grabs the back of her neck and pins her teeth into it.

Amber

Hours have passed since Hakeem left his house. Amber finishes bleaching the kitchen floor, leaving no signs of Camille's blood. Her and his grandma wrap Camille's body in bed covers and leave her in the basement. Amber dumps the bucket of dirty water outside the back door then walks back in the kitchen sink. As she washes her hands, she stares at the corner of the room where Camille had died and zones out. Letting the hot water run for a few minutes, steam from the fountain rises to her face.

Suddenly the sound of grandma's voice breaks her trance. "Amber, come here and give me a hand." She shouts from the living room. Amber shakes her head back then turns the faucet off. She grabs a towel to dry her hands then continues out of the kitchen. Grandma is waiting by the broken sofa. She is finally finished cleaning up all the broken wood that was in the hallway and in the living room. As Amber walks closer to her, grandma says "help me bring this outside." She nods her head then grabs the opposite side of the sofa, the two carry the sofa outside and leaves it on the side of the road. Grandma rushes back to the house while Amber takes her time.

"Grandma, um can't you just use your magic to move this stuff?" She suggests politely. Grandma looks at her then turns her back. Amber feels both embarrassed and insulted, but she continues to follow anyways. She walks to the other half of the sofa and mumbles "I was just saying."

Grandma shakes her head and replies, "You kid's these days are so lazy. Just help me carry this last half." The two lift the sofa and carry it outside. "I'm aware I could have just used magic to move these items. But there was no need too."

"Say's the women with supernatural powers." Amber snickers. The two put the broken half of the sofa next to the other.

She looks at Amber and says, "I'm a witch not a warlock."

"I honestly don't know the difference." Amber replies, dusting her hands off, then continues back up the driveway.

"Some days I wish I didn't know myself." Grandma says under her breath as Amber walks a couple of feet ahead of her.

"Huh? Did you say something?" Amber turns around to ask.

She looks her in the eyes then quickly replies, "No." Amber shrugs her shoulders then turns back around. "Wait, a second." She catches up to her then continues, "I know you think I'm a bitch, getting in the way of you and Hakeem. I don't want to be the bad guy in both of your eyes, but I have no choice but to be. You're a sweet girl and you make my grandson happy, but you can't handle the baggage that comes with our family, and I really don't want to see you end up like my daughter in law or Taryn. So, I'm begging you, after the vampire blood leaves your system, distance yourself from my family!"

Amber puts her head down for a second, then lifts it back up. "Mrs. Exalus, I don't think you're a bitch, but the only way I will end up like those two is if you keep me in the dark. I love your grandson and I give you my word I won't open my mouth about your family, but I can't go home and act like monsters aren't real." She pauses for a second as her eyes became watery. "Three hours ago the mother of the man I love died in front of me, and I have no plans on leaving his side for any reason. If loving him is going to get me killed, so be it! Any other life I live after today wouldn't be real."

She wipes her eyes as she waits for a response. Grandma takes another step toward her and gives her a hug. "God, bless you." She says in her ears then let's go of her. She walks around her and heads back inside.

Amber cracks a little smile and replies, "God never gave me baggage I couldn't carry." When she takes her first step back toward the house, she feels a heat sensation burning in her chest. "Whoa." She grabs her chest.

"Are you ok?" Grandma turns around and asks.

"I think so." She replies sounding unsure. Before she can take another step, the burning sensation she feels in her chest becomes hotter, then migrates to her neck. She slowly starts to back pedal, grabbing her throat gasping for air. "I can't breathe." She struggles to say. As she moves around struggling for air, she notices her surroundings starts to change. The air changes color, it is as if the light that reflected from the sun is a dim red color. Grandma who was just standing next to her, is nowhere to be found. Hakeem's house looks trashed and so does every house lining the block. The more she freaks out and struggles for air, the harder it becomes for her to breathe. She then drops to her knees with one arm on the floor and the other on her neck. Tears fall from her eyes and evaporate before it gets a chance to hit the ground. Suddenly, the ground becomes extremely hot, as if she is kneeling on a frying pan. It becomes too hot for to keep her hand on the ground, so she falls on her shoulder for support. Too weak to push herself back up, she quickly passes out.

CHAPTER 31

Isaiah

"Are you sure this is where he wanted us to come? How long does it take to kill a witch?" Tyriek asks as he walks downstairs holding a bottle of whiskey. Isaiah who is sitting on the armrest of an old sofa staring out the tinted window, doesn't respond. The two were sent to an abandoned loft outside of town. When Tyriek realizes he isn't in the mood to talk, he walks over to him and drops the bottle in his lap. "Don't be so hard on yourself Zay, she killed your mom. You shouldn't feel guilty for wanting revenge."

Isaiah looks at him then takes a swig of the liquor. He looks back out the window gripping the neck of the bottle and replies, "I don't know what revenge is to you, but this is not it." He stands up and takes another swig. "Zechariah should not be fighting my battles while I sit around like a lapdog! If it's not my hands that kill her, her death won't mean anything." Angry, he grips the bottle too hard, breaking it.

"Come on Zay, that was the only bottle of liquor in this dump." Isaiah shakes his head as he shakes his hand to dry. "I hear what you're saying though. Can I ask you a question?" Tyriek continues. He nods his head. "Back at the hotel, Zechariah mentioned freeing the other world to get your mother back. Have you given it any thought that we would literally be raising hell on earth? We'll be partaking in a genocide."

"I did think about it." Isaiah replies then pauses for a few seconds then faces him. "Honestly, I don't give a fuck! I don't know what you saw when you were turned into a vampire, but I saw my mother in a torn apart village. All this time I thought she was in heaven surrounded by doves and fucking angels looking down on me! Come to find out, she was alone in purgatory surrounded by creatures I can't even name! Fuck this world!" Isaiah pokes his shoulder. "I'm bringing my mom back! All this place ever tried to do, is lock me away any chance they got anyways!"

"Damn." Tyriek replies avoiding eye contact. "That's fucking crazy, I still can't believe your grandma killed her."

"I know. What's crazier is if we don't find this before her, we'll end up where my mother is." Tyriek shakes his head as Isaiah senses a weird scent. "He's back." He continues. The front door of the loft swings open, letting sunlight shine through the room. Tyriek quickly runs to the shadow in the corner of the room.

"I see you guys made yourselves at home." Zechariah says entering the loft.

Isaiah looks him up and down then into his eyes. "I expected you to be carrying a body."

"Things didn't go exactly as planned."

"Can someone shut the fucking door!" Tyriek shouts from the corner of the room.

"Oh, pardon me." Zechariah replies sarcastically. "I brought someone special with me." An average height woman with a light skinned complexion walks into the room. She looks like she could be between the ages of 21 to 27. The freckles on her face give her an innocent appeal, but her short red hair screams otherwise. When she enters, she stands in front of the door for a few seconds and locks eyes with Isaiah.

"The door!" Tyriek shouts again. The woman breaks the stare and closes the door behind her. Relieved, Tyriek finally leaves the corner and joins Isaiah's side.

"Who's your friend?" Isaiah asks Zechariah.

"I can speak for myself!" She snaps back, not giving Zechariah a chance to reply.

"So, introduce yourself." Isaiah acknowledges her.

She shakes her head and looks at Zechariah. "Your friend is rude."

"Friend? Who said we are friends?" Isaiah replies.

"Aw, a friendship with no title. You boys are too cute." She snickers.

Zechariah laughs. "Lighten up Isaiah. We may not be friends, but we want the same thing, and this girl right here is the key." Both Tyriek and Isaiah look her up and down.

"She doesn't look too special to me." Isaiah says under his breath.

"Neither do you vampire!" She reaches her left hand toward him then flips it palm side up. Isaiah grabs his stomach then drops to his knees scrunching his face. Confused, Tyriek simultaneously looks at him then both Zechariah and the girl.

"Hey!" He finally shouts stepping toward them. The woman lifts her right hand toward him, levitating him in the air, then extends it out, sending him flying to the wall. Tyriek struggles in the air to get down, which seems pointless if the woman's hands are still raised. She cracks a smile at him, then looks back at Isaiah. By that time, he finds a little strength to force himself up to stand halfway, she slowly folds her left hand into a fist, forcing him back to his knees screaming and wrapping his arms tight around his stomach.

"Enough already!" Zechariah shouts.

She gives him a puppy face and replies, "I didn't even do anything, yet." She looks back at Isaiah then curls her left arm, which brings him down to a three-point position. One arm still wrapped around his stomach tight, as the other hardly keeps him off the floor. His face transforms as he tries not to yell in more pain.

"I said enough!" Zechariah repeats.

The woman lets out a little laugh as she turns her attention back to Zechariah. "Is that an order? I hope our time apart didn't let you forget who's really in charge." She squints her eyes at him.

"No, it didn't." He lowers his voice.

"Good." She looks back at Isaiah then straightens out her arm and loosens her fingers. "I want to hear an apology." She continues He lifts his forehead from the ground and spits a little blood on the floor. When he looks her in the eyes, he cracks a half smile on his face.

"I apologize for thinking out loud. Can you let me go now, your making me want to take a shit." He tries to laugh but can't because of the pain. Her smile quickly fades as she gives him a filthy look.

"Shit on yourself." She replies closing her fingers back into a fist aggressively. Isaiah groans as he wraps his arms back around his stomach in pain. He tries not to scream as he places his shoulder and the side of his head on to the floor.

"What are you trying to prove?" Zechariah asks.

"I think our new friends needed to know their fangs aren't comparable to real power!" Looking at the two vampires struggle, she smiles at them then drops both her arms. Letting go of control on both, Tyriek falls to the floor as Isaiah takes his time to stand up. Isaiah wipes his mouth as he relocks eyes with her.

When he drops his hand, he puts on a fake smirk. "I didn't think I'd come across another witch."

"Your grandma isn't the only one sweetie." She replies.

"That means you could turn me into a day walker, like Zay?" Tyriek asks as he stands up.

"Now, why would I want to do that?" She looks at him puzzled.

"Because we're on the same team." Tyriek implies.

She lets out a loud laugh as she covers her mouth. When she uncovers it, she replies, "we may be on the team, but I have no interest in playing your fairy godmother. Maybe if you show me a bit more loyalty, I'll think about it."

Before he can reply, Isaiah quickly asks, "who are you?"

"Your soon to be queen of the new world. You can call me Lucia."

"Now that we are all acquainted. Let's get to business." Zechariah rubs his hands.

"Hold on, I just have one more question." Isaiah replies then continues, "You seem pretty powerful, why are you waiting for the new world to claim queen? What's stopping you or me from taking over now?"

"You take over? Your funny, only fools run around the streets showing out. You wouldn't finish this week in the path you are heading. You're only immortal if you're smart."

"Nobody knew it was me. And even with their weapons they were no match!" Isaiah pleas.

"The sheep aren't the ones you should be worried about. The Power Circle is, and once their on to you, they will hunt you down and kill you. Even if you are Jason Exalus's son."

Isaiah smirks. "Well they're going to have to come with an army!" He takes a step closer. "I am the coldest creature that ever walked this planet! And if I have to kill every single one of them to prove it, so be it."

She smiles back as she tries not to laugh. "Honey, not to break your spirit but there are far more scarier creatures then you that come out at night. They put down real demons, 10x bigger and badder. And well you, you're just a little boy, a crossbreed of species you have no idea about."

Isaiah's smirk quickly fades away when he felt like she was disrespecting him. "Don't you ever call me a little boy!" He points at her. "I don't care if you were Mother Shipton! You will respect me or forget about finding this Atomizer! I'll do it myself!"

Her smile began to glow. "You're speaking to me like I can't just torture the information out of you" She walks towards him. "I think it's cute you think you're bad. But there's a difference between bad and evil. I know everything about you Isaiah." She runs her fingers up his chest, then wraps her arms around his shoulder. She closes in as if she is going to peck his cheek, but instead whispers "you've never in your life been this close to evil. Now call me out my name again and I will gut your stomach and rip your organs out while you watch." She taps his shoulder then walks away. Isaiah holds his stomach and shakes his head imagining the pain. "Something just came to mind." She stops in front of Zechariah then turns back around to face him. "I want you to come into town with me." She looks back at Zechariah and tells him, "stay here with the help."

"What? Lucia finding this Atomizer means more to me then the both you!" Zechariah barks.

"I know. Do I have to remind you not to question my authority? Maybe if you were successful in killing that old dirt bag you'd be coming along. Now stop acting jealous, we won't be gone too long."

"Why are we going into town?" Isaiah asks.

"If you truly desire power and respect. You won't ask me questions either."

Isaiah nods his head and follows her out the door.

Hakeem

Hakeem stops running when he arrives at the parking lot of the hotel Isaiah and Tyriek were staying. There is a stench of blood that has polluted the air. He hesitates before entering. When he walks inside, his suspicion is confirmed. There is blood all over the lobby and a dead body behind the check in desk. Hakeem is puzzled by the scene as he makes his way up the staircase. When he reaches the second floor, he notices all the room doors are open with blood in front of the entrances. As he walks to Isaiah's hotel room, he looks inside the rooms on his way, there are dead bodies piled on each other in each room. He shakes his head disappointed and continues down the hall. When he gets to Isaiah's room there is nobody there. His room is also filled with dead bodies. Before he can take his first step in, the sound of police sirens distracts him.

He rushes inside and runs to the window. His mouth drops at the number of cop cars he sees driving into the parking lot. Cops are simultaneously hopping out and running toward the entrance of the hotel carrying guns. From his perceptive, it looks like a special unit from the armor they are wearing. They also have k9's with them. "Fuck! I never should have come here." He mumbles under his breath. He takes a second to pounder, then a loud noise comes from downstairs. He can tell it is the front door being kicked down by the officers He can hear multiple footsteps running through the hotel. "I wonder if he left his mask here." He says to himself as he steps away from the window. As he gets on his knees to look under the bed, he hears the footsteps coming up the stairs. "Fuck! I don't have enough time!"

"I think someone's alive in the room down there. I hear movements!" One officer says to the other as they walk down the hallway. "Have your guns ready." Hakeem rushes to see if the mask is left in the bathroom but all he sees are more corpses. He steps back and shakes his head, as he looks at the window the footsteps in the hallway become louder as they are closing in on the door. With no time to think, he decides to make a run toward the window. As the cops kick down the door with their guns in the air, Hakeem jumps through the closed window breaking through the glass and landing on top of a cop car, crushing the roof of it.

"Don't move!" Cops scream with their guns aimed at him. More guns are aimed at him from the window of the hotel room. He stands up cautiously and looks around as machine guns surround him. "Put your hands in the air now!" the cops scream. Two news channel vans enter the parking lot just in time to catch what's going on. "We are not going to say it again. Hands in the air!" Hakeem closes his eyes as he rises with his arms semi in the air. The news reporters jump out their vans and try to get their camera's ready. When he opens his eyes, his hands are all the way up. "Now get down from the car, no sudden movement!" He looks down at the cops then looks at the reporters who are preparing their cameras. "Get down now!"

Hakeem drops his arms then leaps off the car landing behind a cop. The cop tries to grab his arm, but he tosses him on top of the car and runs towards the woods. Gunshots are fired from all angles at him as he flees the parking lot. The news reporters are only able to catch his back as he sprints away in amazing speed.

Not knowing what direction to run to, Hakeem runs deep into the woods. Minutes go by until he notices he has lost the cops miles back. When he finally stops running, he comes across a small pond. Frustrated from what just happened, he walks to a boulder positioned next to it and lets out a roar of rage, punching it a few times. The boulder doesn't break, but the impact leaves large enough cracks for pebbles to fall onto the ground. After the last punch, he pauses to look at his bloody knuckles then his reflection in the pond. A tear tries to sneak its way down the side of his cheek but he quickly wipes it before it passes his nose.

As he kneels to wash his knuckles, a smooth whistling sound flows through the trees. The noise sounds both soothing and annoying. He instantly turns around to see if the sound is coming from the direction he came from, but it isn't. It is hard to pinpoint where the sound is coming from. "What is that?" He stands and walks away from the pond as he tries to tune into his surroundings, but the noise isn't allowing him to focus on anything else. "Shit I wish I knew where I ran too." He looks to his left and right to decide which way is the best way to get back while also trying to avoid the cops. He decides to run through the left side of the woods. Minutes pass when he realizes the sound is growing louder in the direction he is running towards. Not paying attention to the path, he accidently runs off a small cliff and rolls down a hill. Landing face down on his hands, he shakes his head as he slowly gets back on his feet. The fall brings him to what looks like the back parking lot of a construction store. He is surrounded by wood and other labor tools.

"You're clumsy just like your father," says a familiar voice. Hakeem snaps his head up and sees Aaron standing a couple of feet away from him.

"Aaron? What the hell are you doing here?" He looks at him puzzled. Three robe men surface from behind Aaron. One of them is holding a syrinx, that he stops blowing into once he sees Hakeem. The whistling sound stops.

"I'm sorry Hakeem, you guys left me no choice." Aaron looks over his shoulders at the robe warriors and nods his head. Two of three unhood themselves and the one to his right charges at Hakeem first. Hakeem's face transforms as he charges back. The warrior swings first, but Hakeem ducks and grabs his throat. He tries to slam him on the floor, but the warrior's body turns into black smoke as soon as he hits the ground. The smoke levitates around Hakeem's legs, then transforms back into a body behind him. Before Hakeem gets a chance to look over his shoulder, the warrior punches him in the face. He stumbles a little, then charges back at him. Hakeem tries to grab him, but his body turns back into smoke and floats pass his body. The warrior becomes solid again as he maneuver's Hakeem's arms into a lock hold. Hakeem headbutts him and gets himself loose. As the warrior turns back into smoke, two tranquilizers go through him and hit Hakeem in the chest. Through the holes of the smoke, Hakeem sees Aaron placing the gun back to the side of his waist.

He grabs the needles out of his chest and throws it on the ground. His face transformd back into normal as he suddenly becomes light headed. The warrior becomes solid again, then faces Aaron. "I wasn't finished!"

"I am." Aaron replies. While the warrior's back is turned, Hakeem looks for a way to escape. He takes two steps to his right and collapses to the floor. The warrior faces him again and shakes his head. Aaron approaches the two and continues, "I'll take care of him. You and the others kill Isaiah."

CHAPTER 32

Amber

Amber's vision is a bit blurry as she wakes up to an unfamiliar ceiling. She lets out a little groan and places her hand on her forehead. The room is cold and the bench she is laying on feels uncomfortable. When she turns her head to the side, she sees a dungeon door. She quickly sits up and rubs her eyes. Looking around the room, she notices four heads sitting on a shelf, with blood still dripping from the bottom, as if they were fresh. She covers her mouth as her jaw drops open. Panicking, she slides off the bench placing her feet onto the cold floor, then pulls them back up when she realizes she has no shoes on. She then realizes she is wearing nothing but a long dirty white tee shirt.

She starts panicking more, holding her knees to her chest. She looks around the room thoroughly and sees there is only one window to look out of. Removing her hand from her mouth, she slowly places her feet back on the floor. She runs to the window and stands on her tippy toes to look outside, but all she sees are trees that surround the land and a full moon that covers most of the sky. "Where am I?" She thinks, then walks over to the dungeon door. She notices the door isn't shut properly and looks at it suspiciously. She takes one last look around the room then cringes her face at the sight of the bloody heads. Disgusted, she quickly walks out and finds herself in a long hallway which would have been pitch black if it isn't for the candles that are glowing on the walls.

Hesitating, she looks down the dark hallway and whispers "Mrs. Exalus." Her faint voice echoes through the hall. She looks down at the floor and notices a streak of blood leading down the hall. She covers her mouth again trying not to scream. Suddenly there is a loud howl coming from either upstairs or outside that echoes through the halls. She grabs onto the wall nervously, and waits a few seconds before removing her hand and carefully follows the streak of blood. When she reaches the bottom of the hallway there is a choice of turning left or right, the streak of blood leads left while the hallway leading to the right is clean. Not giving it much thought, she chooses to walk down the right side of the hallway. A cold breeze hits her skin as she wraps her arms around herself shivering.

Finally, she sees the staircase down the hall, when she approaches it she hears screams and multiple footsteps running upstairs. She tries to look up, but can't see anything due to the twist of the staircase. Half-way up the stairs, the screams become louder, then a loud vicious growl comes after. She hesitates to take another step, but does so anyways. When she reaches the top of the staircase, she hears a child crying, but from the sounds of it, the child isn't alone. She sticks her head into the hallway from the staircase to see what's going on. Shocked, her mouth drops when she sees a little boy kneeling in front of the door crying. The door is wide open, and outside stands a wolf the size of a bear eating a man guts, with one paw on his face and the other on his leg.

Instantly, another wolf jumps inside the room and bites the child's head. She cries out covering her mouth as the wolf feasts on the boy. She hides back in the staircase and cries silently. When she wipes her eyes, she hears noises coming from downstairs. She has trouble making out the sound over the wolves feasting, so she takes two steps down to hear better. Her heart sinks when she hears what sounds like a heavy door falling to the ground, followed by a loud growl that echoes through the halls up the staircase.

The loud growl that echoes sends chills down Amber's spine. She trips up the stairs as she steps back in fear. Trying not to make any noise, she breaks her fall by grabbing hold of the railing. The sound of heavy footsteps running toward the stairs follow the howl. Amber quickly turns around and tries to rush up the stairs discreetly. When she reaches the door, she sticks her head out into the hallway again to see if it's safe, but the werewolf is still chewing on the little boy's remains. She turns her head and notices the other direction is clear, slowly stepping on to the floor, she quickly slides her back against the wall. The werewolf doesn't hear her, so she continues to carefully slide down the hallway, while nervously keeping her eyes on the werewolf. As soon as she feels the wall come to the curve, she sees another werewolf jump through the entrance of the dungeon, hitting the wall face first.

Her eyes shoot open as the noise causes the other werewolves to turn in their direction. She quickly hides behind the corner, panting, unsure if she was seen or not. All three werewolves howl at each other, one trying to sound louder than the other. Then suddenly, the sound of heavy footsteps makes its way towards her from the hallway. She begins to breath harder, overhearing every step. Just as it is inches away from entering the room, there is a cry for help coming from outside. Not only does the werewolf turn around to run outside, the other two wolves by the entrance leave the premises as well, chasing the source of life. She slowly opens her eyes when the footsteps are gone. Her jaw drops as she covers her mouth and her eyes widen when she sees the room is filled with corpses.

Blood and organs are laid out everywhere. Her legs get weak as she feels woozy, so she places her hands back onto the wall to catch herself from falling. She takes another look around the room and notices shattered glass on the floor in front of an open elevator and a staircase next to it. After a few moments, she finally pushes herself off the wall and slowly walks towards the middle of the room. She looks back at the entrance where the wolves were and sees the body limbs of the child and a bloody trail leading outside to another pile of body limbs. She turns her head back nervously to the rest of the dead corpses in front of her and stares at the elevator. She cautiously steps over a corpse and makes her way halfway through the room. Not getting far, she accidently slips over a man's liver and falls on top of him. Disgusted and covered in blood, she lets out a little scream. As she tries to get off the floor, she slips again but this time in between the corpses.

After struggling to get up, she makes her way to the elevator. As she approaches it, the sound of heavy footsteps resurfaces. She nervously turns to face the entrance and freezes at the sight of the werewolf walking towards her. There is a thick glob of saliva surrounding its mouth as it approaches the room. Her heart begins to beat out of control, as her feet are glued to the floor. The wolf enters the room and sniffs the dead corpse in front of it as if it doesn't see her. After the third dead body is sniffed, it lifts it's head up in her direction. She holds her breath and doesn't move as the two make eye contact. The werewolf sticks its head back into the pile of dead corpse, unbothered.

The werewolf finishes sniffing and makes its way to the staircase. As soon as it enters, Amber lets out a deep breath of relief and slowly rests her back onto the wall of the elevator. Placing her head down, the elevator doors shut on her. Confused, she begins pressing all the buttons to get out, but nothing works. Before she knows it, she is on the third floor. The doors open, and there are no signs of life. She is horrified of the dark hallway and the sight of broken lights hanging from the ceiling. She folds her hand in a fist, then slowly walks out. Paranoid, she walks down the quiet hallway. When she turns the hall, she faces a big metal door that is bent to the side. Half of the door is hanging to the floor. She hesitates to take another step, until she hears laughter coming from inside.

Curious, she whispers "hello, is someone there?" No one answers, but the laugh grows louder. She hides behind the door and peeks inside. There is a young woman standing in front of three people. She can't make out their face with their back turned to her, but she is able to clearly see the face of the young woman and she looks beautiful.

As the laugher stops, someone says "Queen Lucia, the Exalus cousins are finally dead. The citadel is ours, what's next?"

She smiles at the small crowd and replies, "bring me the child!" As the crowd bows their heads towards her, the woman's eyes scan over them and makes eye contact with Amber. She tilts her head to the side slightly and stares at her. When Amber realizes she's been spotted, she quickly ducks and turns around not knowing there is a werewolf towering over her. Terrified, she screams then passes out.

Grandma

Grandma enters Hakeem's room with a tray in her hand, and a hot wet rag on one side and a mug with tea on the other. She places the tray on his desktop and picks up the wet rag. When she looks over at his bed, she sees Amber tossing and turning. Amber is in a deep uncomfortable sleep. The amount of sweat that leaves her body, leaves Hakeem's bed damped. She touches the side of her face and places the rag on her forehead. "You're going to be ok, I need you to be strong." She then faces Hakeem's desktop and crushes some herb into the tea. She stirs the tea with a spoon then sits on the bed next to her. "This won't wake you up, but it should ease your thoughts. Whatever you're going through, you will survive."

Amber continues to toss around unconformably, with the rag on her forehead.

She places her arm under Ambers head and slightly lifts it up. She opens her mouth gently and feeds her the tea. After swallowing, Ambers head begins to toss out of control, until she drops back onto the bed and vomits the tea on to the bed covers.

Grandma gives her a puzzled look. "Why aren't you digesting this?" She stands up and ponders with the mug in her hand. "This is supposed to go down smooth, unless." She pauses for a second then stares at her. "Unless you're pregnant."

Andrew

The high school bell rings ending Andrew's math class. He walks out behind a crowd of students putting on his bookbag. As he makes his way to the cafeteria, he notices Emira standing in the hallway with her arms crossed staring at him. She approaches him and tells him, "we need to talk, now!" He nods his head and follows her inside the cafeteria to an empty table.

"What did I do?" He asks, sitting on the opposite side of her. Before she replies, two of her friends walks by their table and laugh.

"It's not what you think! We're talking about homework!" She defends herself. The girls just laugh some more and walk away.

"We don't have class together." Andrew smirks.

"Shut up and take that smile off your face!" He quickly puts on a serious face. "You need to tell your best friend, that him and his freak cousin need to stay away from Amber!" She points down at the table aggressively.

"What are you talking about?" Andrew looks at her puzzled.

She looks around, then leans towards him. "Listen, I know it was Isaiah who robbed that bank yesterday. He came here after and tried to attack us for no reason. The only reason why I'm not reporting him in, is because after all of that, Amber still choose to spend the night at Hakeem's house."

His mouth drops. "Isaiah robbed the bank and attacked the both of you yesterday?" He asks surprised.

She shakes her head. "God! Andrew, are you always high? Have you not been aware of anything that has been going on?"

"I'm not always high." He scratches his head. "Now that I think about it, I did see him after the fire alarm here yesterday. He came to confront Taryn over something personal. He had this look on his face, like he might have actually hurt her if I wasn't there."

"You stopped him?"

"Yea, I walked her to her car. We were supposed to meet at The Shack after, but she never showed."

"Why isn't she in school today?"

"Honestly, I haven't heard from her since yesterday." He pauses for a second, "I don't know."

She leans her head back and rolls her eyes. "I'm so happy you're not my best friend. You need to go find her! I don't trust Hakeem's cousin."

"I don't trust either of them." Samson comments as he walks by the table at the end of her sentence. The two look at him as he sits down next to Emira.

"Nobody invited you." She replies.

"Don't be so defensive Emira, I'm only agreeing with you. I'm happy you're starting to open your eyes. I think the person who robbed the bank is his cousin too. He's the only guy in this town with dreads!"

"That's not true." Andrew replies. The two look at him and gives him a questionable facial expression.

"Did you even watch the video?" Samson asks him.

"No." Andrew stands up. "I'm not going to entertain this theory, Isaiah isn't capable of robbing a bank!" He looks at Emira and continues, "I saw Taryn's car and her sister is here this morning. If she was in trouble she wouldn't have let Justina drive to school. Now I'm getting on line before all of the hot lunch is finished."

Samson stands up and shows him his phone. "Wait, just watch this! And tell me what you think." Once Samson pulls up the video, an updated news alert flashes on top of his screen. "Hold on a sec, let me just see what this is about." He clicks the alert and sees "Hotel Massacre" as the headline. He skims through the first two paragraphs of the page and sees a video. Emira and Andrew look over his shoulder as he clicks play.

The table is quiet as the video starts. "Good afternoon all viewers, you are now tuning in with channel 14 news and we are here at the Montecer Hotel where there has been a massacre this morning. There has been a total count of 28 dead bodies. The suspects are still on the run. The authorities have reason to believe that one of the killers is the same person who robbed the bank yesterday. The video we are about to play, are from the cameras inside the hotel that was recording during the murders. We must warn you, this video is violent and graphical. You shouldn't watch if you are under the age of 18. If you know any of these people please call the cops! If you see them in the streets, do not approach them, call the cops!" The video continues to play. Both Andrew and Emira's mouth drop open, when the first thing they see are Isaiah and Tyriek walking out of a hotel room.

"I knew it!" Samson gloats. Tyriek attacks the first person he sees in the hallway by biting his neck, as Isaiah kicks open the room next to theirs. None of the cameras are angled to see inside any of the rooms, but it does catch Tyriek kill anyone who runs out of the rooms. Most of the video is fast forwarded and slowed down at the parts where their faces are visible. After the two leave the hotel, the camera fast forwards a couple of hours until it shows a man enter the hotel and call the cops at the sight of all the dead bodies. The man doesn't stay for long, and as soon as he leaves, Hakeem arrives. Andrew's heart drops at the sight of him. The video shows him walking upstairs and entering Isaiah's room. It then shows cops arriving shortly after and ambushing the same room he walked into. Then the video ends.

"What the fuck did we just watch" Emira asks.

"Proof. I was right about these freaks from the start." Samson replies.

"Oh my God, I need to call Amber!" She panics as she runs out of the cafeteria.

"How? How is this possible?" Andrew mumbles in disbelief.

Samson smirks as he dials 911. "I'm going to make sure he pays for what happened to Chris!"

Andrew slowly steps away speechless, and walks out the cafeteria. He looks nauseous as he makes his way to his locker. He places his head on it for a few seconds and thinks to himself. "I don't understand. I know Hakeem, well I thought I did." He takes his phone out of his pocket and hesitates to call him. After a couple of seconds looking at his name, he does so anyways. The phone goes straight to voicemail. He lifts his head up from the locker then calls Taryn, her phone goes to voicemail too. Shaking his head, he puts his phone back in his pocket and runs down the hallway to the staircase.

He runs upstairs to the second floor and passes two classrooms until he finds himself in front of Justina's class. Her classroom door is shut, so he places his head in the window of the door and waves to her as the teacher has her back faced to the blackboard. When she notices his hand movements, she looks at him puzzled. "Ms. Grant, may I use the bathroom?" She asks. The teacher nods her head and hands her the bathroom pass. When she leaves the class, she looks him up and down and whispers "what do you want?"

"Nothing, is Taryn ok? Why isn't she in school today?"

"She didn't come yet?" Justina looks puzzled. "I guess my dad let her stay home."

"So you physically saw her at home this morning?" He asked with a concerned voice.

"Yea, why are you acting weird? You look like you aren't feeling too good yourself."

"It's nothing." He sighs. "I was just worried, she hasn't returned any of my calls. I just wanted to make sure she was safe."

"Um, ok. Is that all?"

"Yea, so you said she should be home, right?" She nods her head and walks back into class. Andrew turns around and runs back downstairs. He grabs his car keys out of his locker and runs out the school.

CHAPTER 33

Grandma

Grandma walks back into Hakeem's room with paper towels and pats down the wet area of the bed while Amber is still tossing and turning. When she finishes, she looks over at Amber and places her hand over hers. Smiling, she says "you don't know yet. But there's a blessing manifesting inside of you. If we fail, that baby will grow to be our savior." Suddenly, the sound of cop sirens disrupts the silence that was within the house. "This can't be good," she shakes her head looking at the window. She stands up and peeks through the blinds and sees a mob of cop cars speeding toward the house from both directions of the street. Her mouth drops as she slowly back pedals from the window. She looks at Amber then back at the window, then runs out the room. When she gets downstairs, she places her hand on the front door and closes her eyes. She chants a spell, and a blue fortress quickly spreads across the walls and the windows of the house then disappears.

She closes all the blinds just as the cops enter the driveway and surround the entire street. As she runs to her room, all she hears is car doors opening and guns being loaded. "I don't have enough time!" She panics, as she searches through her bag for her pouch. While searching, there is a loud knock on the front door that makes her look more thoroughly. When she finally finds it, she opens it and takes out an amulet. She places it around her neck and quickly runs out of the room carrying her bag. As she runs in the hallway, she hears the officers simultaneously try to bust through the doors and windows. She goes upstairs and before entering Hakeem's room, she overhears the officers planning to blow the front door down. She continues to walk in, suddenly the sound of helicopter propellers vibrates through the room. She quickly closes the blinds before anyone can see though.

"Someone is definitely in the house." An officer says to the other. Another cop takes out a megaphone and speaks into it. "Hakeem Exalus, if that's you inside, come outside with your hands in the air. You're surrounded. We give you until the count of five."

Grandma stands over Amber and places her hand on hers again. "I can't bring you with me, but I promise, I'll be back for you. Me and Hakeem." She tightens her grip on her hands as the cop starts counting, then bows her head and let's go.

"One, two, three." The cop counts. When he gets to four, she places her hand over the amulet and closes her eyes "Five!" She whispers two words then teleports out of the room. The barrier surrounding the house leaves with her, just as the cop's begins shooting through the windows into the living room and front door.

Isaiah

"Nice car." Isaiah breaks the silence in the car. Lucia looks at him as she takes the exit off the thruway to enter town.

"Not my car." She replies, looking back at the road.

He smirks then looks out the window. "So, what's your story?"

"My story?"

"Yea, you don't look much older than me, but the way you talk, the way Zechariah respects you, I can tell you've been around just as long as my grandma." He faces her.

She smiles. "Don't let my beautiful face fool you. I've been around way longer than her."

"So why does she age naturally? As far as I'm aware, I thought vampires were the only creatures that don't age."

She stops at a red light and gives him a deadly look. "Stop comparing me to her. I am capable of magic beyond her comprehension."

Looking back in her eyes, he nods his head. "So why didn't you go with Zechariah to kill her?"

"Who said I want her dead?" He looks at her puzzled. "If you ask me, she's more valuable alive for the time being." The car becomes quiet, then the light turns green.

When she continues to drive, he replies, "I'm still going to kill her."

She smirks. "When the time is right, you will but until then you won't lay a finger on her without my permission." He grins his teeth, then looks back out the window as they drive pass local stores. "Back at the loft, you asked me what's stopping me from taking over." She pauses. He slants his head toward her and stays quiet. "Time." She continues. She parks the car in front of a coffee store and faces him. "I lied to you when I said you weren't special. You and your cousin are the first creatures to ever see the treasure of Ozora. That makes you more dangerous than any vampire or demon."

"The treasure of what? I don't know what you're talking about" He looks at her puzzled.

"When you died, the Atomizer wasn't the only thing you saw. There were four gold talismans that appeared to you. I know so, because the Atomizer is only one of the treasures of Ozora."

"How do you know about all of this?"

"My ancestor is the one who created them. She was an ally to your ancestor clan and helped lead the revolt. Stories tell, she supplied all the men with enchanted weapons that were used in the war. After most of the demons were locked in purgatory, there were rumors of her crafting talismans that were powerful enough to annihilate the rest. She died the same night she made them. Horrified of the idea, she was ambushed by her own tribe who secretly plotted against her once word of the talismans got out."

"What?"

"Even though they were enslaved by demons, friendships were made during the revolt. Not all demons were necessarily bad, some fought side by side with humans. The tribe honored their friendship with the demons and hid the talismans in the deepest corners of earth, till this day not one of them have been found. The tribe of Ozora were soon executed for their actions and brought the secrets of the locations to the grave with them. Luckily, Ozora was aware of the risk she was taking, so she sent a message to your great father earlier in the day, letting him know she didn't trust her own tribe or any others. She enchanted the talismans with his DNA. Enabling your bloodline to be the only ones who could locate and use or destroy them if anything happens to her. It was that same year your great grandfather faced his death setting out to find it. The Atomizer and the rest of the treasure eventually faded away into becoming a myth. Told to scare demons, to keep them submissive."

Isaiah looks at her amazed. "Wow, this really goes deep."

She leans back and turns her head to the windshield. "Listen. I have a plan, but it has to stay between us. Zechariah, Tyriek, Hakeem nor your grandma can know." He nods his head. "It won't be easy but if you remain loyal, I give you my word your mother will be freed and your name alone will bring fear to the hearts of both humans and demons." She looks him in his eyes as he nods his head again. She leans over and whispers in his ears. His eyes widen during the whole message. When she leans back into her seat, he faces her speechless. "Are you down?"

"What you're saying sounds insane, but if you can show me anything that you proposed is true then yea, I'm down."

"My pleasure. Come inside with me for a cup of coffee." She smiles. The two get out the car and walk inside the café. They grab a booth by the window as she flags down a waitress. "You want something to drink?" She asks him.

"I don't drink coffee." He replies taking a seat.

"Me neither." He smirks at her as she sits down across from him at the table. "Have you ever heard of mind control?"

He nods his head. "You're going to show me another magic trick?"

"No, I'm going to show you something you didn't know you could do." The waitress comes to the table and asks for their order. "Can I just have a cup of water, we're not ready yet." She nods her head and walks back to the kitchen. Both Isaiah and Lucia look around the half empty café then back at each other.

Smiling, he asks "so you're telling me I can control people?"

"For a short period of time, yes."

"How?"

"When she comes back, I want you to bite her wrist then lock eyes with her."

"That's it?" She nods her head toward him as the waitress walk back out the kitchen carrying the cup of the water. The two look at her as she approaches the table. Lucia's eyes fall onto Isaiah as the waitress places the cup of water in front of her. He quickly grabs the waitress's wrist and sticks his fangs in her veins. She screams causing a scene in the café. The two employees behind the counter and the two customers on line turn their attention to their booth. Isaiah quickly let's go of her before people notice, and locks eyes with her.

"You're a freaking creep!" She screams out loud.

"Tell her forget what you just did." Lucia taps the table.

"Forget I just bit you." He says staring into the waitress' eyes. The angry waitress instantly becomes calm as she stands in front of the booth waiting to hear her next order. "I can't believe this!" He laughs.

"Stephanie is everything ok?" Her coworker asks walking around the counter.

"Tell him everything is fine. Then go bandage your wrist. I'll let you know when I need you again." Isaiah continues. She nods her head and turns around.

"I'm fine." She replies to her coworker as she passes him and heads into the kitchen.

"Are you sure? Blood is dripping down your hands." He looks at her concerned.

"Yes, I cut myself by accident." She covers the wound on her wrist. He stares awkwardly as she heads inside the kitchen. Keeping his eyes on the two in the booth, he walks back around the counter and takes the next order.

"Is it me or does that guy look familiar?" One customer whispers to another.

"The power of mind control is only temporary. Once the bite wound heals so will her full consciousness." Lucia says, tapping the cup of water with her nails.

Isaiah sighs. "Of course, there's a catch. How long does that usually take?"

"A day or two, three the most. You can also communicate with her telepathically." He nods his head at her with a half-smile on his face. "Oh boy, I could only imagine what you're going to do to that poor helpless girl." Suddenly, a loud whistling noise covers the rest of her sentence.

"Whoa, what's that noise?" He cuts her off to ask as he looks around the café and out the window.

"What noise?" She looks at him puzzled.

"You don't hear that whistling sound?" He asks, placing one hand over his ear. As he stands from the table, he notices he is the only person in the store that can hear it. The whistling sound begins to grow louder. He walks out the café frustrated to see if he can hear where the sound is coming from. As he takes a couple of steps out the café, Lucia approaches him from behind and grabs his elbow.

"Stop! It's a trap. They found you!"

"Who?" He faces her.

"Warriors of the Power Circle! Never follow that sound, it will be the last sound you'll ever hear. Go back inside the café and let them come to you." He looks her in the eyes then back around the street to see if he could find the source one last time. He gives up and nods his head. As they walk back inside, one of the customers take a good look at Isaiah.

"Hey! That's the serial killer from the hotel!" Everyone in the lobby starts to panic.

Lucia shakes her head as she walks around Isaiah. As everyone takes their phones out to call the cops, she raises her hand and says "sleep." Everyone falls where they were standing.

"Why am I the only person that can hear this?" Isaiah asks, looking at Lucia puzzled.

"Because you're the only demon in the café. They're not trying to catch us, they want you." As the two look at each other, a waiter walks out the kitchen and drops the tray of coffee he is carrying at the sight of everyone on the floor. When the waiter makes eye contact with the two at the entrance, he tries to turn around and run. Isaiah beats him to the kitchen door and bites him in the neck. As he screams, Isaiah pulls back from his neck and locks eyes with him. Not saying a word, the waiter regains his composure then nods his head and continues into the kitchen. "What is that about?" Lucia looks at him intrigued.

"You'll see. How strong are these warriors?"

"Strong, but they're still human." She replies walking toward him.

"This should be interesting."

"Yes it will, I want to see if you're all talk."

"Cool, so sit down somewhere. I'll handle this by myself."

"A little cocky, aren't you?"

"No, just." He can't finish his sentence; the whistling noise grows extremely louder. He grabs both of his ears and growls. Looking at the window, he sees a man in a black robe playing a syrinx. When the two make eye contact, Isaiah takes a step forward. Lucia looks behind her to see what he is looking at, and when she sees the warrior, she takes a seat in the booth nearest to her. When Isaiah takes another step, black smoke crawls underneath the entrance door. The man in the robe stops playing the syrinx once the smoke forms into a man. Isaiah removes his hands from his ears as his eyes shift to the warrior standing across from him. The café is quiet. "Did you come here to look at me or did you come here to fight?" Isaiah asks anxiously.

The man pulls his hood down and looks at all the customers laying on the floor. Shaking his head, he says "it's a shame, what a disappointment you have become." The robed man standing outside enter the café following another man.

Isaiah smirks. "There's only three of you? That little music show is disappointing."

The other two men take off their hoods. "It only took one of us to take down your cousin. I doubt you're any different."

His smirk quickly fades away. "You ambushed Hakeem? He's on your side!"

"No, he's not. All of you vampires are the same. Feeding off us to survive. You hold no value to this world anymore, but to be honest I would have preferred to kill you first."

Isaiah folds his fist as his face transforms. "Now's your chance!" Just as the warrior takes a step toward him, Stephanie the waitress runs out the kitchen crying. Isaiah yolks her by the neck and holds her tight to him. "You won't mind if I have one last meal?" He asks the warriors sarcastically.

Everyone gets defensive. "You're an animal! Let her go, now!"

He smirks at them then looks back at the waitress. "As you wish!" He replies tossing her toward them. As the warrior catches her, she pulls out a butcher knife from her apron and stabs him in the gut. His mouth drops as he fall to his knees. She pulls the knife out and stabs him in the jaw. The other two warriors are shocked as they witness their partner's body fall to the ground. One of the warriors' charges at her and hits her unconscious. He kneels over his partner and holds his head as the rest of his body lays lifeless.

"I didn't know you guys die so easy. He received the easy way out, the two of your deaths will be way slower and painful. You're going to wish you never laid a finger on my kin!"

The warrior places his partner's head gently on the floor then stands up. With his eyes full of rage, he yells "I'm going to kill you!" Then charges towards Isaiah. Isaiah swings first, but hits smoke as the warrior disappears and reappears behind him. He kicks Isaiah in the back of his knee, then elbows his temple. Causing Isaiah to fall next to an unconscious customer. The warrior picks up the knife the waitress used to kill his partner and runs towards him. As he tries to stab Isaiah, Isaiah uses a customer as a shield then grabs his hand. Pulling him down, Isaiah climbs on top of him and tries to punch him, but hits the floor, as his body turns back into smoke and reappears behind him. He grabs Isaiah by his hair and tosses him across the café onto a booth.

He pulls the knife out of the customers back and charges toward Isaiah. As the two tangle, the other warrior approaches Lucia who is sitting down enjoying the show. "You're blocking my view!" She scowls at him.

As the warrior swings the knife at Isaiah, he rolls off the table and elbows him in the gut. Before Isaiah can hit him again, the butcher's knife is impaled through his chest. Isaiah stands speechless looking down at the handle sticking out of his chest. "Fuck, I missed!" as the warrior steps back.

Isaiah slowly pulls the knife out as he grins his teeth in pain. "That was the only chance you had to kill me." He grips the knife and points it at him. "I'm going to tear your throat out!"

"You're father never did this much talking."

"When this is over, you can reflect with him how different we are." Isaiah replies then charges towards him. As he swings the knife, the warrior turns back into smoke and reappears behind him. He quickly turns around and swings again but the warrior stays in the form of smoke. Frustrated from swinging, he backs up and waits for him to form again. "Stop doing that! And fight like a man!"

The warrior smiles as he becomes solid again. "Don't tell me your tired already." Isaiah grins his teeth and charges at him again. The warrior turns into smoke allowing Isaiah to run through him. As the warrior begins to form again, the waiter opens the kitchen door and tosses a knife at his back. Direct hit. The warrior stumbles as he turns around to see who's behind him. Isaiah approaches him as he falls to his knees in pain, struggling to reach for the knife in his back. The two make eye contact, before Isaiah stabs him in the neck and licks the blood off the knife.

"Now it's your turn!" When he turns around to face the other warrior, to his surprise he is laid out on the floor in front of Lucia. She is still seated in the booth, holding the amulet the warrior was wearing. "Show off." He smirks.

She smiles back. "All you had to do was remove their amulets. They can't transport without it."

"The two of you will burn for this! They will send more warriors when me and my brothers don't return!" The warrior shout as he lays paralyzed.

"I left him alive for you." She says to Isaiah.

He walks over and stands over him sliding his index finger down the knife. "Every warrior that seeks me out will be joining you and your brothers in hell. Your justice will never be honored." He kneels over him then grabs him by the throat. "Tell me why did you guys kill my cousin and I'll reconsider giving you a slow death." The warrior doesn't respond. Isaiah begins to carve a deep cut down the side of his face. As the warrior screams, Isaiah moves his head to the side and does the same to the opposite cheek. The warrior cries out in pain as Isaiah stabs him in the leg and uses the handle as support to stand back up. "Tell me who's idea it was to kill my cousin! Was it my grandma's?"

The warrior grins his teeth as he tries not to make eye contact. Isaiah pulls the knife out of his leg and stabs his hand. He cries out in enormous amount of pain then screams, "he's not dead! We kidnapped him! We only need one of you to find the Atomizer, and we chose him. Until this Atomizer is found you will be hunted down until you're a pile of dust."

Isaiah smirks then looks back at Lucia. When Isaiah turns back to face him, he kneels over him and replies, "I want you to give the Power Circle a message." His face transforms as he leans in and bites him.

CHAPTER 34

Grandma

The impact of grandma's transportation sends everything in the room out of order. When her body fragments finally regenerate, she is still holding the bag from the Exalus house. She tosses the bag onto a chair and runs out the door. When she opens the door, the few people that are walking by stop and stare. She storms pass them and heads straight to the elevator and presses the up button. Waiting anxiously, she looks at the staircase next to her and decides to use that instead. There are three floors in the citadel, not including the dungeon. Her dorm room is located on the second floor. By the time she gets to the top floor she is out of breath. Taking a second to breathe, a couple of people nod their heads at her as they walk pass to go downstairs.

The third person to pass her stops and does a double take. He looks like he is a few years younger than her and not trying to make conversation, she places her head down and continues to walk through the hallway. "Hey Adeline, is that you?" The man asks as he reaches for her shoulder.

She turns around and gives him an awkward smile. "Hey Carter. I didn't see you."

"I didn't get a chance to give you my condolences. I heard about William and Jason. And now your grandchildren, if there's anything you need, please let me know. I'm here for you."

She nods her head and replies, "thank you, I appreciate it"

"I mean it!" He holds onto her hands.

"I know you do Carter. I don't want to be rude but the elders are waiting for me. Can we talk another time?" She asks pulling her hands back to her side. He nods his head then continues in the opposite direction. Walking quickly down the hall, she bumps into a few more people before coming to a stop in front of a metal door. A green laser light scans her face as a robotic voice confirms her alias. Within seconds, the metal doors open.

As she enters the room she hears a deep voice greet her. "We've been expecting you." She nods her head as she continues to the middle of the room. She stands in front of a round table of five elder men. "We are highly disappointed in you Adeline, we truly expected better leadership," said the man sitting to the far right of the table.

"You carelessly allowed both of your grandchildren to die intoxicated with vampire blood in their system. Not only jeopardizing the mission but completely ending your own blood line. The Exalus blood line," said the man sitting to the far left of the table.

"There was nothing I could have done." She replies.

"Adeline do not speak out of turn. You will have your chance to speak." The man sitting in the middle cuts her off and continues. "They were under your supervision! They don't know how important this mission is, but you do! Your son's put away their foolish grudges to obtain that container of blood. They died believing Hakeem and Isaiah would be the key to a new beginning."

"But not only did you fail them, you encouraged this act of

abomination by deliberately going behind our back and giving them the ability to walk in the sun. If we knew this was what you were planning, we would have had them killed the same night you pleaded for them." Said the man sitting left to the man in the middle.

"Are you aware Isaiah turned someone into a vampire?" The man seated in the middle asks.

"I..." She stutters.

"This morning the local news in that town aired a video of him and his friend tearing apart innocent families staying at a hotel last night. We cannot stand for this!" The man in the middle slams his fist. "If other demons become aware of his behavior freely in society before we find the Atomizer, towns will become bloodbaths! We will not put any more lives at risk! Now, you will be held accountable for Isaiah's actions. You will no longer be active on this mission nor are you allowed to leave the citadel until further notice. We haven't come up with a punishment for your behavior yet, but you will be informed shortly. Do you have anything to say Adeline?"

"I'm sorry for how my decisions turned out, I never anticipated this from him. You're right, I should be held accountable for his actions, but Hakeem should not have to be daggered because of Isaiah's stupidity. Let him live until the Atomizer is found. There's a bigger threat than them walking around town. A demon named Zechariah attacked us this morning and killed Camille!"

The room grows quiet. "We're sorry for your loss Adeline, truly. Before the warriors return we will have them sweep the town for him. As for Hakeem, we are aware he isn't the same as Isaiah. Therefore, we kidnapped him before he had a change of a heart. Even with the knowledge of the Atomizer's whereabouts, we can't access its true power without an Exalus warrior."

"You kidnapped him?" She looks at them puzzled. "Where are you holding him?"

"He's downstairs in the dungeon with Aaron. In a few hours, they will be setting out to find the Atomizer." The man seated in the middle replies.

"You have to let me leave the citadel with them, please!"

"No, but you may have your final words with him downstairs, you are not by any means to leave." The room is silent again.

"May I have one more request before I am dismissed?" The man in the middle nods his head. "Hakeem's girlfriend Amber is conceived with the heir of an Exalus. My bloodline doesn't end with Hakeem and Isaiah. If you won't let me leave, can you at least send someone to escort her here?"

All the men look at each other intrigued. "Provide us with an image of her, and we will escort her here safely."

She bows her head slightly, "thank you," then walks out of the room.

Hakeem

"Here, drink this." Aaron says as he tosses a packet of blood into the dungeon cell next to Hakeem, who is laying on the floor dehydrated. He groans as he slowly reaches for it. Aaron steps back out and quickly shuts the door, he stands beside the window and watches Hakeem sink his teeth into the packet. After draining the bag, Hakeem quickly gets back on his feet and runs toward the door. He tries to force the door down but the door doesn't budge. Stepping back, he sees Aaron watching him through the window and punches the glass in hopes of breaking it, but that doesn't budge either.

"Why the fuck am I here!" a frustrated Hakeem asks.

"Just calm down and I'll fill you in."

"You fucking ambushed me and kidnapped me." He begin to pace back and forth then looks back at the window. "Give me one reason why I shouldn't take your head off!"

"It was the only way we could ensure that you'd come here. We couldn't risk you straying away like Isaiah. If we wanted to kill you, we would have while you were unconscious."

Hakeem grins his teeth. "That's not a good enough reason!"

Before Aaron can say another word, Hakeem's grandma enters the hallway. Aaron turns his attention towards her and says, "Adeline you made it."

"My grandma is here?" Hakeem looks at him puzzled. "Let me talk to her!"

She gives Aaron a cold stare as she approaches him. "I presume you spoke to the elders already?" He asks as she gets close to him. Grandma doesn't say a word as she stares him in the eyes. The hallway is quiet. He breaks the deadly stare by looking at Hakeem who is also staring at him and says, "I'll just leave you two to say your last goodbyes, I'll be back when we're ready." He looks back at Grandma for confirmation, but her facial expression doesn't change. He nods his head and continues pass her.

"Grandma what are you doing? Where's Amber?" Hakeem looks at her puzzled.

"Most likely at the hospital by now, the cops just raided the house for you. I have no doubt they found your mother downstairs too. If it wasn't for my amulet, I would have got caught too."

"Damn!" He places his head down. "Why would Amber be at the hospital?" He lifts his head to ask.

"Not too long after you left the house, the vampire blood started kicking in. She was unconscious when the cops came and there was no change as I was leaving."

"I have to see her before we leave! I didn't get a chance to say bye! I have to say bye to Andrew and Taryn too!" His voice cracks.

"We don't have much say in what we can and can't do in our current circumstance. Isaiah's ruthless behavior robbed us of our free will. Even after you carry out this mission, I will be paying the price for his actions." He grins his teeth as he closes his hand into a fist. "Listen." She softens her voice. "I don't agree with them kidnapping you, it kills me seeing you in this cell. And it breaks my heart knowing this will be my last time laying eyes on you. If I could trade positions with you, believe me I would. I love you and I hope you know that. And despite Isaiah's reckless behavior, I love him too, but the world needs this Atomizer to be found. Amber needs this Atomizer to be found. There's no better time to tell you this, but she's pregnant."

"What?" He replies puzzled.

"She's pregnant Hakeem. She's carrying your baby."

It takes a moment for him to gather his thoughts. "How do you know this?"

"I fed her a special herb tea that was supposed to ease her fever, but her body rejected it."

"That doesn't prove anything!" He stutters.

"That's exactly what it means!"

He places his hands on his head then covers his face for a few seconds. "How do you expect me to go through with this? To abandon her at a time like this? Abandon my child?"

"You're not abandoning them, get that out of your head! You are making sure what happened to your mother this morning doesn't happen to your child, Amber or any other innocent being. You have an opportunity to really save the world. Secure a normal life for your child. That's all your father ever wanted." Grandma replies.

He grins his teeth and puts his head down again. "Make me a promise then. Promise me, my death won't be in vain. That you'll make Amber understand!"

"I promise."

He sighs. "Tell Aaron I'm ready."

Tears start pouring out of her eyes as she replies, "I love you Keem!"

"I love you too grandma."

Grandma

She places her head down as she walks away from the dungeon cell. Wiping the tears from her eyes, she walks down the hall passing cells that people are guarding. Avoiding eye contact, she makes her way to the entrance of the staircase. As she walks up the stairs, she makes sure her eyes are dry before she reaches the top.

Aaron is waiting on the wall between the entrance of the citadel and the staircase for her. As soon as she gets to the first floor, he steps from the wall and approaches her. "Are you really going to continue to give me the cold shoulder? This isn't my fault!"

"This isn't your fault? You have the nerve." She grits her teeth.

"I was only doing my job Adeline, Isaiah is out of control!"

"So you go behind my back and have Hakeem kidnapped?"

"He needed to be here! He has no place in the streets and you know that! You should have never allowed him to entertain this idea of keeping a personal life. That was supposed to die when they did."

"Well consider our friendship dead along with them!" She replies then turns to walk away.

"It doesn't have to be this way." He reaches for her. As she turns back around, the front door of the citadel opens. Both her and Aaron's eyes shoot open when they see the bloody warrior walk through the door. His facial expression shows that he has been put through a lot. He carries in two big brown coffee bags with blood dripping from the bottom of both. "Jacob, what are in the bags?" Aaron manages to ask. He drops the bags on the floor and two heads roll out the bag. Grandma covers her mouth shocked, as Aaron's mouth hangs speechless. Aaron is stunned when he realizes the two heads belongs to the other two warriors. Trying to find words, he stutters "how was he capable of this? Did you kill him?" The warrior stands emotionless and doesn't respond. "Jacob!" He steps closer.

The warrior pulls out a sharp blade and waves it in his face. Aaron back steps quickly and stretches his arms out defensively as grandma steps from behind to beside him. The warrior looks Aaron in his eyes and says, "you really thought you could kill me?"

"What are you talking about?" Aaron looks at him puzzled.

"You're a bunch of cowards, sending warriors to do an Exalus job!"

Staring at the warrior, grandma notices a bite mark on his neck. She grabs Aaron's hands and whispers "be careful, he's under possession. He's not thinking for himself."

"How?" Aaron replies, while not taking his eyes off him.

"Death is coming, there's no corner you can run to, no God you can pray to. I will find all of you and rip your throats out. The hotel massacre will be nothing compared to the citadels. And tell my grandma once I find the Atomizer and free my mother from purgatory, we will be looking forward to a family reunion," the warrior grips the blade handle and stabs himself in the thyroid.

CHAPTER 35

Amber

"Mr. and Mrs. Irizarry!" The doctor greets as he enters the hospital lobby. Amber's mother is sitting on the sofa with Emira and three other classmates, while her father who is tense sits on the armrest. The lobby is filled with worried students, everyone faces the doctor once he appears. "Can I speak to the two of you in private?" He asks. Amber's father nods his head as her mother rises from the sofa. Her parents follow the doctor outside of the lobby and into the hallway. Before they get further, he stops to introduce himself. "My name is Dr. Murray, and your daughter seems to not be responding to any of our medication. We ran some blood tests on her and oddly enough, no known drugs came up in her system. We did indicate that she's in the beginning stages of pregnancy and what she is going through could possibly be related to this. We will run a few more tests, but I don't want the two of you to worry, I am 100% positive she will wake up from this."

"What? She can't be pregnant. Your blood test came back wrong!" Her father yells.

"Mr. Irizarry, I understand your frustration. But we ran multiple blood tests on her, there's no question about it, she's pregnant." Her father grits his teeth as her mother shakes her head, disappointed. "Do you want me to give you two a moment?"

"When can we see our daughter?" Her mother asks.

"You can see her now. Due to our hippa policy, by law we can't share that information with her friends. I had to tell you privately, but now that we have spoken, I can allow the two of you and a select few to go into her room."

"Only Emira." Her father says to his wife. She nods her head with approval. "We only want one of her friends to accompany us, Emira." He replies to the doctor.

Doctor Murray nods his head, "before I forget. I assume the officers filled you in on the investigation on the death of Camille Exalus. They are going to want to question her when she wakes up. When I get Emira, a detective is going to have to come too." Both parents nod their heads. When Dr. Murray comes back from the lobby, he is followed by Emira, one detective and one officer. He leads the group down the hall to her room, the police wait outside as he escorts the rest inside. Immediately, tears fall down her mother and Emira's eyes when they see her laying in the hospital bed. Both parents sit on one side of her bed as Emira sits on the opposite side.

After Dr. Murray walks out, her father looks at Emira and calls her name. As she wipes her eyes, she gives him her attention. He continues to ask, "why wasn't Amber in school with you? She told us last night she was staying over your house."

"I. I don't know." She stumbles over her words.

"Did she even spend the night at your house?" He becomes furious.

"No." She replies, avoiding eye contact.

"How many times did she lie to us about staying over your house?" He looks at her puzzled.

Scratching the back of her head, she avoids making eye contact again. "This was the only time I'm aware of Mr. Irizarry."

He grits his teeth as he shakes his head. "Why would Hakeem kill his mother?" Amber's mother asks.

"I keep asking myself the same question. This isn't the Hakeem I know." Emira replies facing her.

"He was also at the hotel when the massacre happened." Her father continues.

"Emira, did Amber tell you that she was pregnant?" Her mother asks.

"She's pregnant?" Emira replies, covering her mouth. The room is quiet as the parents put their heads down. "I didn't know. I don't even think she knows, Mrs. Irizarry."

Angry, her father bends his hands into a fist and yells, "that bastard raped my daughter!" Emira keeps her head down to avoid any more questions. As Amber's father continues to curse Hakeem, Amber's head begins to turn side to side. Her mother stand's up and grabs her hands, stopping her husband mid-sentence.

"Get the doctor!" Her mother shouts at Emira. As Emira gets to the door, she over hears Amber's mother cry in joy. Amber opens her eyes. Amber instantly flinches back in bed as she remembers the last things she saw. Her parents launch themselves at her suffocating her with hugs. She is both relieved and confused. When Emira sees the celebration, she shuts the door and joins the group hug.

"I can't breathe guys." Amber says smiling.

"I'm never letting you go!" Her mother replies holding her tighter.

"Amber, I'm disappointed in you!" Her father says, letting go of her. Emira and her mother slowly let go of her too.

"What did I do?" She looks at him puzzled, then continues, "what am I doing here?" She looks around.

"You lied to us about spending the night at Emira's house! You allowed this boy to drug you and impregnate you!" Her father replies.

Her mouth drops as she grabs her stomach. "Whoa, I am not pregnant! And Hakeem did not rape me, what are you talking about?"

"Amber, please. The doctor just took your blood test, you're pregnant! Hakeem's been taking advantage of you!" Her father replies.

"Emira, please tell my dad Hakeem is not this dark character he draws him out to be. I don't know why he's assuming he raped me!"

Emira shakes her head at her. "I really don't know Hakeem anymore."

"The cops found you in his bedroom unconscious while his mother was dead in the basement!" Her father interrupts and continues, "not only did he kill his mother, he's associated with the sociopath who slaughtered the families at the hotel!"

"What! Hakeem did not kill his mother!"

"Good your awake!" Doctor Murray says, interrupting both Amber and her father. Both him and his nurse cut in front of Emira to stand beside her, leaving the police by the entrance. "Nice to finally meet you Amber, I'm Doctor Murray."

She ignores his introduction and replies, "I want to go home!"

"Once we know you're stable and your baby is healthy, I see no reasons why you can't go home." Dr. Murray replies.

"Enough with this pregnancy talk, I am not pregnant! People don't just wake up pregnant!"

"No, people don't." He pauses to look at Emira, the detective then the officer. "Can you guys give us a moment of privacy." He continues. The three nod their heads and leave the room. Once the door shuts behind Emira, he turns his attention back to Amber. "I know this is a lot to wake up too. I need you to take a breather and let reality sink in."

"I don't need to do anything! I'm not pregnant! I'm going home with or without your approval!"

"Amber stop!" Her mother shouts.

"Amber, I'm not here to make up stories about you. I'm only here to help you." Dr. Murray replies.

"I passed out, now I'm awake. What else can you help me with?"

Doctor Murray shakes his head. "Fine, but before you leave, may I just suggest you take another pregnancy test? Maybe this time it'll come out negative."

Before she can reply, her father quickly answers for her. "Yes, she will!" She looks at him and shakes her head.

"Ok then, I'll let the detective in so you can be on your way."

"Thank you." Her mother replies. He and the nurse nod their heads and walk out the room. As soon as the door opens, the detective and the officer walk in. The detective introduces himself as he shakes her father's hand.

"Good afternoon, my name is detective Ashor Marino. We have some questions to ask Amber regarding Hakeem Exalus." She nods her head as he stands over her bed. "What's your relationship with Hakeem?"

"He's my boyfriend."

"Was, she is no longer seeing him." Her father corrects her.

"Dad!" She scrunches her face at him.

"Listen to your father, Hakeem isn't the greatest influence on your life." Detective Marino replies.

"He didn't kill his mother." She says firmly to the detective as he approaches the seat on the other side of her bed.

"Were you awake when she was killed?" He asks.

She pauses then looks at her parents as if she needs their permission to answer. She knows she can't tell the truth. "No, I wasn't." She looks down.

"Then how can you be so positive he didn't." He replies suspicious.

"Because, I know"

He nods his head then takes his cell phone out of his pocket. "I want you to watch something." He goes through his apps, until he finds the video of the hotel massacre. When he clicks on it, he hands the phone to her and lets the video play. She covers her mouth stunned at the sight of Isaiah. "Do you know who they are?" He points at Isaiah and Tyriek.

"No, no I don't!" She quickly shakes her head.

He shakes his head disappointed and lets the rest of the video play. Watching the graphic video makes Amber sick to her stomach, when the horror finally ends, her eyes widen at the sight of Hakeem entering the hotel. The detective takes the phone away at that point.

"Amber, we need your cooperation. We can't allow these murderers to roam our streets. Do you know the people he went seeking out? I need you to be honest with us." Still covering her mouth, she slowly shakes her head.

He shakes his head again, disappointed. "Amber if you lie to me again, you leave me no choice but to view you as an accomplice to his crimes, and instead of going home with your parents you will be coming to the station with us. Emira told me the fellow with the dreads is Hakeem's cousin. Now I don't understand your relationship, but from watching your loving parents and with the number of concerned friends you have in the lobby, I'm convinced you're nothing like them. Do not go down this road of self-destruction."

She shakes her head and hides her face in her palms.

"Shouldn't we have a lawyer here if that's the case?" Her father asks.

"Not necessarily, she's not under investigation unless she gives us a reason she needs to be, and our conversation is in your presence." Detective Marino replies.

Her father nods his head as his wife asks, "if she's not under investigation, may you just give her some more time to get her thoughts together. I don't think she's thinking straight yet."

Detective Marino nods his head and replies, "I understand. I'll give her a couple of hours, but I won't be the only detective seeking her out. This man hunt is very serious, and as of right now Amber is the only person with ties to Hakeem." He reaches into his wallet and hands her parents his contact card. They shake his hands as Amber keeps her head down.

"We will give you a call." Her father says to him.

"Thank you, I can't stress this enough. The more time we waste, more innocent lives are being endangered."

CHAPTER 36

Andrew

"Please be home," Andrew says to himself tapping on the steering wheel as he turns into Taryn's driveway. He parks behind her father's car and gets out the driver seat. "Great, he's here." He says sarcastically under his breath. He walks up to the door and the rings the doorbell. He waits a few seconds and hears no response, so he rings it again then knocks. When he knocks, the door slightly opens as if it was never shut. Sticking his head inside, he says "hello, it's me Andrew. The door wasn't shut." The house is quiet. "Taryn! Mr. and Mrs. Czarnecky! Is anybody home?" He walks in and shuts the door behind him.

The first thing he notices entering the house is blood next to the welcome mat. He quickly grabs his phone out of his pocket and holds it tight. He takes his time as he continues to walk in, when he sees the butcher knife laying on the kitchen floor, he grits his teeth and runs upstairs. He sprints to Taryn's room and her door is already opened. When he steps inside, he sees both of her parent's corpse laying on top of each other in front of her bed. He grabs his stomach and vomits on the floor. Wiping his mouth with his arm, he grabs the side of the wall to stay stable. "Fuck" he pants under his breath. When he unlocks his phone, he over hears sobbing and sniffing coming from the bathroom. "Taryn is that you?" He pushes himself off the wall and puts his phone away as he walks out the room. "Taryn it's me Andrew, are you ok?" he asks, opening the bathroom door.

Taryn is sitting on the floor on the opposite side of the room, knees pinched to her chest with her arms wrapped around her legs and her face down crying. "Taryn!" He runs to her, drops to his knees and hugs her. "Thank god you're alive. I thought I lost you!" Taryn hugs him back tight but doesn't respond. "Let's go get some help."

He replies, looking her in her eyes. She tries to avoid eye contact as she wipes her tears. "Come on, let's go before whatever did this comes back!" He stands up holding her hand. She looks him in the eyes then pulls her hand back to her side. "Are you ok? Do you want me to carry you?"

More tears fall down her cheeks as she shakes her head. "It was me, I killed them." She says under her breath.

"You what?" He looks at her puzzled.

"I didn't mean too. I swear, I, I had no choice."

"Taryn, I know you and your father had differences, but murder? Your parent's bodies are torn apart." She shakes her head again and places it back between her legs. He puts his back against the wall and sits on the floor. The bathroom is quiet. Lifting his head up to exhale, he faces her and asks, "when did you and Hakeem decide on living the rest of your lives as fugitives?" She keeps her head down and doesn't respond. "If you want me to help you, you have to fill me in on the madness that's going on. Who influenced you to do this? Isaiah? You killing your parents the same day him, Tyriek and Hakeem massacred an entire hotel can't be a coincidence!"

"What? Where did you hear this from?" She asks as she lifts her head up and wipes the last of her tears.

"It's all over the news and the web. There is video of Isaiah and Tyriek feasting on guests like they are into cannibalism." He pauses for a second, then tilts his head back. "Strange, the wounds on the victims at the hotel look exactly like the ones on your parents." He struggles trying to stand up. "Oh my God, you're one of them! That's why Isaiah came to school looking for you. The reason you left me hanging at The Shack yesterday," He says.

"No, I'm nothing like him!" She stands up.

"I knew you my whole life Taryn. Before today you were never capable of hurting anyone, not even that bastard Chris! Now your parents are victims to a random rage?" Before she can reply, she hears a car entering the driveway.

"Did you tell anyone you were coming here?" She looks at him puzzled.

"Only Justina when I left school. Why are you going to kill me too?"

"Andrew stop! Someone is outside, can you look through my room window to see who it is?"

"I don't hear anything Taryn." As soon as he says that, the doorbell rings. The two look at each other, then she begs him to check again. He walks out the bathroom and into her bedroom, when he sees her parents on the floor again he closes his eyes and keeps walking. The doorbell rings again. When he looks through the window blinds he sees two officers in front of the house. "Oh shit. It's the cops!" He panics, moving away from the window.

"What? Why?"

He gives her a blank stare and replies, "we're going to jail, I'm going to spend the rest of my life in a cell for being affiliated with you."

"No, you're not, you need to calm down." The doorbell rings two more times followed by loud knocks.

"What are we going to do?" He looks at her nervously.

"Answer the door for me and find out why they are here."

"Why do I have to answer the door? This is your house!"

"I can't go outside. I'll explain everything after you do this for me." He grits his teeth. "Please Andrew."

"Fine, they're going to arrest us regardless who answers the door." He shakes his head.

"No, they're not, there's no way they know about my parents. Just don't let them inside and we'll be fine." She replies as he walks pass her.

When he gets downstairs he covers the blood stain on the floor with his sneakers and opens the door slightly enough for the officers to see him, but not the inside of the house. "Hello." He introduces himself first.

"Good afternoon, I'm officer Guzman, and this is my partner officer McGrath. May we speak to Taryn Czarnecky please".

"I'm sorry, but she's not here."

"Are her parent's home?" Officer McGrath asks.

A nervous facial expression falls upon Andrews face. "No, they're not home either."

"Hm, may we ask why you're here then?" Officer Guzman asks.

"What?" He pauses to think, then replies nervously, "Oh, I'm watching the house until they return."

Officer McGrath squints his eyes at him. "Aren't you Andrew Lorelli? Shouldn't you be in school?"

"I finished my classes early today" He looks at him puzzled. "Is there a reason why you know my name?"

"We need you to come down to the station with us. We have a few questions to ask you," Officer McGrath continues.

His heart drops as he stutters, "Why? why do I have to go to the station? I didn't do anything."

"We know you didn't." Officer Guzman replies. Andrew is relieved for a moment, "but, we understand you and Taryn are really good friends with Hakeem Exalus. I'm sure you are aware of his involvement in the hotel massacre this morning. We found his mother dead in the basement shortly after and his girlfriend Amber Irizarry unconscious on his bed," He states.

"Mrs. Exalus is dead too?" Andrew asks, closing his eyes, upset.

"Too? Was anybody else you know killed within the last 24 hours?" A curious officer Guzman asks.

Andrew's eyes widen at the question. "No, I was including her along with the rest of the innocent lives taken at the hotel. Is Amber ok?"

"Yes, luckily we got her in time before she became another victim. She's currently at the hospital. It's very urgent that you cooperate with us on finding this monster before more lives are lost." Officer McGrath replies.

"I'm sorry officers, but I wouldn't be any help to anyone. I haven't spoken to Hakeem in several days."

"But if you call him, he'll answer." Officer McGrath replies.

"He hasn't returned my calls in days, he's not going to answer for me today. I'm sorry."

He tries to shut the door, but officer Guzman places his shoe in the entrance. "You don't mind if we look around the house, do you?"

"Yea, I actually do. I was told not to let anyone in when no one is home."

"We just want to make sure everything in the house is normal. Are

244

you hiding something from us?" Officer Guzman stares in his eyes.

"No." Andrew replies nervously.

"Then let's have a look, if everything checks out we will be on our way before anyone notices. I don't think we have to inform you how serious of a crime it would be, if you lied to us about Hakeem's whereabouts or worse, if you were hiding him." Officer Guzman leans closer to his face.

"You don't have to inform me of the law, just like I don't have to inform you that I don't have to let you in without a warrant."

An upset Officer Guzman backs up from the door, then looks him up and down. "When Taryn comes home, tell her to come to the station as soon as she can."

"Come to the station with her." Officer McGrath adds.

Andrew nods his head. "Will do." As soon as they turn around to walk away, he immediately closes the door, almost slipping on the blood he is stepping on. He closes his eyes and takes a deep breath. When he opens them, he sees Taryn sitting on the stairs looking at him. "I need to know the truth now! Hakeem killed his mother too, so now I know this couldn't have been an accident! Are you guys performing some kind ritual?"

She stands up and walks down the three steps. "No Drew, we are not performing rituals. I honestly don't know why Hakeem would kill his mom. She was the sweetest person I knew."

"Enough Taryn! If this isn't a ritual, then what the fuck is going on? I'm your best friend, I deserve to know the truth!'

"Something happened to us Drew. You're not going to believe me but you have to promise me you'll keep it a secret."

He nods his head slowly. "What happened?"

"I'm a vampire."

"Really, Taryn? A vampire? I just stood here and lied to the cops for you and you're going to stand here and bullshit me?"

"I'm not lying! We all are." She steps toward him.

"I thought we were friends." He looks at her disappointed. "Good luck selling this vampire story to your sister." He turns around and reaches for the doorknob. As he opens the door and sheds a small light from the outside in, she quickly closes the door on him.

"I said I'm not lying!" She shouts with one hand on the door.

Andrew faces her freaked out. "Whoa! You were just standing by the stairs; how did you move that fast?"

"I'm a vampire!" She pleads, as her fangs come out and red veins race down her eyes.

CHAPTER 37

Isaiah

"Those warriors really thought they stood a chance against me." Isaiah laughs. "I wish I could've seen their facial expressions when the last warrior showed up carrying the other warrior's heads."

"Are you going to gloat the whole ride back?" Lucia replies, not amused.

"Yes, how can you not be impressed by that? You don't see shit like that every day!"

"When you've been alive as long as I have, you'll need more than that to impress me." He lets out a little laugh as he looks out the window. "The sun should be settling any moment now, it's only a matter of time before you and the boys set out to find the Atomizer." She continues as they approach the abandoned loft.

"You're not coming with us?" As he looks at her quizzically.

"No, I have other matters to attend to. You'll be going without me."

"What could be more important than finding this Atomizer?" She smirks and doesn't respond. "How can you talk this big bad ass game, but not show your face at the showdown!"

"I told you what you have to do. You truly don't need me there to hold your hands, unless you have some kind of mother fetish going on." She snickers.

"I don't need a chaperone! All I'm saying is, if this was as important as everyone proclaims it to be, I don't see why you wouldn't want to be there. You should want to secure the mission more than anyone with what's at stake."

"I'm five steps ahead of everyone, and I am well aware of all the possible outcomes that may happen tonight. And I am confident you will succeed."

"How can you be so sure?"

"Because I know what's at stake for you, you won't fail." She replies, then looks him in the eyes. "I'm surprise you still doubt me."

"I don't doubt you." He replies, avoiding eye contact.

"Good." She parks the car in front of the abandoned loft.

"Let's get this over with," he says under his breath, glancing over at the front door to the loft. She turns off the car and takes the key out of the ignition. Before the two get a chance to get out the car, an owl lands on the hood of the car and stares directly at them. Isaiah looks at the owl then back at Lucia, who has already opened the door to get out.

"Were you following us?" She asks angrily. The owl shakes his head then begins mutating. In a matter of seconds Zechariah is sitting on the hood of the car. Isaiah gets out and walks around the car. Zechariah jumps off the hood and faces Lucia. "I told you stay inside!" She points at him.

"I did, but that vampire kept staring at my neck. I felt uncomfortable." Zechariah replies sarcastically.

Isaiah smirks. "You know we only drink human blood."

"I never underestimate the thirst of you creatures." He turns to face him.

"You shouldn't, and you know better than to underestimate me. Disobey another direct order from me and I will rip that tainted eyeball out of your skull. I want to see you try and change into anything after that!" She continues.

Zechariah looks back at her and puts his hands in the air. "Don't be so hostile!" He replies with joy. "We're finally going to find the Hell Atomizer. No more hiding in the shadows, all my brothers and sisters will be free! And every demon that fell victim over the centuries will be free to avenge their death and take over the land they were pushed out of!" He smiles.

"Sounds like it's going to be a party." Isaiah replies.

"Yes, a huge party which we all will be the host of. And you will be reunited with your mother." He faces Isaiah again and places his hand on the hood of the car. Looking him in the eyes, he continues, "I'm happy I didn't have to put my hands on you for your cooperation."

Isaiah fixes his face and steps closer to him. "Good thing you didn't try. You would have had two losses this week." The two stare at each other with great intensity.

"No need to fight over me boys, let's pregame for this party." Lucia says, walking pass the two and into the loft. Zechariah breaks the stare by following her. Isaiah waits a couple of seconds then follows them.

When she opens the door, Tyriek is laying on the floor staring at the ceiling. He turns his head to face everyone as they enter. "About time you guys came back. I was getting ready to take a nap." Tyriek says, sitting up from the floor.

"If you fall asleep now, you won't recognize the planet when you wake up." Zechariah replies.

Isaiah smirks as he walks around Zehariah to stand by his side. "When we find the location, how can you be so sure we'll even get there tonight? For all we know this damn Atomizer could be in South India!"

"Don't be so simple minded, your best friend is a witch."

Zechariah replies, looking at Lucia. "If this Atomizer was in India, every stone would be turned by sunrise until we found it."

"So, when we find this Atomizer, will you turn me into a day walker?" Tyriek asks, getting off the floor.

"I have one more mission for you after we find the Atomizer. If you come out successful, I'll turn you into a day walker." She replies.

Zechariah shakes his head as he folds his arms against his chest. "You're always up to something."

She looks him in the eyes and smiles, she doesn't reply but instead she looks over at Isaiah. "Let's get started."

"What do you want me to do?" He asks walking toward her.

"Lay here on the floor, I'm going to enter your mind." Isaiah nods his head then lays down on his back. She takes out a small needle from her pocket and injects herself in the thumb, a small amount of blood spills out. She kneels over him and places her thumb on his forehead, drawing a line from his hairline down to the middle of his eyebrows. Fangs pop out of his mouth, once the blood touches his skin. "Relax." She smiles in reaction to his fangs. He closes his eyes as he tries to control them. Once they go away, she closes her eyes too. She takes a deep breath and continues, "concentrate on the image of the Atomizer, I haven't done this in a while." She places her fingers on his temple and starts humming. After a few seconds, her eyes shoot open and they are now pitch black. After a minute goes by, she closes her eyes again then bows her head down. Placing her forehead on his. Isaiah aggressively closes his hands into fists, then slowly loosens them. When she lifts her head, she slowly opens her eyes and removes her hands from his head. "I know where it is."

"Where?" Zechariah asks, impatiently. Isaiah opens his eyes and slowly sits up, placing his hand over his forehead.

She lets out a little laugh as she stands on her feet. "It's closer than we thought, it's right here in America!"

"Where?" he asks again.

"In a deep cave, the infamous Cathedral Caverns."

"Alabama? Isn't that a state park?" Tyriek asks looking at them puzzled.

"The entrance of it is, but inside there's a land beyond the average tourist limit. Land that not even the owners know about."

When Isaiah gets off the floor, he licks the blood that he touched off his finger. "Why do you taste so weird?" He interrupts to ask.

She smiles at him and replies, "I'm what evil taste like." He looks her in the eyes then takes another taste.

"Take us there, I can't wait any longer!" Zechariah shouts.

"Gather together." She instructs. Everyone forms a circle around her and bows their heads. In seconds, they disappear from the room.

Hakeem

"Alright, I'm finished." Hakeem places his pencil down, folds the piece of paper and hands it to his grandma.

"Can I read it?" She asks. He shrugs his shoulder, looking away. She takes the note and puts it in her back pocket. "I'll read it later." He nods his head then looks up to the ceiling. She gives him a hug and holds him tight. "I love you so much! I regret ever letting you drink that blood!"

He stretches his arm out and hugs her back. "At least we get to say our last goodbye in person." She hugs him tighter. After a few seconds go by, she finally lets him go and steps back. "What's the chances you think I will come across Isaiah there?"

"I highly doubt it. The elders didn't even share the location with me, there's absolutely no way he can find this on his own."

He nods his head. "How was he able to control the warrior?" He looks puzzled then continues, "You never told me we had abilities like that."

"I wasn't certain until I saw it for myself, vampires using mind control was always a myth. I don't know how he obtained the knowledge to use it."

"As bad as those warriors deserved an ass whooping for kidnapping me, they didn't deserve to die like that. I was thinking about what you said earlier. You're right, it is going to have to be me who puts an end to this. Isaiah is out of control. I saw all the dead bodies at the hotel with my own eyes. Families torn apart. That's not what our family was built on, that's not what I want my child to be raised around. And if this is the only way I can take Zechariah down, so be it."

She smiles, "your father would have done the same."

"I know he would of." He looks down.

The dungeon door opens in the middle of their conversation. It is Aaron with five men behind him. "Sorry to interrupt, but it's time to go." The two stop talking and looks at him.

She steps away from Hakeem and approaches Aaron. "Where will you guys be taking him?"

"I'm not allowed to share that information with you." Aaron replies.

"Can you stop being stubborn for a moment and be a friend. A real friend. This is the last time I'm going to see my grandchild. I just want to know where I'll be losing him." Her eyes become watery. Aaron grits his teeth as he avoids eye contact and tightens his fist.

Hakeem steps up behind her and continues, "if you want my full cooperation, tell us."

Aaron bites the bottom of his lips and hesitates to reply. "It's in Alabama, the Atomizer is in Alabama. It's a six-hour flight away, well two hours, thanks to our new enhanced jet system." She nods her head and faces Hakeem, before she can say anything, Aaron continues, "we have to go."

The two take a moment to look at each other, then Hakeem places his hand on her shoulder. "Goodbye grandma."

"Goodbye Hakeem." She replies, placing her hands over his. He removes his hand and walks pass her towards Aaron.

"Are we going to have to restrain you?" Aaron asks, holding large handcuffs.

"No, I gave you my word. You have nothing to worry about."

Aaron nods his head then puts them away. "Good, follow me then." He steps away from the door giving Hakeem space to step out. Once he walks out, the two walk down the hallway with the five men behind them. When the group make their way upstairs, everyone that is either socializing or walking by, stops and stares at Hakeem. The room grows completely quiet. They continue to walk through the lobby as everyone keeps their attention on him.

"No one here is a fan of vampires huh?" Hakeem asks as they step outside.

"No, and with everything your cousin did. Hell no." The group walk around the citadel to a field of grass and a shed the size of a house further in the back. Aaron unlocks the shed door and opens it. Inside is an all-black jet, with its entrance open. "Meet Sophia!"

"You can fly this?" Hakeem asks admiring the jet.

"Heavens no." Aaron replies.

"I'll be the one flying this sexy thing!" The pilot approaches them from behind the jet. Aaron nods his head at him and leads everyone inside. Once seated, the pilot presses a button that opens the roof of the shed. "Hold tight guys, this is going to be a bumpy ride." He turns on the engine and shouts, "next stop, Alabama!" In a matter of seconds, the jet levitates out of the shed and speeds off in the air.

CHAPTER 38

"I can't believe it; all those vampire movies were real. Are you guy's descendants of Dracula?" Andrew asks Taryn, seated on the stairs.

"They're not real Andrew, stop with the silly questions."

"My questions aren't silly, you're a freaking vampire! My best friend is a vampire, I don't know what to believe in anymore." He looks her in her eyes as she sits next to him.

"I don't know what to believe in either, 24 hours ago none of this shit existed to me. After you left me in the parking lot yesterday, Isaiah came after me again and fed me his blood." She pauses, then continues, "he snapped my neck, I was dead, physically dead. All I remember was darkness, and when I woke up, I was in Hakeem's arms in the school sewers!"

"That bastard!" Andrew replies, jumping to his feet, "I can't believe he would do that to you! He crossed the line for the last time." She nods her head slowly with a look of depression on her face. "Wait, when he came to school yesterday it was broad daylight. Why can he walk in the sun and you can't?" He looks at Taryn puzzled.

"I don't know, Hakeem can walk in the sun too. Maybe it's something I haven't acquired yet. Drew you must promise me, this stays between us! Nobody can know about this!"

"You have my word, plus I lied to the cops already. If they find out, I'm going down as an accomplice, I should be the least of your worries." He pauses then continues, "how do you think Justina will take all of this? You murdered your little sister's parents."

"She can't find out. You have to help me get rid of the bodies." She stands up.

"You want me to touch their bodies?" He stutters. "Keeping this to myself isn't good enough?"

"I don't have enough time to hide their bodies, clean my room and come up with a story. I need your help!"

"Ugh, where's Hakeem?"

"There's no time, the sun is setting, that means school should be ending in a few." She grabs his arm and pulls him upstairs. He gives in and follows her and when they get to the top, he stops in front of her bedroom and stares at the corpses as Taryn goes to the hallway closet for sheets. "Hold this." She says, handing him covers. He begins to breathe heavy holding it tight. She runs to the bathroom and comes back with two pairs of rubber gloves. She puts on hers, as she places the other pair on top of the covers for him.

He puts everything down and picks the gloves up. "I think we are supposed to put these on before touching the sheets."

"Forget it." She shakes her head. "We're going to have to burn their bodies."

He swallows his spit as he looks at the corpses' again. "Ok, we'll burn them." He mumbles, not taking his eyes off them.

"What are you looking at?" She looks at him puzzled. "We don't have time!" He shakes his head to regain focus as she reaches down and grabs the covers from his feet. She lays one of them next to her father and the other on her mother. "Help me roll my dad over. Push his top half, I'll push the bottom." She continues, looking back at him. He nods his head and steps closer to her father's corpse. She kneels first and places her hands underneath his knees, Andrew kneels and prepares to touch his shoulders, until he notices his eyes are still open.

"I can't do this, I'm getting dizzy just by looking at him." He sits back and places his hand over his forehead.

She shakes her head, disappointed. "Go outside and pop my dad's trunk, I'll take him downstairs myself. His keys should be in the kitchen."

He gets up and goes downstairs. He grabs the keys and heads to the car, when he opens the car door there is a bottle of vodka sitting on the driver's seat. He picks it up and takes a swig, but not a single drop comes out. He peeks inside of it and shakes his head when he notices that it is empty. By the time he places the bottle down, Taryn is standing at the house door with both parents in each arm, wrapped up in covers. "Jesus Christ." He mumbles.

She has one parent under her arm and the other in the air. "Open the trunk!" She instructs, walking outside. He pops open the trunk and inside contains a full box of empty alcohol bottles. He lifts the box up and places it in the front of the car. Taryn looks around the driveway to make sure her neighbors aren't looking while she carries her parents to the car. She drops her mother in the trunk first, then shoves her father in after. Once the bodies are squeezed in, she shuts the trunk and looks Andrew in the eyes. "Can you take his car to your house? I'll drive your car back after I clean my room."

Andrew hesitates to answer, then nods his head. "Don't take too long. I don't know how long I can keep this in my driveway." She nods her head as he takes out his car keys and hands it to her. She continues around him as he gets in the car, by the time he starts the car and puts it in reverse, she has already made it inside and has shut the door.

It takes Taryn no longer than 45 minutes to clean her house. She makes sure there isn't a drop of blood anywhere. By the time she is finished it is five o'clock and dark outside. Justina still hasn't come home from school, so Taryn figures she stopped at her friend's house when school was over. Instead of waiting, she changes her clothes and leaves the house with Andrew's car. On her way to his house she decides to take the route the hospital is on. Approaching it, she notices Emira walking out the front entrance with a small crowd of students from the school. She quickly looks forward avoiding eye contact with any of them. Once she passes them, she can't help but notice someone climbing out of the hospital's third floor window and falling on the side of the building. Once she stands up, she instantly notices that it is Amber.

Taryn turns into the parking lot and drives to the side of the building she just saw Amber falling from. As Amber prepares to run through the parking lot, Taryn cuts her off with the car and asks, "where are you going?"

Amber

An hour before her escape, all the students that were in the lobby came into Amber's room to greet her.

"Thank god you're alive! I thought you were a goner!" Students are saying as they jump on the bed with her. Smiles and laughter go around the room as everyone is filled with joy. Amber puts an insincere smile on her face to blend in, as everyone tries to comfort her.

"I told you there was something wrong about that freak! To stay away, but you didn't want to listen!" Samson says, entering the room. Once the door shuts behind him, all the laughter quickly stops.

"He did say that." One girl said to another. "I can't believe Samson was right, Hakeem is a monster," the other girls whispered.

Amber's smile quickly fades away. "Stop! Everyone stop talking! Hakeem's not a monster, he's not a killer!" She shouts with one hand on the side of her head.

Samson makes his hand into a fist, as his face cringes into anger, "how can you lay there and lie to us in our face?" He points at her and continues, "we saw it for ourselves, him and his cousin fed on families. Drained them dry, he drugged you and planned on doing the same if it wasn't for the cops! The goddamn monster even killed his own mother! And you're still covering up from him!"

"You know what Samson, I watched the video too. And I didn't see Hakeem touch one body. So, if Amber is saying he's not a monster, I believe her." Emira replies, stepping in front of Amber's bed.

"His cousin didn't leave any survivors for him, if you're going to tell me he's not a freak like his cousin, tell me, how did he get away when the cops surrounded the room?" Samson looks at her puzzled. Emira closes her mouth and looks over her shoulder at Amber for an answer, but she is silent. "I thought so, he's no different than his dread head cousin and let's not forget about the bank robbery he was a part of!"

"He was a part of the bank robbery?" a girl asks.

"Yes, ever since he came to our town, we've been dealing with unusual shit!" Samson replies.

"Get out of my room Samson! Everyone get out!" Amber shouts. Everyone looks at each other with a confused expression and walk out. Samson shakes his head at her and walks out the room too. When Emira begins to leave, she tells her to stay.

"We'll wait for you outside," one of the girls say to her on the way out of the room. Emira nods her head at them then returns to Amber's bedside.

Amber looks at her parents and tells them, "you two can get out of my room too."

Her father crosses his arms as he gives her an unpleased

expression. "We're leaving the hospital together. Don't get any funny ideas, we'll be waiting for you in the lobby." He nods his head at her mother, and the two walk out.

The room is quiet after they leave. "Thank you for having my back, I know everything looks crazy but I promise you Hakeem isn't a murderer."

Amber breaks the silence but Emira cuts her off. "I didn't stick up for you because I believed you, I did it because you haven't been awake for nearly an hour and Samson is already down your throat gloating how right he is. I saw what Isaiah tried to do yesterday at school. And I saw what he did at the hotel, I don't know what happened at Hakeem's house, but he clearly wanted to finish what Isaiah started. Amber promise me you'll stay away from him, even if he will be the father of your baby. You don't need him in your life. There are plenty of successful single mothers in this world."

Amber bites her bottom lip as she sits back against the pillow. She wants to defend him some more, but she realizes it is useless. "May I see your phone? I still haven't received a new one." She extends her hand out.

"Who are you going to call? All of your friends are here." Emira asks, taking out her phone.

Amber shakes her head and replies, "just let me use it!"

As she hands her the phone, a nurse opens the room door and interrupts the two. "Are you ready to take the pregnancy test?"

"Yes, I'm ready." Amber replies, holding onto the phone. "Are you bringing my clothes so I can change back into?"

"It'll be here for you when you return from the bathroom."

She nods her head and crawls out of bed. "Amber I love you, but you're not peeing on a stick with my phone in your hand. That's gross, how about I give this back when you come back." Emira says, taking the phone from her and putting it back in her pocket.

Amber shakes her head and replies, "fine, don't go anywhere."

"I won't."

The nurse hands her a cup of water and the pregnancy test as they walk down the hall. "Have you ever taken one of these before?" The nurse asks. Amber shakes her head. "The instructions are on the back of the package." She continues. Amber follows her to the bathroom with her face glued to the back of the pregnancy test. "Here we go, come find one of us when you're done." She smiles and closes the door after her, leaving Amber standing in the middle of the bathroom.

After 20 seconds, she finally takes the test out of the package. As she holds it, a flashback of the mysterious woman claiming Hakeem and Isaiah to be dead and wanting the baby to be brought to her, hits her. Following another flashback of Hakeem's grandmother warning her of what she may see with vampire blood in her system. She closes her eyes and takes a deep breath. "That dream felt so real. Lord please don't let that be what the future holds for us." Tightening her grip, she opens her eyes and walks to the toilet. After she finishes, she walks out the bathroom and grabs the first nurse she sees walking by. "Here, I wasn't sure who I was supposed to give this too." She hands her the test. The nurse nods her head and starts guiding her back to her room, but Amber insists she can get back on her own.

She can't help but notice how busy the hospital is, nurses and doctors are running room to room. Seems like there isn't one room left unattended. On her way back, she takes a glance into the waiting room and sees her parents waiting in the lobby along with

Samson, other students and several other civilians. More officers are waiting in the lobby as well. "They're here for you." A deep voice replies from behind her. She turns around and looks at him puzzled. "Sorry to intrude, you must be Amber. I'm Joel." The tall gentlemen stretches his hand out for a handshake.

She steps back slightly and looks at his skinny hands. Ignoring it, she replies, "how do you know who I am?"

"Don't be alarmed, I'm not a creep or anything." He places his hand back to his side and continues, "I couldn't help but overhear all the commotion when you arrived."

She nods her head and gives him a serious facial expression. "Thanks for the heads up, but my situation is already situated. They're not here for me."

"They lied to you, if you leave this hospital they'll detain you until Hakeem is captured."

"You overheard this?" She asks, folding her arms.

"No, it's common sense. There's only so much they can ask you while you're lying in bed. Once you are released they're going to interrogate the shit out of you!"

"Ok, I heard enough." She waves her hand, annoyed and walks pass him. "Thanks for the warning, but I'll be going now."

"Don't leave!" He shouts. She stops and turns around as he lowers his voice. "Don't leave the hospital. It's not safe, the baby you're carrying means too much to this world. You need to stay here; real help is coming." She looks at him puzzled, then turns around and continues to walk away, "You'll die if you leave!" He continues.

After Amber turns the corner, she runs to her room. Emira is still sitting in the chair. When Emira notices her heavy breathing, she jumps from the seat worried and asks, "are they here?"

"No," She paces herself. "There was a creep down the hallway." She shakes her head walking towards her clothes on the bed.

"You want me to say something to the cops for you?"

"No, forget about it. Let me see your phone." She puts on her jeans then buttons it.

"Amber, I don't think it's a good idea."

"What?" She replies, holding the hospital gown in her hand.

"Amber, I'm your best friend. If you don't want to talk to me or your parents, the only other person you'd call is Hakeem. And by the way you've been defending him, I know you're going to call him!"

"Emira, he's innocent." She pleas.

"You were unconscious in his bed Amber! Downstairs was his dead mother! Nobody would have known if Samson didn't call the cops! I wouldn't be here talking to you if it wasn't for him. Even though he's an asshole he was right, those cousins are too dangerous to be around!"

"Isaiah yes, Hakeem no. Emira, I'm telling you Hakeem did not kill his mother, I was conscious for that."

"Then who did?" Emira looks at her puzzled. "Why haven't you said anything yet? It's like you're living in your own world."

"I don't know who it was!"

"Of course you don't, you know what, I don't even know why I even defended you. You're fucking delusional!"

Dr. Murray knocks on the door and then opens it, interrupting the two. "Can I come in?" He asks, before sticking his head further in the room.

"Just one sec." Amber replies. tossing the gown and grabbing her shirt.

"Good luck Amber, I'm leaving." Emira says, heading toward the door.

"Wait, don't leave yet! He's giving me my results." She replies, putting on her shirt.

"I'm not staying, I won't allow you to use this opportunity as a ploy to suck me into being used later."

"Emira!" Amber pleas. She passes the doctor awkwardly as she leaves the room. "Fuck." She says under her breath.

"Should I just come back?" Dr. Murray asks, standing at the door.

"No, I'm ready." She exhales deeply shaking her head. "You can come in."

Dr. Murray nods his head and enters. "The test came back positive again. You are pregnant." Amber nods her head slowly and doesn't respond. "I know you want to be discharged from the hospital. Are you sure you don't want to spend one more night here? You've been through a lot, it doesn't hurt to make sure your baby is still healthy."

She nods her head again and looks the doctor in his eyes. "On my way back from the bathroom, I noticed more cops in the waiting room. They wouldn't happen to be here for me?"

Dr. Murray bites the bottom of his lip, contemplating if he should give her an answer. "Yes, they are going to take you if you don't agree to stay. They think Hakeem may still try and contact you.

That's why I encourage you to stay because where they're taking you is no place for someone in your condition."

"But they can't take me against my free will. I didn't do anything!"

"I know you didn't, but you're the only lead they have to finding him. A lot of people died while you were unconscious. If it wasn't for the fact that we found out you were pregnant, they would have taken you once you awoke." She looks down at the floor and doesn't respond. "I'm going to tell everyone you changed your mind. That you will be staying." Dr. Murray continues. She nods her head. He turns around and leaves the room. Once the door shuts, she turns around and runs to the window. She opens it but the mesh window is sealed shut. She pauses for a second to think, then storms out the room. When she gets out, she quickly puts on a calm face and walks down the hall. She stops in front of the doorway that leads to the waiting room and is relieved Joel isn't there. She sees Dr. Murray talking to her parents and her friends along with the officers.

After a couple of seconds pass she sees everyone wave to each other then walk out the entrance as her parents follow the doctor back inside. She panics and quickly walks further down the hall. Just as they enter the hall, another doctor with a group of nurses pull a patient on a rolling bed out of a room in front of her. She places her back against the wall to allow them to pass and then she sneaks into the empty room without anyone paying her attention. Just her luck, she feels a cold breeze behind her and notices the window is open. She closes the door and runs to it. She looks outside to see if anyone is walking by and sees no one. Placing her legs out the window, she holds onto the ledge and wastes no time in letting go. When she lands on the floor, she sprints through the parking lot.

She doesn't get far when she's blinded by a car light cutting her off. When she steps back, she realizes it's Andrew's car. Relieved, she looks into the driver side and sees Taryn. "Where are you going?" Taryn asks.

CHAPTER 39

Alabama (Cathedral Caverns)

Isaiah

"Everyone with a ticket, please report to the entrance for the last tour of the day." A deep voice announces over the speakers. A blue light flashes in the woods outside of the state park. Lucia, Isaiah,

Zechariah and Tyriek appear at once. Everyone but Lucia, touches their chest and looks around amazed at their current surroundings.

"This is it." Zechariah says under his breath, with a wide grin on his face.

"It's up there, inside the cave." Lucia replies, pointing in the way of the cave.

Zechariah steps away from the group and walks the trail alone. "Let's go!" He barks. Tyriek looks at Isaiah and Lucia and scratches the back of his neck then follows him.

Lucia lays her eyes on Isaiah and nods her head at him, giving him permission to follow them. "How am I going to find you when this is over?" He asks.

"You won't, I'll find you." She steps back and disappears in front of him. He grits his teeth, then follows the other two walking the path toward the toll booth. Zechariah wastes no time before transforming into a bird and flying into the cave, leaving Tyriek on the path.

Tyriek stops and turns around to wait for Isaiah to catch up. When he does catches up, Tyriek says, "I guess we're on our own."

"Just like juvey," He replies, passing him on the path. As the two approach the booth, they are able to run inside undetected. They are amazed at how the cave is molded. Water drips down the rocks on the walls, as they hear the flow of a river above the grounds. When they get to the bottom of the stairs, they are stepping on puddles of water that fall onto the ground. "It's here, I can feel it's presence. Its making my blood warm!" Isaiah says, leading Tyriek over a bridge and down a path that leads them to a long hallway.

"So, does this mean you know where you're going? I mean we're here, is there something that's supposed to be sticking out?" Tyriek asks, looking around.

"Honestly, I'm not sure, but if we walk like this, we'll never find it. Let's speed this up." The two sprint full speed down the rest of the path, passing the tour guide group, knocking them off balance. Before they know it, they are at the end of the cave. "Did you see anything suspicious?" Isaiah asks, looking around.

"No, I didn't."

"Me neither, let's double back. We must've missed something."

Tyriek nods his head. Before the two sprint off again, the bird Zechariah transformed into, lands on the platform in front of them. He transforms back to his human body and says, "don't waste your time. It's not going to be in the bloody Davey Prince's hall!"

"Where else can it be? I didn't see any doors." Tyriek replies.

"How about you two stop looking with your eyes, and let your ears guide you."

"Our ears? What the hell are we supposed to be listening to?" Tyriek replies, then looks at Isaiah for back up. Isaiah takes another look around the cave then closes his eyes. Tyriek shrugs his shoulders then does the same. A few seconds pass when Tyriek says, "I hear conversations, footsteps. I think it's the tour guide." He pauses, then continues, "Damn, I can hear all the way up to the entrance."

"Tune that out!" Zechariah replies.

Suddenly, the word "death," echoes through the cave.

"You heard that?" Isaiah asks, opening his eyes.

"That wasn't the humans?" Zechariah replies, looking around, puzzled.

"I heard it too, what was that?" Tyriek looks around.

Isaiah twitches his nose and closes his eyes again. As he lifts his head toward the ceiling, the word "leave," echoes through the air. He opens his eyes and points to a hole the size of a tennis ball in the ceiling.

"It's coming from there!"

Zechariah transforms back into a bird and flies to the hole. As he flaps his wings around, he realizes he can't fit through. He quickly transforms into a silverback gorilla and grabs ahold onto one of the stalactites. He is able to hang from it for a moment as he punches the hole to make it larger. The impact causes the stalactite he is hanging from to collapse along with a few next to it. He quickly holds onto the inside of the hole as everything else falls onto the floor.

Isaiah and Tyriek avoid everything that hit the ground. When they look up to the ceiling, they see him tearing through the hole with big pieces of stones dropping as he fits his top half through. The entire tour guide runs towards the direction of the noise. Zechariah then transforms into a smaller creature to fit inside and finds that the actual tunnel isn't as small as the entrance to it was.

When the tour guide sees Zechariah's transformation, they freak out and run the opposite way. Isaiah and Tyriek watch him waste no time dig his way through the upper level of the cave. Isaiah bends his right knee then jumps high enough to grab ahold of the bottom and climbs through the hole too. When Tyriek sees what Isaiah just did, he follows. The three climb several miles up into the tunnel in incredible speed.

As they approach the top, a bright light shines through the small hole of the cave. When Zechariah breaks through it, there is a tall creature with a dark skin texture standing in the middle of the room staring at him. The creature isn't muscular, but still looks threatening. Zechariah transforms into his human form as he stands on his feet and shortly thereafter, Isaiah and Tyriek climb through. The three observe this mysterious creature before saying anything. "What you're looking for is not here, leave," it says with a serious facial expression.

Zechariah smirks. "Are you serious?" He tilts his head. "Get the fuck out my face!"

"I won't repeat myself," It steps towards them. Five more of the same creatures creep from out of the shadows beside the group and behind them.

"We're not leaving without it!" Zechariah shouts looking at the creatures surrounding them.

"I'm giving you a chance to leave alive. There's no peace beyond this point, what you're looking for will only bring forth death!" It replies.

"I didn't ask you for an opinion!" Zechariah barks.

"Who are you to deny us access to the Atomizer?" Isaiah asks, stepping beside Zechariah.

"We don't go by a name. I am the overseer." The creature takes a whiff of Isaiah and becomes intrigued. "What's this? Your blood is tainted, an Exalus in a demon flesh. You allowed yourself to become a vampire!"

"Yea, I'm an Exalus and a vampire." Isaiah walks toward it and points as he continues, "now you can either be a part of this new world or die with the old one." He stares it in the eyes.

Hakeem

"Hold on tight guys, we'll be landing shortly!" The pilot says as he flies over the woods that lead to the Cathedral Caverns. Aaron sits in the seat across Hakeem and stares at him as he looks out the window.

"May I have a word?" He asks. Hakeem faces him and nods his head. "I just want you to know I appreciate what you're doing for us. I wish all demons were as level headed as you. Maybe then we wouldn't have to resort to such extreme matters." He pauses, then continues, "the Elders filled me in on your girlfriend, I know there's nothing I can say that can change the circumstances, but I want you to know we sent some of our best men to your town. I give you my word, her safety will be our top priority!"

"Have your men return back to the citadel! If you really want to do me a favor, you'll leave her alone and never seek her or my child out again."

Aaron nods his head. "I understand your hostility toward us. From your perspective, we may have come off a little vindictive, but you should remember this is what your father stood for and his father. Fortunately, I was able to meet them both. So, I'm not bs-ing when I say you are your father's son."

Hakeem quickly cuts him off. "Listen, I'm not doing this for you. I'm doing this for my unborn child, I don't want to hear you try and justify your actions with having relationships with my family. When I die tonight so will your ties to this family."

Aaron leans back in his seat, speechless.

"Aaron, you may want to look out the window. Looks like we're late to the party." The pilot says as he flies over the cave. Both Aaron and Hakeem look out the window and see people sprinting out of the attraction.

"He's here. Land the goddamn plane!" Aaron shouts. The pilot waste no time flying closer to the ground. As soon as he lands, everyone stands up and ambushes the door. When Aaron unbuckles Hakeem's seat, Hakeem pushes him to the side and runs off the jet. All the warriors that came, stand in front of the entrance of the jet and watch as everyone scatters in fear. When Hakeem runs pass them, they look at his back puzzled, then chase after him.

As he enters the cave, he hears footsteps and fighting echoing throughout the halls. He continues to run down the path until he spots the man size hole in the ceiling. He looks around for a possible ladder, but finds nothing. When he hears the warriors catch up, he takes another look at the ceiling. Groans and other sounds of pain come echoing down the cave. He grits his teeth, bends down and jumps to the ceiling. To his surprise he is able to grab ahold of the tunnel. He wastes no time continuing to climb as the warriors shout after him.

CHAPTER 40

When Hakeem reaches the top of the tunnel, he sees dead creatures all over the platform. A cold chill runs down his bones as he stands up and looks around. The room is empty, no doors, stairs or passageway. He is confused. Voices break the silence of the room which leave him even more confused. He can hear Isaiah talking to someone, but the sound is coming from all corners of the room. As he steps away from the hole he crawled out of, he turns to the left side of the room.

Even though there is nothing in sight but a rocky wall, a sudden urge makes him want to touch it. As he approaches it, he realizes the wall begin to fizzle as if he is looking at a mirage. He extends his hand out and watches it disappear as he puts it through the wall. He quickly draws it back to look at his palm, then does it again as he walks through it. On the other side of the wall, there is a thick fog that covers the dark forest and a trail of green ooze that awaits him. He looks over his shoulder to see where he entered from, but there is no sign of any wall or door. He realizes he has just entered a different realm. The air behind him, fizzled the same as the wall he walked through.

"Stop! You're making a grave mistake!" A voice cries out in pain, followed by a thrusting sound and slight gag. Hakeem follows the trail as fast as he can, and is shocked at the sight of Isaiah and Tyriek standing beside Zechariah. Zechariah with a smirk on his face is holding the creatures head, while green ooze is pouring from bottom onto the floor.

When Zechariah sees Hakeem, he tosses the head over Hakeem's shoulder. "Nice of you to join us." Green ooze covers his shirt and face. Isaiah looks over his shoulder and is stunned at the sight of Hakeem. Hakeem wipes the ooze off his face then looks at his hand. Angry, his face transforms into a vampire as he roars.

Isaiah quickly jumps on the path in between them and stretches his hand out. "Stop! Let's make sure the Hell Atomizer is here first. You two can settle old scores later."

"What? What the hell is wrong with you?" Hakeem points at him. "You think this is a game? You murdered innocent people this morning and now your teaming up with the demon that killed my mom! I don't even recognize you anymore."

Isaiah is caught off guard by what he just said. He turns his head to Zechariah and asks, "you killed my aunt? You didn't fucking tell me you killed her! That wasn't a part of the plan!"

"I did her a favor, she would have died either way." Zechariah shrugs his shoulders. Hakeem charges pass Isaiah and swings at him. He misses his chin by an inch and is quickly grabbed by his throat and tossed. His back hits the tree everyone is standing in front of, then he lands upside down on his shoulders. As he rolls over to his bottom, Zechariah begins to transform as he walks towards him. Hakeem quickly gets back on his feet, but before he can move, Zechariah towers over him in the form of a yeti and grabs him by the throat again. "Don't look at me like I'm the bad guy." The beast tightens its grip on his neck. Hakeem grabs its hand and tries to peel its oversize fingers back, but the beast's grip is too tight. It lifts him off his feet, as his back drags against the tree. "All you had to do was walk away like Isaiah. You brought your mother an early death not me." It places its other hand on top of his head and tightens that grip too. "The funny thing is, even after I pop your head off. You're going to come back with the rest of the demons when we open the Atomizer. You'll have to suffer forever knowing you'll never see her again."

Hakeem screams and kicks his feet, as the beast begins pulling his head off his neck. Before it can rip his head off, a sharp metal pipe pierces through the beasts back and out its chest, nearly touching Hakeem's. The beast screams in pain as it drops him. Isaiah pulls the pipe out and backs away. The beast holds its chest as it transforms back into its human body and collapses to the floor. Isaiah stands over Zechariah, waiting for him to move, but he doesn't. He throws the pipe on the floor and faces Hakeem, as Tyriek approaches them. "I'm sorry about your mom cuz, I didn't know."

"What happened to you Zay?" Hakeem looks at him puzzled. "You really let this vampire shit get to your head. You chose a demon over your family!"

"I didn't choose anything over anyone! She killed my mom Keem. Grandma took my life away before and I won't help her do it again!"

"Did you even hear her side of the story?"

"I don't give a fuck about her side of the story! I lived a fucked-up life because of her, and not once was she ever there for me. Not for nothing neither were you."

"Don't pull that card, we were kids." Hakeem steps closer to him. "There was no way I could have helped your situation. Even so, it doesn't justify what you're here to do. Do you honestly believe your mom would want you to destroy earth in the process of bringing her back? It's not worth it!"

"Says who? You?" Isaiah looks at him puzzled, then continues, "you're going to stand here and tell me my mom isn't worth it, that she would rather have us spend eternity in hell with her for being different, then to be able to see the world again?"

Hakeem grits his teeth. "You know what I mean."

"No I don't, tell me what the fuck do you mean!" Isaiah steps closer to him.

"Word." Tyriek instigates.

The two stand face to face. "It doesn't matter what we want, it's not about us, it never was. We were supposed to find this piece of shit, lock the demons away, and go back to our lives. We were never supposed to become vampires! You think grandma wanted us to die? That wasn't her fault, it was yours!" Hakeem pokes his

275

chest.

"I can't look at you." Isaiah shakes his head and tries to walk around him, but Hakeem stops him by putting his hand on his chest.

"I can't let you do this."

"I found another way to bring my mom back, I was never going to open the Atomizer. Just destroy it, but if you feel like you don't belong here feel free to kill yourself. Just don't expect any sympathy from us." Isaiah looks him in the eyes, then knocks his hand away. He approaches the tree Hakeem was held against, and reaches his hand into the hollow.

"Amber's pregnant Zay." Hakeem turns around to face him. Isaiah stops to listen. "I was there when Zechariah killed my mother, I wasn't able to stop him. We don't know what other demons are out here, I wasn't doing this just for grandma. I was doing this for them."

Isaiah puts his arm back to his side and faces him. "Killing yourself won't guarantee them a safe life. Take it from me, you'll be no help to your kid from the other side. We'll face whatever dangers harm our family together. Your child deserves to have you in its life."

A burst of laughter interrupts the serious moment between the two. All threeface Zechariah who sits up laughing. "How can you save them? When you can't even save yourself!" Isaiah and Hakeem put their guards up as he gets on his feet. "You stupid vampire." Zechariah snickers. "I knew Lucia was up to something, but to have you literally stab me in the back, that hurts more than this wound does. Did you really think it was going to be that easy to kill me?"

"Didn't really think you were going to put up much of a challenge." Isaiah replies.

"Who's Lucia?" Hakeem asks, puzzled.

"A coward who's going to face her death real soon, but not before the three of you. I'm going to shove your dead heart down your little girlfriend's throat. Than strangle her with your cousin's dreadlocks."

"Good bluff. Even if you wanted to kill us, you'd ruin your only chance of ever opening the Hell Atomizer. All of this would have been for nothing." Isaiah replies.

Zechariah laughs as he transforms into a yeti. "The witch didn't tell you? All I need is your blood, I can open the Atomizer myself! But thank you for helping me find it." The beast begins to flex then charges at the cousins, giving them no time to react. It grabs both of their heads and lifts them off the ground. It lets out a loud roar, then kicks Tyriek in the chest who is standing stunned. It tosses Hakeem across the foggy forest and Isaiah horizontally against the tree. Isaiah screams as he grabs his back in pain. As he tries to get up, the beast grabs him by the leg and slams him back and forth over his head, as if he were a baby playing with a toy.

When Hakeem gets off the floor, he charges at the beast and launches towards its head. He grabs its face from behind, facing the opposite way and lets out a glorified yell as he slams it over his shoulders onto its neck. The beast loosens its grip on Isaiah's leg and tosses him away. He rolls a couple of feet away as the beast bounces back onto all fours trying not to lay on the floor. As it shakes its head, Hakeem quickly grabs the pipe off the ground, but before he cans point it, the beast lets out a loud roar and charges toward him, transforming into a four-legged beast. This new creature is not a part of the animal kingdom. It has the body of an oversized lion but the face of a panther, its tail is a long furry snake with a mouth of a sarcastic fringe head.

Growling, it jumps on top of Hakeem, reaching to bite his face. Hakeem holds the pipe against the beast's chest, struggling to keep it from fully dropping on top of him, but its tale takes a bite of his leg. Hakeem screams as he drops the pipe lower. Tyriek approaches the two from the side, and tackles it off. The two roll over and down a slight hill.

The beast scratches his chest, with its heavy paws and sinks its teeth into his ribs aggressively. Hakeem approaches them from behind with the pipe, but hesitates to make a move when he sees the tails face and its sharp teeth. Tyriek screams in pain as he is swept on the floor.

When the beast lets go of him, Hakeem quickly tries to poke its tail, but gets pulled in closer when the tail bites the pipe. He tries pulling it back but the tail pulls him in as the beast faces him and scratches his face and arm. Letting go of the pipe, he falls to the floor and quickly rolls over back onto his feet, before it has time to attack again. The beast laughs as its tail throws the pipe away.

"Why don't you fight like a man?" Hakeem asks.

"I'm no man, neither are you!" It replies, as it approaches him. Hakeem steps back trying to keep a short distance between the two. When he sees Tyriek trying to get off the floor, he signals him toward the pipe with his eyes. "You're not even useful anymore. I have your blood on my paws. I could end this now," It slowly creeps towards him.

"Not without this." Isaiah replies holding the Atomizer in the air. It is small, black and shaped like a snow globe. A blue flame is lit inside of it. Both Hakeem and the beast's eyes light up when they see the Atomizer in his possession. "I thought this was made of gold, I mean it looked gold in my vision. I guess I'll be the one ending this," He smirks.

Zechariah transforms back into his yeti form. The blood that was on his paw is now on his hand as he makes a fist. "You imbecile, put that down!" It startes to growl, as if it were charging up.

"Don't break it! We need to open it!" Hakeem pleas.

"Sorry cuz, I made the decision for you. You're going home to your pregnant girlfriend tonight." Isaiah replies, tossing and catching the Atomizer with one hand.

"I'm going to kill you!" The yeti takes a step closer.

Tyriek rolls over and picks up the pipe. "Do it now Zay!" He tries to poke the yetti in the back, but it dodges the blow with a spin and takes the sharp pipe out of his hand then sticks it through his heart. Both Isaiah and Hakeem's eyes shoot open when they see the metal pipe sticking out of his back. Tyriek grabs the tip of the pipe and looks at the cousins. His body instantly lights up in flames and evaporates in dust. The cousins are stunned.

The yeti gets a better grip of the pipe and charges toward Hakeem. He tries to dodge it, but isn't quick enough. The yeti drives the pipe right through his chest, missing his heart by three inches. Hakeem holds the pipe as he falls to his knees, gasping, not able to speak.

Isaiah screams in anger as he cocks his arm back and slams the Atomizer to the ground. To his surprise, it doesn't break. The yeti puts his foot on Hakeem's shoulder and kicks him off the pipe. Letting out a loud roar, he charges toward Isaiah.

When he tries to pick the Atomizer up again, the yeti hurls the pipe at him, intercepting his attempt. The pipe lands between Isaiah and the Atomizer. Zechariah transforms back into the four-legged beast, as it approaches him. It steps on the Atomizer with its bloody paws and cracks it a little. It quickly takes its paw off when it realizes what it has done and steps over it, letting out a loud roar.

Isaiah notices how he cracked it, and a light bulb goes off in his head, but before he can make a move, the beast launches at him. It lands on him, but Isaiah is able to maneuver away underneath him. He gets back on his feet and back pedals away.

The beasts doesn't stop charging, it launches at him and lands on his legs. It bites his ribs and starts toying with him, dragging him around the floor. As he screams in pain, he looks the beast in its huge eyes and grabs ahold of its head. He sticks his thumb in his eyes, popping it.

Zechariah tosses Isaiah as he transforms into a blue ball of light and then into his human form screaming in pain. Isaiah rolls over grabbing his rib cage, which is pouring out blood. Zechariah begins losing color, his skin turns grey and his body becomes skinny. Isaiah struggles to get off the floor, but when he does, he sees Zechariah crawling toward the Atomizer looking weak. Zechariah cries as he crawls, covering his eye socket. When he approaches it, he reaches his hand out, but gets kicked in the face by Hakeem.

Hakeem pulls the pipe out from the floor and holds it over him. Isaiah laughs as he limps over to them. Zechariah rolls onto his back and looks Hakeem in the eyes. "You stupid son of…" Hakeem cuts him off, by shoving the pipe through his head.

He let's go of the pipe then spits on him. When he turns around, he sees Isaiah holding the Atomizer. "Wait!"

Isaiah covers it with his blood, them slams it on the floor again. The Atomizer scatters in pieces, putting out the blue flame.

Isaiah laughs at his accomplishment, then gets grabbed up by Hakeem. Hakeem looks him in the eyes, frustrated with no words to say, he let's go of him and walks away.

"I couldn't let Ty die for nothing Keem. Go home to Amber, I'll bring my mother and him back!" Isaiah shouts at his back, then follows him down the path that leads them back to the caves. Hakeem leaves him and walks through the mirage first. Aaron and his warriors have just made their way to the top of the tunnel, when he resurfaces. They shoot him on sight.

CHAPTER 41

Taryn

"Taryn?" Amber asks, confused standing in front of Andrews car. She walks around the car and opens the door. She hesitates to get in the passenger seat, but does anyway. "Where's Andrew? Is everything ok?" She asks suspiciously.

"Yea, I was just taking his car to his house." Taryn replies, making a U turn in the parking lot. "What are you doing jumping out of the hospital window?"

Amber thinks twice before she answers. "I have to find Hakeem." She replies under her breath. The car is quiet. "Have you seen him?" She faces her.

"No." Taryn slows the car down to look at her. "Listen, about last night, I'm sorry for running off like that."

"You don't owe me an explanation. I get it, if he had told us at the same time, you wouldn't be what you are now. It was probably best you left anyways."

"Why? How did you end up at the hospital anyways? Where did Hakeem go?" Taryn looks at her puzzled.

Amber turns away and looks down. "His mother was murdered this morning, in front of all of us. While me and his grandma were cleaning up the house, I passed out from digesting Isaiah's blood yesterday and woke up here. I have no idea where he is, to make matters worse the whole town thinks he was the one who killed her and is part of this hotel massacre that Isaiah is responsible for."

"What?" Taryn replies shocked as if Andrew didn't already inform her. She shakes her head. "Who killed Mrs. Exalus? Was it Isaiah?"

"No, it was something I have never seen before, a shapeshifter." Taryn gives her a confused facial expression then focuses on the road. "We need to find him before the town does. We have to find him before his grandma convinces him to do something he can never come back from." She pauses. "Suicide."

"Suicide? Why would she try to make him do that? How is that solving the problem?"

"She wants him to find some artifact that will, will lock you vampires and any other creatures in purgatory."

Taryn presses on the brakes in the middle of the road. "What? How can he keep that from me?"

"He was indecisive about the choice before you became a vampire. I don't know where he stands on it today, but the fact you're alive means he hasn't found it yet or he hasn't made up his mind. Which means we still have time."

Taryn nods her head and replies, "you're right." She begins driving again.

"Does Andrew know what you are? Do you think he knows where to find him?"

Taryn thinks about her dead parents in the trunk of her father's car, which is probably in Andrew's driveway by now and thinks twice before answering. "No, I didn't tell him. He hasn't heard from Hakeem in two days."

"How do you know he hasn't contacted him while I was in the hospital? We should go to his house first and see if he can help."

Taryn shrugs her shoulders annoyed. "No! He can't help, leave him out of this!"

Amber looks at her puzzled, then leans back in her seat. "Where will we go first to look then?"

"The mountain top, he took me there last night before we came back to his house. Up there you can see everything in town." Amber turns her head and tries to hide her shady facial expression. They drive 15 minutes away from the hospital and leave town. As they enter the trail heading up the mountain, she continues to ask, "have you thought of something to say?"

"Huh?" Amber faces her again.

"Something good to say, something that'll make him change his mind."

Amber laughs a little as she looks down at her stomach. "Yea, I have something convincing to say. I'm going to offer to run away together. The people at the hospital told me I'm carrying his baby."

Taryn stops the car and gives her an odd stare. "You're pregnant?

"Yea." She smiles. "He has something to live for now. Something to live forever for. I can't do this by myself." The car becomes quiet as the stare Taryn gives, turns into a deadly one. Amber feels uncomfortable and tries to avoid eye contact by looking out of the window. "Why are you staring at me like that?"

"It's not fair, why do you get the happy ending?" Taryn's face begins to transition.

Amber faces her again and becomes scared, "Taryn what the fuck?"

She launches at her and bites her neck, draining her dry.

To be continued…

ABOUT THE AUTHOR

Omar Desmond Hardware, born June 20th, 1991 is an American author. Middle child of three, Omar was the first in his family to be born in America. His roots vary all over Jamaica, but his mother was born and raised in St. Ann Green Hill and his father, Chalky Hill. Omar graduated from Ramapo High School in 2009. Due to financial difficulties, he had to put his goal of getting a higher education on hold and focused his attention on working at various jobs to one day make that goal a reality. Working in between jobs, he was always criticized for his imagination. It wasn't until the summer of 2015, he began to put his creativity on paper. With only one book published, Omar is preparing to flood the world with his thoughts.

Made in the USA
Middletown, DE
31 August 2017